AN ORDINARY MYSTERY

An Ordinary Treasure Hunt

By

D.D. Drew

Book layout by ebooklaunch.com

Other stories by this author as:

D.D. Drew

Welcome to Ordinary

Return to Ordinary

Bret H. Lambert

For the Innocent

Vindicta

Regina Maris

Praesidium

Havoc

Nemeses

ONE

Sunday, July 4th.

The grandfather clock in the family room chimed six a.m.

Anne Hambaugh opened her gold-flecked green eyes and stared for a moment at the textured ceiling. *Just once*, she thought, *I would love to have a lie-in.* She sat up and stretched, accompanying that with rather a large yawn. *My first fourth of July in America,* she continued, swinging her feet out from under the covers and into her fuzzy bunny slippers. *And in two days' time, my first birthday in our new home.* But it really wasn't a new home; rather, it was the two-hundred-year-old home of her father's side of the family, the ancestral home built several miles north of the town of Ordinary by Nathaniel Hambaugh.

She pulled on her plush daisy-print robe as she followed her nose into the kitchen, and to the automatic coffee pot that had just finished creating the morning elixir. She poured up two mugs—hers with cream and sugar, her father's black—and carried them into the family room. She placed her father's mug on the side-table beside his leather recliner, and then she took her own in both hands and went to the huge bay window. She looked out over the lake's tranquil surface and sighed contentedly.

She had been angry when first uprooted from the only home she had known in London, England, but that had been before going to work as a "cub reporter"—in the words of the owner/editor William Bascomb— of the *Ordinary Outlook.* She had solved two mysteries in that short time, the latest just a few days prior. She had put in long hours getting that story written and ready for the weekly journal as she had had only two days. Her contributions in the short time she had been on the journal's staff had brought subscriptions to an all-time high. Today's edition was special in that, not only was it coming out on a major holiday—which was unheard of—but there would be two articles written under her byline. *My article on the American revolution from the perspective of the "losing side" ought to raise some eyebrows,* she thought with a smile.

She had made some good friends and was settling into a routine—of sorts.

"Good morning, Anne," came a pleasant baritone voice from behind her.

"Good morning, Pater," she responded.

"And where is Benbow this morning?" inquired Nathan Hambaugh, referring to the family's stocky brindle rescue mutt.

Anne laughed. "He's having a heart-to-heart with that fat gray squirrel that teases him. The one that lives in the tree beside the driveway."

"Good luck with that!" her father chuckled, sipping his coffee. "So," he continued, "what are your big plans today?"

"Well, quite frankly, Pater," she sighed, "I'm rather pooped! Solving this last case, and then all those hours to get the story ready for today's special edition— I think I'll just have a bit of a rest."

"Probably just as well," agreed her father, watching her across the top of his cup. "You wouldn't be interested, anyway."

A perplexed expression touched her freckled face. "What wouldn't I be interested in?"

"Oh, it's nothing," he said dismissively, "really."

"*What* is nothing really?" she pressed, a hint of frustration in her tone.

"Well," he began, and then stopped. Holding out his empty cup to her, he asked, in his sweetest voice, "Refill, please?"

"Not until you tell me what the nothing is that I wouldn't be interested in!" she declared, exasperated.

Emma entered the family room just then, her own steaming cup in hand. "Oh, Nathan, tell her before she wakes George!"

He laughed lightly, and then nodded. "All right, all right," he said. "Just having a little fun."

Emma kissed her daughter's forehead, kissed her husband's forehead, and then curled up in her favorite corner of the leather sofa. "You are a stinker, dear."

"True," he sighed, winking at his daughter. "Very well, but don't say I didn't warn you."

"Pater!"

"Last night," the interim Chief of Police said, "I got a report of a ghost—or, for the sake of accuracy, an alleged ghost—at the old MacLeod Manor."

Anne looked at her father. Her eyes narrowed. "A ghost," she repeated, flatly.

"I knew you wouldn't be interested." Holding out his cup, he asked, "Coffee, please?"

Wordlessly, she took his cup, proceeded into the kitchen, and filled it. She returned, handed him the now-filled cup, and said, "A ghost?"

"Allegedly."

"At the old manor on the bluff?"

"The very one."

"Overlooking the lake?"

"The very same."

"A ghost."

"You're fixating."

"At that decaying edifice that was abandoned after the mysterious disappearance of the sea captain nigh on two hundred years ago?"

"Yep, that's the one."

Anne looked over at her mother. "Really, Mum?"

Her mother shrugged her shoulders as she sipped her coffee. "That's what George said when the officer brought him home at two o'clock this morning."

"George? Oh, and let me guess! Jorge?" queried the daughter, referring to her brother's best friend. "Again?"

"Again," sighed Emma.

"He seemed pretty sure," said Nathan, lugubriously. "And that's what went into the police report." And then he chuckled. "Maude will love that one when she sees it tomorrow morning!"

"So," murmured Anne, turning back to look out over the lake, "there's an *alleged* ghost at the old manor."

"Nothing as exciting as spies, and government secrets, and stolen jewels," her father said.

"Or general murder and mayhem," added Emma, shaking her head.

"No, nothing as exciting as all that," admitted Anne, thoughtfully. "Even so," she added in a contemplative voice, "it could be rather fun . . ."

"What happened to being pooped?" asked Nathan, playfully. "What happened to having a bit of a rest?"

Anne spun about on her heel, her eyes wide and her face flushed with excitement. "What? With a mystery to solve? Surely thou dost jest!" And then a broad smile appeared that seemed to set off her uncombed wavy red hair. "I can hardly wait to tell the others!"

As the teen hurried from the room, Emma Hambaugh glanced over at her husband. "You *are* a stinker, Nathan."

"Maybe so," he sighed, contentedly, "but Anne loves a good mystery!"

❧❧❧❧❧❧❧❧❧

The town of Ordinary, founded in 1793, by people seeking respite from persecution in Europe, was nestled in a wooded mountainous area on the edge of a beautiful lake. It was reminiscent of an old English town with its Common—an elongated stretch of thick, rich lawn, where the townsfolk would picnic on warm spring days—complete with a magnificent Victorian-era gazebo which served as the centerpiece of all public celebrations. The four one-way streets which surrounded the Common were known, collectively, as the Circus Maximus; it was a nickname given in the late 1930s by the youth of that era. At the west end of the Common, and across the appropriately named West Street, was City Hall. The two-story building, built of locally quarried stone, also included the volunteer fire department, the small police department, and, in the basement, the local weekly news journal. Along the streets that bordered the three other sides of the Common were a variety of small businesses. Taking up the entire east end, on East

Street, was the Only Ordinary Bed-and-Breakfast, and its various outbuildings, such as the now-unused Ordinary Livery. Carter's Ordinary Clothiers, Marvin's Ordinary Market (commonly referred to as 'MOM's'), The Ordinary Theater, and other such businesses were found along the entire length of South Street. The various dining establishments occupied the entire length of North Street, what the local citizenry affectionately referred to as Restaurant Row.

The most popular dining establishment with the town's youth was an eatery known as the Ordinary Malt Shoppe. A family owned and run business, it was a safe place for people of all ages to converge, plan (or plot), and enjoy a deliciously simple meal. Darlene Dunlap, a founder's descendant, the nineteen-year-old daughter of Conrad, and granddaughter of Colby (the current proprietor of the establishment) worked at the family-run malt shop when not attending the junior college in nearby Clovertown. With pad and pencil in hand, she walked up to the corner booth at which sat four teens, one of whom wore the immaculately-pressed uniform of the Ordinary Police Department.

Nineteen-year-old Harvey Freeman was a cadet with the police department who had hopes of joining as a fully-fledged officer when he turned twenty-one. In pursuit of that dream he was taking criminal justice courses at the same junior college Darlene attended. Putting down his glass of water and wiping its condensation from his hand with a cloth napkin, he said, "I've less than an hour, Anne, so say your piece so I can get back on patrol."

"He's so dedicated," said Constance Bascomb. Connie to her friends, she was the sixteen-year-old daughter of the owner/operator of the town's weekly news journal *The Ordinary Outlook*.

"And *so* handsome in that uniform!" swooned seventeen-year-old Tammy Coleman, batting her eyelashes at the blushing lad.

"You two are terrible!" laughed Anne. "Let's give Darlene our order; I'm sure she has better things to do than listen to you lot!"

Smiling at the quartet, Darlene said, "Actually, if you call doing the dishes something better to do. So, what'll it be?"

They quickly placed their orders, and, after she had gone, Anne asked, "Is the MacLeod Manor haunted?" Three sets of eyes focused on her, and three mouths hung open. No one spoke for several seconds so she tried again. "I asked ..."

"We heard," said Connie, recovering first.

"We just can't believe what we heard," added Tammy.

"I just felt a cold shiver," muttered Harvey, unhappily.

"*Why* do you ask?" queried Connie, her brown eyes searching her best friend's face.

"Well, apparently George and Jorge were up there last night ..."

"And they saw a ghost?" asked Tammy, incredulously.

"*Alleged* ghost," corrected Harvey. "There's no such thing as ghosts."

Connie and Tammy, both born and raised in Ordinary whereas their two friends were recent arrivals, looked at the six-foot-six-inch blond. "Oh?" they said in unison.

Anne leaned forward in her seat. "Do tell!

The two girls looked at one another, looked at Anne and Harvey, and both shook their heads.

"But, why?" asked Anne, surprised.

"Lunch is coming," Tammy explained.

Darlene placed the correct plate in front of each patron, and then, before leaving, said, "There is a rumor going around town that a ghost was seen at the old manor."

"There is no such thing—"

"Is there?" asked Anne innocently, cutting off Harvey's denial. "What are people saying?"

Their waitress shrugged. "I don't know, really. I've just heard snippets here and there from some customers this morning. Weird." With that, she returned to her duties.

Wiping hamburger juice from his chin with a napkin, Harvey growled, "There is no such thing as a ghost!"

"Have you ever seen one?" asked Connie.

"No."

"There you go, then," said Tammy firmly.

"There I go *where*?" Harvey gaped.

"You have no foundation for your claim," explained Connie, giving Anne a wink.

"I ..." he started, and then stopped. "You guys are no fun to have lunch with!"

"Well, ghost or not," said Anne, "it would be fun to look into. We could do the research, ask some of the old-timers, stay the night ..."

"Oh, no!" declared the cadet emphatically, all but throwing his half-eaten hamburger onto his plate. "Not just 'no,' but hellllooooo, Pastor Pettigrew!"

Pastor Archibald Pettigrew, the senior pastor at God's Ordinary Church, stopped at their booth. "Well, hello, you four!" he said, beaming. "Going to the Common this afternoon for the Independence Day festivities?"

"Wouldn't miss it!" they responded together.

"I'll see you at the dunking booth, then," he told them. "Yours truly is the willing victim!"

"Harvey has to work," Tammy said, "but the rest of us will do our best to dunk you!"

"Since it's for a good cause, of course," added Connie.

"Excellent!" declared the pastor. "Excellent! Oh, and Anne, I read your article this morning in the *Outlook*, that was quite well written! And there were some things in it that aren't covered in our history classes today."

"Like the losing side's opinion," snickered Tammy.

"Even so," said the pastor, "it was a most enjoyable read!" And with that, he sauntered off to talk with people at another table.

"This will be your first Independence Day festival here, Anne," said Connie. "It'll be great fun!"

"Oh, I dare say," admitted Anne, smiling. "Great fun!"

Finishing his lunch, Harvey told his three female companions, "I've got to get back to work. I'll cover the tab today, someone else can get it next time." He smiled at them before he headed for the cashier, "See you at the festival!"

After he had gone, the trio returned to their own meals. Between bites of her BLT, Anne said, "Who do we talk to about the old manor?"

"I could search for information on the internet," offered Connie.

"That would be one source," agreed Tammy, "but I doubt you'll find much about it. The crazy sea captain moved it forever ago. If you find anything it'll be about when it was in Scotland, and that it was moved in 1800-and-whenever."

"True," acknowledged Anne, "but that could give us—or me—some excellent background material for an article."

"I'll start on it tonight," Connie told them happily. She loved online research.

"And there's bound to be something in copies of the *Ordinary Outlook* around the time it was brought over," said Tammy, "and when the captain and his wife vanished."

"Also, true," nodded Anne. "I wonder if Maude Raynes would have anything to share with us. Being the central person at the police department, and within easy shouting distance of City Hall, she might know quite a bit."

"Possibly," admitted Connie, wiping her mouth.

"And what about Elisa Rialdi?" asked Tammy, washing down the last bite of her tuna sandwich with root beer. "She was the librarian here for, like, ever; she might know something."

"All excellent suggestions!" declared Anne, enthusiastically.

Tammy hesitated for a moment, and then, as she set her empty glass on the table, asked, "This isn't to involve people trying to, you know, kill us, or anything, right?"

"How could it?" Anne responded. "The major players have been dead for hundreds of years."

"Except for the ghost," interjected Connie. The other two teens looked at her with bemused expressions. "Well, you know what I mean!"

"Assuming that the 'ghost' is not really a ghost," Tammy said, "what is he—or she, or it—after?"

"My understanding is that Captain MacLeod left behind a sizable fortune," explained Anne, "a treasure, if you will, so I imagine that is what is being sought."

"It's probably not the first time," murmured Connie thoughtfully.

"People have been looking for his loot off and on ever since he vanished," Tammy told them. She looked at Anne. "Your aunt was a teacher, and history was one of her subjects, so maybe she knows something?"

Anne smiled. "You are brilliant!"

"Well, yes, that's true," admitted the seventeen-year-old modestly, a mischievous smile on her lips.

"I expect that she'll be at the festival," continued Anne, "we could ask her there."

"And Mrs. Raynes will probably be there, also," Connie added. "With any luck, we can mine both sources today."

"We'll probably have to go by Miss Rialdi's house," said Tammy. "I don't know that I've *ever* seen her at the Independence Day festival."

"That can be our assignment for tomorrow," Anne told her friends. "In the meantime, let us finish our lunch, and then enjoy your festival."

"It's half yours, too!" laughed Connie. "After all, your dad is one of the troublesome colonists!"

The three had a good laugh over this. They finished up their lunches, thanked Darlene Dunlap and her family for another excellent meal, and stepped out onto the sidewalk. Across from them was the Common, and, what with the influx of tourists for the festival, to get there, they had to cross a busy Circus Maximus.

ଔଔଔଔଔଔଔଔଔଔ

Andrea Somerfield-Hambaugh, a founder descendant and a member of the city council, was the fifty-three-year-old wife of Raymond Hambaugh, and the sister-in-law of Nathan and Emma Hambaugh. With her short auburn hair streaked with silver and her laughing hazel eyes, the recently retired school teacher was a woman happy with her life. She enjoyed being involved in the community, and every year for the last thirty years, she had helped, in one way or another, to put together the annual festival. She also helped with the festivals at Thanksgiving, Christmas, and Easter. And now that she was retired—after almost thirty years she had been ready—she had more time and energy to put into these events. Along with substitute teaching when she was needed and tutoring the youth who needed a little extra help, she managed to keep herself busy.

She thoroughly enjoyed keeping busy, but she also thoroughly enjoyed her quiet time which often entailed losing herself in a good book with her huge, golden-eyed, black cat, Enchante, firmly on her lap. So, when Andrea saw the three teenagers strolling across the lush green grass of the Common to where she stood beside the kettle-corn vendor, she knew she was about to get involved in something exciting. Albeit, her role would be small, but it would still be ever so much fun!

"Hello, you three!" she called out as they approached. "You look like you're on a mission."

"Hello, Aunt Andrea," Anne returned the greeting, smiling broadly. "And I dare say you are probably right!"

Handing out three small bags of kettle-corn, Andrea said, "I absolutely enjoyed your articles this morning, Anne. The one on the history of Independence Day from the perspective of the British was brilliant!"

"Oh, thank you!" responded her niece. "I hope I didn't upset too many people."

"I've heard only good things from the folks I've talked to thus far."

"That's a relief!"

"It's obvious you three want something from me, so, what can I do for you?"

"Well, Pater mentioned this morning about a ghost-sighting at the MacLeod Manor," Anne said, "and I've decided to do an article on it—the manor, not the ghost—so we were hoping that you could provide some insight that we wouldn't find on the internet, in the library, or in the old copies of the *Ordinary Outlook*."

Andrea let her eyes drift to where the manor stood, up on the bluff, hidden by deep woods. "Well, certainly I would love to share what I know," she told them, "but this isn't really the place. Tell you what. Come by the house tomorrow about mid-morning, that will give me time to piece together what I can. Would that work?"

"Definitely!" the trio responded.

The older woman winked at them. "I'll see you then, then!"

"One down," said Tammy with an air of satisfaction. "Now all we need to do is find Mrs. Raynes."

"She may not appreciate being pestered with this sort of thing on a day she's away from the office," Connie suggested.

Anne thought for a moment, and then said, "I think she'll be fine with this. After all, it isn't really work related."

"Well, maybe," responded Connie, clearly not convinced.

The trio wandered about the festival. It was early in the afternoon and the Common was not yet too busy. They participated in a few of the booths; Anne impressed her friends at the shooting booth and annoyed the attendant. At the dunking booth, Tammy put her pitching skills to the test, dunking Pastor Pettigrew several times … for a good cause, of course. Connie made an impressive showing at the ring toss which netted her a dinner-for-two certificate that she decided to give her father. They whiled away several hours, all the time keeping an eye out for Maude Raynes.

It was she who found them.

They were getting an ice cream cone each when the sixty-seven-year-old police department secretary/records clerk/dispatcher sauntered up behind them. "Rumor has it," she said, startling all three of them enough so their cones almost dropped, "that you're looking for me."

"Yes," replied Anne in a nearly apologetic voice. "Yes, we are."

"Well, here I am," Maude said.

Taking the older woman by the arm, Anne led her away from the crowd to an area that allowed them some privacy. "We were wondering what you could tell us about the MacLeod Manor," the teenager said.

"You mean, about ghosts and buried treasure and the like?" asked Maude, amused.

"Yep, just that like," Connie chuckled.

Maude shook her head and sighed. "I thought you kids had better heads on your shoulders."

"It's George's fault," said Anne. "He and Jorge were up at the manor last night—"

"Trespassing," interjected Tammy with a slight snicker.

"—and were picked up by the police," Anne continued without missing a beat.

"And they claimed to have seen a ghost, am I right?" concluded Maude.

"Right," admitted Anne.

"And you want to know if there's a history of that sort of thing, am I right?" the older woman went on.

"Right, again," nodded Anne.

"And if I said there were other sightings, what then?" queried Maude.

"There were other sightings?" gasped Connie. "I don't remember any of that! And Dad never put that into the journal!"

"It's not something he *would* put in the journal," Maude explained. "Unsubstantiated sightings? No, no, your father didn't believe in that kind of journalism. He only printed what was corroborated by facts."

"I don't remember hearing anything about ghosts," Tammy said. "There was always some talk of the old guy's treasure, and a whole lot of speculation as to its whereabouts, but never anything about spooks."

"What *can* you tell us about the manor?" asked Anne. "Or MacLeod, for that matter?"

"What is out there is all common knowledge," Maude told them. "He started out as a cabin boy at the age of twelve—or thereabout—in the family shipping business. He quickly moved up through the ranks to become the captain of his own ship at the age of twenty-something, and not because he was family. His family, funnily enough, couldn't stand young Angus. Anyway, he went his own way after purchasing his own ship and made his fortune as a tradesman, shipping anything and everything to wherever it needed to go. He was known to be fearless, and—by the standards of his fellow seamen—he was known to be reckless. Captain Angus MacLeod went places that others felt were far too risky, but he always came back, and he always reaped the hefty rewards. That was how he amassed his fortune. When he retired from the sea—at fifty, I believe—he married a young lady—Elaine, I think, or something like that—who was easily half his age—some sources put her as young as eighteen—and they took up residence in his family's ancestral home in the Highlands. By then, he was the last of the direct bloodline to inherit the family's wealth and property. It was a few years thereafter, while visiting the U.S., and, specifically, the Lake Ordinary area, that he decided to move the whole kit-and-caboodle from Scotland to the bluff overlooking the lake. He was pushing sixty by the time it was all said and done. The manor was rebuilt here but not without mishaps, apparently there were a few mysterious deaths. The work was almost complete when MacLeod and his wife vanished."

The three teens looked at the woman with their eyes wide and their mouths open.

"You know quite a bit!" declared Anne gleefully.

"One hears things," shrugged Maude, a small smile on her lips.

"There goes my online research," mumbled Connie.

"I had no idea," said Tammy.

"Well, you ladies have fun," the older woman said, "I'm off to the kissing booth."

"Really?" asked an astonished Anne.

With a wink, Maude explained, "I take the money."

The three teens watched her go, and then began to talk among themselves when they spied a tall figure in an immaculate uniform. Harvey Freeman was walking toward them in an officious manner, his face set and stern. He stopped in front of them and looked down—at six-feet-six-inches, he was taller than the tallest of them, Tammy at five-feet-nine-inches.

"How goes it?" he asked.

"Oh," said Tammy, smiling, "it goes."

"I saw you talking with Mrs. Raynes," he continued. "She was helpful?"

"Oh, quite!" declared Anne.

He nodded. "I'm glad." Glancing over his shoulder from the direction he had just come, he added, soulfully, "George and Jorge are over at the shooting gallery hitting everything but the targets."

"In that case," Connie quipped, "we should stay here!"

"Harvey," said Anne, "have you seen Elisa Rialdi anywhere at the festival?"

He took a moment to ponder, and then replied, "No."

"Have you learned anything further on the ghost?" she added, watching his face.

"What ghost?" he declared, exasperated. "There is no such thing as ghosts!"

"Then what did George and Jorge see?" inquired Tammy.

"Who knows?" the cadet responded hotly. "Probably just some nut in a sheet!"

Anne's eyes wandered thoughtfully to the place where, hidden by the woods, the manor stood. "Has anyone else reported seeing a ghost up there of late?"

"No."

She put her eyes on him. "Has there been any … scuttlebutt … on the streets about *any* goings on up there of late?"

He opened his mouth to reply in the negative, and then promptly shut it.

"There *has* been!" exclaimed Connie, her brown eyes wide.

"No!" he responded, emphatically. And then he added less emphatically, "Well, not really, no. Just mutterings here and there, but nothing along the lines of George and Jorge."

"Mutterings such as?" pressed Anne.

Harvey Freeman nervously cleared his throat and glanced around for a means of escape. There was none. Everyone, visitors included, was behaving. Finally, he sighed and muttered, "It's nothing."

"Tell us about this 'nothing,'" Tammy urged, grinning mischievously.

"Well, there was a middle-aged couple in town earlier in the week," he explained, grudgingly. "They saw the sign pointing toward it outside town and asked about it. I'd told them what little I knew: that it was abandoned, decrepit, and kind of spooky. I also told them that, because of hazards brought on by its age and lack of upkeep, it was off limits to the public. They'd joked about it being a perfect setting for a haunted house around Halloween."

"Hmm," murmured Anne. "Quite."

"Off limits to the public," he repeated. "That includes you three."

"But if we had permission …" began Connie.

"The owner's dead," Harvey interjected. "Who's going to give you permission?"

"Oh, yeah, I forgot," the teen sighed.

"How are we supposed to find the ghost if we can't go there?" Tammy asked.

"There are no such things as ghosts!" declared Harvey.

"Even so," Anne murmured, "something—or someone—frightened George and Jorge last night."

"Technically speaking," said the police cadet, "it was early this morning."

"Nevertheless, there is obviously *something* going on up there," said Anne adamantly, "and I fully intend to find out what!"

"You're not permitted—"

"Fiddlesticks!" countered Anne, firmly. "There's a mystery that needs solving, and I am going to solve it!"

"But—"

"Preferably with your help, Harvey," she said, "or without your help, if necessary!"

"I'm doomed," he muttered, no longer standing ramrod straight. "It never fails … you're going to get me fired …"

"I'll put in a good word with the chief if you cooperate," Anne told him, smiling sweetly.

"I am *so* going to get canned!"

"Oh, ye of little faith!" laughed Tammy.

"Don't quote me Shakespeare," grumbled the tall teen.

"The Bible! That's what Jesus said to his disciples when they seemed to doubt His divinity," corrected Tammy, who then sighed, "Really, Harvey, I despair of you sometimes!"

"Whatever," he sighed, defeated.

"I'll talk to Pater this evening," Anne said. "In the meantime, I think we should go and have a word with the two who were actually involved."

"Do you think that's wise?" asked Connie. "I mean, while they're armed?"

"As long as we stand perfectly still, they won't hit us!" joked Tammy with a chuckle.

"That's probably true," admitted Harvey as he fell in with the three younger teens.

The foursome weaved through the rapidly growing crowd of festival attendees, bumping and jostling some, and being bumped and jostled by others. The sounds were loud and varied. There were the calls of those running the dozens of booths and rides competing with the chatter of the multitudes. No one could really understand much of what was being said—or shouted—but that didn't stop anyone.

It took a bit longer than intended to find the two fourteen-year-olds as they had moved on from the shooting gallery. When at last they were located, it was at the booth selling hand-dipped caramel apples. They were hemming and hawing as they looked over the collection of sweet goodies, trying to make up their minds. The four older teens watched with amused smiles as the younger ones struggled with their decisions.

"Get the biggest," whispered Connie, just loud enough to be heard.

The two boys turned, startled.

"That's what I've been saying!" George declared, recovering first.

"But if we do not eat it all, then there will be waste," Jorge said, a thoughtful furrow on his brow.

"So, we'll just have to eat it all then," George told his best friend, firmly.

"But I do not know that I can eat a large one," explained Jorge.

"Here's a thought," sighed Harvey. "George, you get a large one, and Jorge, you get one that's more your size."

Tammy looked at the cadet. "You are as wise as Solomon."

He glanced over at the auburn-haired teen and shook his head. "You're a nut."

"Ah!" she replied. "But I'm a *happy* nut, and that's what matters!"

"Shall we get back to the matter at hand?" Anne asked, mildly annoyed. She returned her attention to her younger brother and his best friend. "I would like to hear your side of the story, oh brother mine."

"Story?" he inquired as he chewed on a piece of a particularly large caramel apple.

"Your little adventure last night," prodded Harvey, "up at the manor where you *were not* supposed to be."

"Ah!" the youth said, swallowing his masticated morsel. "I say, these are quite good! Have one?"

"No, thank you," sighed his sister. "Look, you two, let's go over to the other end of the Common—where there are fewer distractions—and have a chat."

"I need to hang around this end," explained Harvey.

"To maintain the illusion of the presence of law and order?" responded Tammy, smiling.

"What did I ever do to you?" he countered, and off he walked.

"You really shouldn't tease him so much," said Connie. "You know how sensitive he is."

"But it's so easy!" laughed Tammy.

"Come along, you two," Anne said as she started off with the two boys, "if you want to be in on this."

The five teens walked the length of the Common to the north end where the crowd was much smaller. They found an empty park bench directly across the street from the Ordinary Bed-and-Breakfast, a colorful, mid-19th century, Victorian-style two-story brick house with a deep, open veranda across its front. It was currently under the management of Tammy's aunt, Ruth Gilman, a forty-six-year-old retired Marine Drill Instructor. The boys were settled onto the bench before the grilling.

"All right, you!" Tammy Coleman started off in her best tough-cop voice. "Where was you on the night of the 3rd? And no funny business, see?"

Anne Hambaugh looked over at her friend with a blank expression on her face. "What, pray tell, was that?"

"Jimmy Cagney?"

"Oh, no," said Connie Bascomb, shaking her head sadly. "No, no, no. Not even a poor facsimile thereof. No."

Anne laughed. "It was a nice try, though!"

"Thank you," responded Tammy. "I do try."

"Can we get on with the inquisition?" asked George Hambaugh. "We've mischief to get up to waiting."

"That I do not doubt," Connie sighed.

Anne took a seat on the bench beside her brother. "For starters, what prompted you two to go to the manor?"

"Well, the last time we were up there," George explained, "a couple of weeks ago, we were caught—"

"I recall the 3a.m. return," Anne murmured.

"—so, we went back to finish that, er, adventure."

"It was *his* idea," added Jorge Bustamante, nudging his best friend in the ribs.

"*That* I believe, *too*," chimed in Connie.

"All right, you went back to finish your initial adventure," acknowledged Anne. "Then what happened?"

"Well, we were doing all right," her brother said, his hazel eyes lighting up as he spoke. "We had ridden our bikes there—"

"In the middle of the night?" Tammy asked, doubtfully.

"*Also*, his idea," added Jorge.

"Ah, *mi amigo*," said George, "who was it who went on about a hidden treasure?"

"I didn't mean to go hunting for it in the middle of the night!" declared Jorge.

"We would have been caught had we gone looking for it during the day!" countered George.

"But you *were* caught," Tammy pointed out.

"Twice," added Connie, smirking just a little.

"Yes, well, that *is* true," conceded George with a slight shrug of defeat.

"You were looking for the hidden treasure," prodded Anne. "Where?"

"Where?" repeated her brother.

"I mean, did you have some type of clue—"

"Or a map!" interjected Tammy.

"A treasure map is good!" added Connie.

"And very handy," agreed Tammy.

"The whole 'X' marks the spot thing!" Connie went on happily.

"You two are *not* helping," sighed Anne, addressing her two grinning girlfriends.

"Oh!" Tammy exaggerated.

"Sorry!" said Connie, over-dramatically.

"Are we done?" asked George, hopefully.

"No, you are most definitely *not* done," his sister said, flatly. "Did you have any kind of clue that told you where to look?"

"No," said Jorge. "I mean, not really. The rumor had always been—at least, for as long as I can remember—that there was a clue to the treasure's whereabouts within the walls of the manor. That was what we went to find: that clue."

"But you had no clue exactly where that clue was, right?" Tammy asked.

"That is true," admitted Jorge.

"So," murmured Connie, thoughtfully "you had no clue to the clue."

"Yes," replied George.

"So," added Tammy, suppressing a smile, "what you're saying is … you were clueless."

"They aren't the only ones," muttered Anne. "Are you two quite finished? I would like to learn what they knew sometime during the reign of the current monarch!"

Her two friends burst into laughter while the two boys, with perplexed expressions, looked at all three older teens.

"The thing is," George finally said, "that we went up to explore the old place, and if we stumbled across the rumored clue, well, all the better, right?"

"We were in there less than fifteen minutes," added Jorge, "when we saw something move in the deep shadows."

"A ghost?" asks Tammy.

The two boys looked at one another, and then at the seventeen-year-old. They shrugged their response to her.

"Then," said Anne, "you didn't actually *see* anything."

Her brother took a deep breath, and then released a troubled sigh. "That's just it, oh sister mine, we don't know *what* we saw … or *didn't* see."

Anne looked over at Jorge. "What do you think it was?"

"You know," he replied, "it's hard to say. It may have been nothing, you know? Or, it may have been *something*. It was a movement in the deep shadow—"

"Where?" asked Anne. "Where was this deep shadow? Where were you when you saw it?"

"We were in the main foyer," her brother answered. "I guess you call it the grand hall, like what *Grandmere* and *Grandpere* have at the old family estate near Tewkesbury, in Gloucestershire County."

"Where?" asked Tammy.

"Never mind," Anne said to her friend. To her brother she nodded, "Very good. Now then, this foyer, what could you tell about it?"

"It was wide," said Jorge.

"And high," added George.

"We were using small flashlights, you see," Jorge told them, "and they didn't cast much of a beam."

"And mine was dead, anyway," George explained, "so we had only the one."

"Did you shine the light on whatever it was that moved in the shadows?" asked Tammy.

"George saw it, and by the time I brought the light around, it—whatever it was—was gone."

"Was it a person?" asked Anne.

The two boys shrugged.

"What are you thinking, Anne?" inquired Connie.

"Well, if what they saw was another person who was—more than likely—on the same quest as our stalwart explorers here," answered Anne, "then that would solve the 'ghost' mystery."

"Did you see anyone while you were there?" queried Tammy, looking down at the boys.

"No," said Jorge.

"How did the cops know that you were there?" asked Connie.

The boys sat in thoughtful silence.

"It would seem that someone *was* there at the same time you were," Anne said, confidently. "Someone who did not want you there."

"Because you guys were cramping their style!" declared Tammy.

"So, they called the cops to get you removed!" added Connie, excitedly.

"But we saw no one!" insisted Jorge.

"That is not the point," said Anne, gently. "He, or she, or even they, saw you and wanted you two out of the way. A simple anonymous phone call brings the local constabulary and the problem—that being the two of you—is solved."

"Does that mean there *is* a treasure to be found up there?" George asked, somewhat dejected.

"Who knows?" responded his sister.

"That's been the story for, well, forever," Tammy told him.

Connie, usually the less adventurous of the three girls, looked in the direction of the MacLeod Manor. "So, who do we talk to about getting permission to investigate?"

Anne smiled. "We might as well start with Ordinary's Chief of Police."

Tammy laughed lightly. "You do have an 'in' with him!"

TWO

Interim Chief of Police Nathan Hambaugh brought his patrol car to a stop behind City Hall at his designated parking space. He had done a slow swing along the Circus Maximus and had managed to avoid being hit several times by vehicles backing out of spaces, and he had managed to avoid hitting several people who had darted out into the one-way street. Seated in his car where it was safe and quiet, he allowed himself to breathe. His memory drifted back to when he was a youth and his family would attend the Annual Ordinary Independence Day Festival. He remembered the rides brought in by the small, touring carnival, and all the booths with inexpensive prizes just waiting to be won. An inadvertent glance into the rearview mirror reflected a smiling man now of sixty-two. He had been eighteen when he had last attended the festival; forty-four years had passed.

A sad sigh escaped him.

He tried to remember why he had so abruptly left Ordinary all those years ago. He knew there had been a major disagreement with his parents—specifically, with his father. They had always had differences of opinions on things, whereas Raymond had been almost a clone of their father. He had the same disagreements with his older brother. What he could not recall was what the knock-down-drag-out had been about!

All that led to being happily married to his beautiful wife (although her parents almost did not allow that to happen) and being the proud father of two wonderful kids. Still, he had to admit, his son caused him more than a few gray hairs. But then, his son was very much like him when he was a young teen: adventurous, exploring, and usually in trouble. A little laugh escaped him as he got out of the police vehicle and locked the door, and then, just like that, the little laugh vanished.

His father had told him to grow up.

After his last minor run-in and being brought home in the middle of the night, his father had pushed him—none too gently—into a chair and shouted his displeasure. His father had been livid, and his voice awakened his mother and brother, who all sided with his father.

Why won't you grow up! his father had shouted in those early hours of the morning. And it had gone on and on. His list of failings, the trouble he had caused the family, on and on.

It was then that he had decided, at the age of eighteen, to leave home and to never return. He decided to cut all contact with his family and make his own way in the world. His one regret had been how much such a decision would—and did—hurt his mother, but he had no choice. His father had been very clear: *grow up or get out*!

So, he got out.

His immediate departure the following morning resulted in his enlistment in the United States Army, eventually leading to his becoming a member of the elite Green Berets. It was 1966, and he grew up fast in the jungles of Vietnam. That experience led to a very successful career in the military, followed by a successful career with the U.S. State Department.

And now, he thought, as he unlocked the back door to the city hall building, which also housed the Ordinary Police Department, *here I am, back home again*. He felt a tear run down his cheek; that had not happened even on the day he left home. *Forty-four years*, he thought with a sigh. It was as he walked the silent hall toward his office that he wept for what he had lost, and what he had denied his children. They never knew his parents—their paternal grandparents—because of his stubbornness. And when his parents had passed on—many years before, now—he had denied himself their mourning. As he sat in the chair at his desk, he admitted to himself, for the first time, that his father had been right; he had not grown up—not entirely—but, instead, had remained selfish and immature.

He closed his eyes and prayed through his body-shuddering sobs.

His cell phone vibrating on the desk in front him forced him to regain control of his emotions, to wipe his red eyes, and to wipe his nose. It was his daughter calling; he could not let on that he had been crying for an unchangeable past. Picking up the device, he pressed the green button to receive the call.

"Hello, Anne," he said. "What sort of trouble are you getting everyone into?"

"Pater!" she declared. "I would *never*!"

He smiled. "I know. What's up?"

"Can we investigate the Macleod Manor?" she asked.

That question caught him off guard, though he did not know why. It only stood to reason that, in exploring the ghost story, she would want to do this. "Well, I don't know," he replied. "The only way I can see that happening is if you are part of the police investigation into the whole trespassing and ghost-sighting thing."

"Oh, thank you!" she blurted out happily.

"Wait a minute!" he laughed. "I said '*if*!"

"Oh, Pater," sighed a suddenly dejected teenager.

"Is Harvey with you?" queried her father.

"No, we frightened him off," was her response.

"Why does that not surprise me?" he muttered before he realized what he had just said.

"Pater!"

"All right, dear heart, don't get your knickers in a twist," he laughed. "I'll talk to Harvey about investigating all the shenanigans going on at the manor, and you can accompany him as a member of the press to ensure the transparency of the investigation."

"Oh, that *is* good, Pater!" she declared happily.

"I thought you'd approve," he admitted. "When would you like to go up there?"

"Tomorrow, I suppose," she told him. "We want to go by Elisa Rialdi's house and speak with her."

"And Mrs. Raynes?"

"We tracked her down here and spoke with her already. She was a wealth of information! We're hoping that Miss Rialdi will also provide us with some background information. I would like to know as much as I can before going up to the manor to minimize our stumbling around in search of answers."

"That certainly makes sense," her father agreed. "All right, you go do your background legwork, and I'll have a word with my cadet."

"Thank you, Pater."

"You're welcome."

They exchanged 'I love you' and disconnected. He sat there looking at the phone in his hand. How different she was from him—for which he was grateful—and how like him was his son—for which he had mixed feelings. He loved his children, even when they pushed his buttons.

After a minute, he dialed Harvey's cell number. It was answered on the second ring. "Hey, Harvey," he said.

"Hey, Chief!" responded the nineteen-year-old, cheerfully.

"I have an assignment for you."

Silence.

"Are you still there?" the chief of police asked, unsure.

"Yes, sir." It was not a cheerful reply this time.

"I want you to lead the investigation into the shenanigans that have been going on at the MacLeod Manor," explained Nathan Hambaugh.

"Yes, sir." It was still not a cheerful reply. If anything, it seemed less cheerful than the previous one.

"The boys weren't the only ones up there," the chief went on. "I want you to find out—if you can—who else was there. Who made that call that got the boys picked up? Think you can handle that?"

"Oh, yes, sir," was the unhappy response.

"Harvey," said the chief, "is there a problem?"

"Well, sir, it's just that … well, your daughter …"

"Spit it out, lad," the older man encouraged.

"I don't want to spend the night up there, sir!"

Nathan was quiet for a moment, and then said, "Well, hopefully that won't be necessary. Plan on starting your investigation tomorrow."

"Yes, sir."

"Oh, and, Harvey …"

"Sir?"

"The press will be with you."

"Anne."

"I'm afraid so."

There came a long sigh, followed by, "Yes, sir."

"Harvey, this isn't a 'just because' investigation," the chief told him. "There is something going on up there, obviously, and someone is behind that something. I want to know who and why."

"The 'why' is easy, sir: treasure."

"More than likely, that's true," agreed the chief. "And just maybe, during the course of this investigation, we can solve that little mystery. Frankly, I'd like to let the world know that there is *no treasure* and be done with that nonsense."

"I'll do my best, sir."

"I know you will, Harvey, and I'm grateful to you."

"Thank you, sir."

The call ended on that exchange.

Nathan Hambaugh placed his cell phone on the desk in front of him and stared at it for a moment, and then his gold-flecked hazel eyes wandered out the window to the tree-shrouded bluff that overlooked the lake. He pursed his lips as he pondered the whole MacLeod legend. When he had been a boy the legend had been alive and well, and on more than a few occasions he had been escorted home by a local officer. *In a way*, he thought, *it would be a shame to put that legend to rest.* He smiled at the memories, and at how much George was like him!

ᴄᴏᴄᴏᴄᴏᴄᴏᴄᴏᴄᴏᴄᴏᴄᴏᴄᴏᴄᴏ

Harvey Freeman stared blankly at the phone in his hand, slowly shaking his head. "Why me?" he forlornly muttered.

Returning the device to his pocket, he resumed his foot patrol, although this time it was more like an aimless meander. His focus was most certainly not on the task at hand, but, rather, occupied with tomorrow and all that day would entail. He gave the wooded bluff a black look of displeasure. And then he sighed, surrendering to the inevitable. He tried to look at the bright side; he would be investigating, on his own, a crime—albeit, a minor offense—that would illustrate to everyone—particularly his mother and step-father—that he could be a good police officer. They wanted him to go to work at the Ordinary Savings & Loan Bank, following in their footsteps, but he could think of nothing more boring than being a teller. His mother was a senior teller; Wolfgang Radke was the new bank manager.

The nineteen-year-old moped as he meandered through the throng of revelers. No one seemed to notice his unhappiness. He had managed to completely tune out the noise and commotion that encircled him … until he was bowled over by a runner. He let out a yelp of surprise as he pitched forward, landing face down on the lush lawn of the Common. It was then that he heard people shouting … mostly at him.

"Get that guy!" one yelled.

"He snatched a purse!" bellowed another.

"Get your backside up, boy!" shouted a third. "Go get that thief!"

Harvey quickly scrambled to his feet, brushing himself off as he looked for the runner.

"Over there, boy!" hollered Voice Number Three. "Are you blind, boy?"

The young cadet turned hotly toward the voice: Abner Newby, the thirty-five-year-old owner/operator of Ordinary Bait & Tackle Shoppe, and the local loud-mouth. Without a word to the older man, Harvey took off at a full gallop after the fleeing runner.

Although the runner—wearing a plain, black hoodie—had a sizable lead, Harvey was younger, faster, and determined to get the person who knocked him down in front of the gathering of the entire townspeople. While the distance between the two was steadily decreasing, Harvey was beginning to doubt he would catch the fleeing thief. They had run most of the length of the Common when, suddenly, the hooded figure turned southward, weaved through the parked cars, and jumped into a waiting lime-green AMC Gremlin. In a billowing, black cloud of exhaust, the vehicle lurched once and then roared eastward out of town.

Harvey came to a stop on the sidewalk, leaning against an old pickup truck and breathing hard. He watched as the getaway car quickly disappeared. He tried to recall as much as he could about the runner, but there was nothing: jeans, sneakers, and a dark hoodie … His eyes settled on the handbag in the street where the Gremlin had been. With a sigh, he walked over and picked it up. There was no cash, but the driver license identified the owner as Marjorie Nielson, the forty-year-old wife of Ordinary Police Sergeant Bradley Nielson and mother of Mitch Cavenaugh, and the receptionist/clerk at the Ordinary Cemetery.

"Great," he mumbled, despondently. "Brad will be just *thrilled* that I let the purse-snatcher get away."

As he headed back toward the main crowd at the western end of the Common, he saw five young people nearby looking at him. He straightened up and walked over to where they were, two standing and three sitting.

"Hey," he muttered his greeting.

"Hey, yourself," responded Tammy Coleman. "You were making up some serious ground there, Harv!"

"A lot of good it did," he sighed, though inside he appreciated the review.

"Well," added Connie Bascomb, sympathetically, "he *did* have a head start."

Holding up the purse, he said, "Explain that to Mitch's mom."

"I'm sure she will understand," Anne Hambaugh said, encouragingly.

"She might, but Brad will be fit to be tied," Harvey countered, shaking his head.

"There's no way *he* could have done any better," Tammy gently admonished.

"Yeah, well ..."

"Ugly thing, that getaway car," George added, hopefully helpfully.

"Not too many lime-green 1975 AMC Gremlins around, I would expect," Jorge Bustamante commented. "It might be easy enough to track down."

Harvey looked down at the quiet Hispanic teen. "You're right ..." he murmured, his blue eyes lighting up. "You're right, by George!"

"Jorge," said George.

Caught unaware, Harvey stammered, "What?"

"You said 'by George,'" explained George, "but you should have said 'by Jorge.'"

"I ..." began Harvey, and then he finished with a long sigh, "Never mind."

"Does this happen often?" Anne inquired.

"What? Confusing me?" growled Harvey.

She laughed lightly. "No, silly, I meant purse-snatching."

"Sorry" he replied, somewhat sheepishly. And then he continued, "Often, no, but on occasion, especially at a gathering like this: large, outdoors, easy escape routes." He looked carefully at her thoughtful freckled face. "Why?"

"Oh, I was just wondering," she said, dismissively. "Odd that he would knock you down."

"Not really," Tammy spoke up. "It actually gave him time to create distance between him and Harvey."

"Ah!" declared Connie, grinning. "Method to the madness!"

"Something like that," agreed Tammy.

"So, it was a team effort," murmured Anne.

"'Team effort?'" queried the cadet.

"The actual purse-snatcher," pointed out Anne, "and the driver."

"In the ugliest getaway car ever!" laughed George.

"Which could be to Harvey's advantage," Jorge said.

"Well, right now it's my best clue," the police cadet sighed. Holding up the purse, "But right now, I have some stolen property to return." Looking down at Anne, he added, "I spoke with Chief Hambaugh, by the way." And, with that, he walked away.

"Poor guy," Connie said, watching him go. "Finds out he has to work with us on this mystery and gets knocked over by a purse-snatcher, all in the same day."

"Yes," agreed Tammy with a little grin. "Some guys get all the luck."

ଓଓଓଓଓଓଓଓଓଓ

The home of Elisa Rialdi, Ordinary's seventy-seven-year-old retired librarian, was a quaint cottage, a small, two-bedroom house built in the early 1950s on the lake at the southern end of town. It was not an extravagant structure, as was more common of the houses built by her affluent neighbors. On five acres of lush woodland, the encroaching neighborhood of the well-to-do was kept at bay. The drive from the main road to her front door was a gentle curve, with an entrance and an exit, through the cool trees. Tammy's white 1967 Mustang convertible rolled to a stop at the picket fence that wrapped around the small house.

"Is it all right if we all go in?" the seventeen-year-old driver inquired, hopefully.

Anne looked at the serene home, thought for a moment, and then said, "It should be fine. Did I mention that she has a dog?"

"I knew she had a dog," Connie chimed in. "What kind of dog does a retired librarian keep around the house?"

"Chihuahua?" suggested Tammy.

"No," Connie said, shaking her head. "A cockapoo, I think."

Anne looked at her best friend. "A *what*?"

"A Cockapoo. You know, a cross between a cocker spaniel and a poodle," explained Connie.

Anne smiled. "Ah! Um, I think not." She opened the gate of the picket fence. "Do follow me."

The trio walked toward the front door, but before reaching it they were met by a large dog with a solid, muscular build, a thick white coat, a large head and a black nose. It did not come across as being a vicious dog but considering its size—and the fact that it had firmly planted itself in front of them—Tammy and Connie were not eager to test that theory. They stopped at the midway point while Anne continued.

"He is a Maremmano-Abruzzese Sheepdog," she explained to her silent friends. Holding out her hand to the huge head with its wet, black nose, she murmured, in a soft voice, "Do you remember me, Amico?"

The front door to the cottage opened, and a petite woman with dark eyes stood before them. Her dark, silver-streaked hair was in an attractive pixie-bob haircut. In one hand she held a leather-bound book that was showing its years. Elisa Rialdi looked at Anne and smiled. "But of course, he remembers you, Anne," she said in a light, pleasant voice. "Amico has a remarkable memory." She looked at the other two teens. "It's quite safe to approach." Adding mischievously, "He's been fed."

Connie and Tammy did as they were told, allowing the impressive white dog to sniff their hands. This ritual concluded, Amico returned to his place of concealment to await the next unsuspecting visitor. The three teenagers followed Elisa into her home, to the sitting room filled with artifacts from her lifetime of travel. They sat quietly as their hostess put together a tea tray, complete with delicious, light, homemade biscuits.

"Now then," said Elisa, having ensured that everyone had been properly served, "what brings our town's pre-eminent journalist and her cohorts to my door?"

Tammy chuckled. "I don't think I've ever been described as a cohort before."

"It sounds better than being called a crony, though," Connie told her, smiling.

"True," admitted Tammy. "Very true."

"You will have to forgive my comedy relief, Miss Rialdi," sighed Anne.

The older woman was smiling at the three teens seated on the tapestry-upholstered divan. "It's good to have friends like that, who keep life enjoyable, if not interesting. One can't be serious all the time."

"Oh, yes, I know," agreed Anne, with a slight nod, "but, even so…"

"Let me see if I can guess why you're here," Elisa said, sitting back in her matching tapestry-upholstered armchair. "You want to pick my brain about the legend surrounding the Angus MacLeod and the MacLeod Manor. Am I right?"

Anne's smile widened. She loved this woman. "You are so right!"

With a lovely little laugh, Elisa said, "Well, I'm not just a pretty face, you know!" Sipping her steaming tea, she asked, "What do you want to know?"

"Connie and I have lived here all our lives," Tammy said, quickly, "and there's always been the story of the old sea captain, and his manor, and his treasure, but it's one of those things you always hear about but never really do anything with."

"It wasn't something discussed in school because, other than being local folklore," Connie continued, "it really had no bearing on the greater schemes of worldly things. It wasn't a part of world history, you know?"

"But *all* history—no matter how seemingly infinitesimal—is a part of world history, my dears," Elisa told them, gently. "Perhaps not a large part, or even a significant part in the grander scheme of things, but a part nonetheless."

"Oh!" declared Anne, taking notes. "Can I use that in my article?"

"Of course, my dear!" laughed Elisa. "Goodness, but you girls have brightened my day!"

"I'm glad," said Anne. "We've spoken with Mrs. Raynes about what she knows, and with my Aunt Andrea, but, as the long-time librarian—and the closest this town has to a local historian—we wanted to speak with you as well."

"'Local historian?'" queried Elisa, surprised. "Oh my, no pressure there!"

"We learned quite a bit from our other sources," admitted Anne, "mostly general information, but I was hoping that, perhaps, there was something *not* generally known about the Legend of Captain Angus MacLeod."

"Oh, good title for your article!" declared Connie.

"Something not generally known," murmured Elisa, thoughtfully. She sat quietly, sipping her tea and pondering the question. "You know that he had only one eye, I suppose …"

"Really?" perked up Tammy.

"Or so the story goes," admitted Elisa. "He was not a handsome man and, while I have not seen it myself, there is supposed to be a portrait of the old sea captain hanging somewhere in the manor … or perhaps it's now in our local museum."

"We'll look for that when we go to the manor tomorrow," murmured Anne, making a note.

"The manor has not been untouched since the couple vanished," went on Elisa, "and the things that are there—the books, artwork, and such—have probably not weathered well. The heat of the summers and the dampness of the winters are not kind to things like that. But no one has been able to find even a remote next-of-kin to whom to turn it all over."

"I expect that any next-of-kin would not want the responsibility," said Connie. "The cost to renovate and upgrade it to code would be enormous, I'd expect."

"That is true," agreed Elisa with a nod. "At the same time, it has great potential as a tourist attraction or country hotel. But that is neither here nor there. You want to know its deepest, darkest secrets."

"It has secrets?" asked Tammy, sitting up straight and almost spilling her tea.

"Doesn't every abandoned, centuries-old manor house?" said Elisa enigmatically, adding a playful wink. She got up from her armchair and went to the floor-to-ceiling built-in hardwood bookcase that occupied one entire wall. It was not all books, but, rather, a serene combination of leather-bound books and unique antique *objets d'art*. "Oh, dear," she murmured as she extracted a thin volume, "I've fallen behind in my dusting!"

The three teens sat quietly as they watched the older woman return to her chair.

"I picked this up little book while in Scotland many years ago." She paused as she recollected. "Thirty years ago, give or take a decade. But, anyway, I came across it in a small, out-of-the-way book shop in the small fishing town of Pittenweem."

"'Pittenweem?'" Connie and Tammie asked in unison.

"I've heard of it," said Anne, "though I've never been. It's on Scotland's east coast, I believe."

"Right," nodded Elisa. "In the East Neuk of Fife, if my memory serves me—which it doesn't always. The name comes from the ancient Pictish language, for those who may not know," she explained, giving two of the teens a wink. "It means 'The Place of the Caves.' It's a quaint little town, with its red-and-white architecture and crow-stepped gables."

"It sounds lovely," said Connie, dreamily.

"Oh, it is!" admitted Elisa. "Anyway," she continued, holding up the thin volume, "I came across this book quite by accident. It's a journal, actually, handwritten a very long time ago by members of Angus MacLeod's family. That I found it in Scotland and not out here has always been a mystery to me."

"It's also possible," said Anne, "that, over the many decades, it somehow found its way from here back to Scotland. Acquired—legally, or otherwise—by person or persons unknown, it could very well have made the journey."

"That is a distinct possibility," admitted Elisa, nodding. "And that would certainly explain things."

"So, what's in it," inquired Tammy, just slightly impatient.

"It's a glimpse into his family's history," Elisa told them as she opened the volume, and then she looked into its pages in silence. "The last few entries are, I believe, done by the hand of Angus MacLeod himself as there is a mention of his travel here, and his decision to uproot. It isn't an easy read, being hand-written in the Scottish of nearly two centuries ago."

"Does he indicate *why* he decided to literally uproot house and home?" asked Anne. "From the sound of him, it wouldn't be something done on a whim, or with no reason."

"To that I would have to agree," nodded Elisa. "It's hard to believe that he was driven away as he seemed to have feared nothing."

"That we know of," added Connie.

"Maybe it was his in-laws," suggested Tammy. "His wife was considerably younger, right? They may not have been too keen on that, or very forgiving."

The three others looked at the teen.

"What?" she retorted around a mouthful of tea biscuit.

"Sometimes," said Connie, "you just amaze us with what comes out of your mind and mouth."

"I really don't know how likely that is," said Elisa, "but it's as good a reason as any. I am inclined to think, however, that it had something to do with clinging to his riches. Perhaps the government wanted more than he thought was their fair share, or, perhaps, distant family members may have been appearing out of the woodwork wanting what they felt they were entitled to."

"Whatever the reason," murmured Anne, "it happened over a period of a few years. I mean, disassembling the manor and marking each stone, then the shipping, and then the reassembly literally stone-by-stone."

"He does write a little about that," Elisa responded, tapping the open journal. "He never seems to say much, nor very often, but he does comment on things. He writes about the workers who are disassembling his ancestral home, and none too kindly. There is the rare comment about his wife, not unkind, but also not flattering. Angus was an odd man, and not an easy one to read."

"What was his wife's name?" asked Connie, finishing her tea.

Elisa Rialdi flipped back a few pages, perusing them carefully. "Eleanor," she finally answered. "Eleanor O'Ceallaigh."

"She was Irish, then," murmured Anne.

"Is that significant?" Tammy asked.

Anne shrugged. "Probably not. I just find it interesting. Why not a local lass, I ask myself?"

"Maybe because all the local girls knew what an old curmudgeon he was!" laughed Connie.

"More than likely," agreed Elisa, chuckling. "That, and he would have her away from the influence of her family. The immediate influence, at any rate."

"So," said Anne, "he moved the whole kit and caboodle here to a bluff overlooking the lake—or loch, if you're Scottish—then what?"

"He didn't seem to have very kind things to say about the workers reassembling his manor, either," Elisa told them as she scanned the last few pages. "At least one died, apparently, from a fall, which did not help matters. Another vanished near the end of the project and Angus was accused of killing the fellow. He does make mention, at one point, that he suspects they—or some of them, at any rate—are after his treasure, so he must hide it."

"Where?" asked the three teens in unison, eyes wide with excitement.

Elisa read quietly for several moments, and then told them, "He doesn't say."

Three hopeful faces fell.

"Well," said the older woman, "you really wouldn't expect him to, would you? Had he, then whoever found this journal would have found the treasure, and there would be no legend today."

"She has a point," commented Tammy.

Anne was quiet for a moment, and then asked, "What does he say about his treasure?"

"If I am reading this final entry right," responded Elisa, "he writes: the key to the treasure is in the time."

"I hate riddles," moaned Tammy.

"I know, right?" sighed, Connie.

"'The key to the treasure is in the time,'" murmured Anne, thoughtfully. "Time. Time. Time as in timepiece, perhaps?"

"His treasure is in a clock, maybe?" asked Tammy, hopefully.

"Or, the key—as in *clue*—to his treasure is in a clock!" exclaimed Connie.

"There is one other thing," said Elisa Rialdi, her voice soft and enigmatic. "I spent much of my life traveling—when not working in the library—and I have seen and heard many strange things. Most I dismissed as fairy tales because they were so fanciful, but there is one that I was never able to dismiss. It may very well have had to do with our dear sea captain, Angus MacLeod." She hesitated, as if debating with herself on whether to tell what she knew. Finally, she said, "I heard a tale while I was traveling in Central America many, many years ago. More years ago, as a matter of fact, than I care to remember. Sometime during the reign of Moctezuma II—which was between 1502 and 1520—a jewel-encrusted gold statuette of the goddess Tlaltecuhtli—the one who gives and devours life—had been made for one of his consorts—either Teotlalco or Tlapalizquixochtzin."

"What?" said Anne, suddenly. "A jewel-encrusted statuette?"

A frown touched Tammy's brow. "As in Dashiell Hammett's *The Maltese Falcon*?"

"Is this on the level?" asked Connie, her brown eyes wide.

"Yes. In a way. And very much so," Elisa answered each of the questions. "I know how it sounds, which is why I've never spoken to anyone about it—not that there has been much opportunity—but it's true. At least, I think it is. Now, you must keep in mind that what I am sharing is just a story I heard a very long time ago. Quite honestly, I had forgotten about it until just today while we were discussing Angus MacLeod and his manor. What jarred my memory is that buried in the journal—his part of the journal—he makes a single mention of an *ìomhaigh*."

Three young faces stared at the retired librarian.

"It's Scots Gaelic for statue," she explained gently.

"And you think that his statue is this … this … Aztec goddess?" Tammy asked in disbelief.

"Well," said Elisa, "perhaps. On occasion the statuette would surface, usually through the violent end of its current owner, and then disappear again with its new owner. Angus MacLeod's last voyage—before his sudden retirement—was to Central America, where he picked up a hefty cargo worth a fortune. There were those who said that his last run was sufficient to set him up for life, and maybe that's true, but I am not so sure. You see, one thing Angus was was greedy. For him, enough was never enough. This was why he took on the most perilous, most suicidal, shipping runs."

"So, while in Central America," Connie mused, "he came across the owner of this statuette and … purchased it?"

Elisa shook her head. "The story I heard was that almost two hundred years ago a European seaman learned of the whereabouts of the statuette and *took* it."

"He stole it?" Anne queried, surprised.

"Yes, but not before a struggle," Elisa nodded. "Now, keep in mind, the goddess Tlaltecuhtli required many human sacrifices to sustain her—"

"So, someone always died when she changed hands," finished Anne, solemnly.

"So goes the legend," nodded Elisa.

"But how likely is it that Captain Macleod is the unnamed European seaman that pinched the statuette of what's-her-name?" pressed Tammy.

"That was MacLeod's last voyage," Elisa replied. "He was not very old when he suddenly gave up the sea and went into seclusion. He came out of seclusion on three noted occasions: the first being long enough to take a younger woman as his wife; the second to travel to America—as in: Ordinary—and the third to move all his worldly possessions—including the manor, to the bluff."

Connie thought for a moment, and then asked, "*If*—and it's a very big 'if'—Angus MacLeod was the seaman who took the statuette, and *if* the statuette he took was, indeed, this Aztec goddess, and *if* he was able to move it undiscovered from Scotland to here …" She hesitated. "I lost track of where I was going with that."

"Does the sudden disappearance of MacLeod and his wife mark another change in ownership?" inquired Anne. "And if so, who got the statuette?"

"I don't know the answer to that," admitted Elisa, smiling at the young investigative journalist. "But I suspect that if anyone can piece together that puzzle it is you, Anne, and your friends."

"I'm still having trouble getting my brain around this whole stolen mysterious statuette thing," sighed Tammy. "It sounds like a sappy storyline from some old movie."

"Just beware of the Fat Man," said Elisa in a serious voice.

Connie sat up straight. "There's a Fat Man?"

Elisa laughed lightly. "I doubt it, but it sounded good, didn't it?"

"And we mustn't forget his clue," Anne reminded her friends. "'*The key to the treasure is in the time.*'"

The four sat in silence as they pondered what they had learned over tea. They sipped the hot brew and nibbled on the cookies, and they contemplated what the sea captain had meant.

Finally, Anne said, "We will just have to go up to the manor tomorrow and see what we can find."

"Probably the wisest course of action," agreed Elisa, closing the journal.

The three teens rose from their seats, thanked their hostess for the tea and the information she could glean from the leather-bound volume, and bade them farewell. Once seated in Tammy's convertible, they began to talk excitedly among themselves.

No one noticed the lime-green Gremlin parked up the road, partially hidden by a massive bougainvillea.

❧❧❧❧❧❧❧❧❧❧

Harvey Freeman found Marjorie Nielson to be both grateful and thankful for the return of her purse. She also admitted the thief did not get much as it was her 'back-up' purse used primarily for carrying the odd thing: tissues, a pen or pencil, breath mints, and the like. That way, she explained, there was no money for her to spend. She had made it a point to ask if he was all right after being run over and then chasing the man most of the length of the Common. He hoped that her husband, when he found out, would be equally understanding, if not grateful. But he wasn't going to hold his breath. Sergeant Bradley Nielson was known to have a rather intimidating personality when it suited him.

The nineteen-year-old stood away from the teeming throng of humanity that moved across the Common in—what seemed to him—an undulating wave. Leaning against an oak tree that had been there since before Ordinary was founded, he divided the remainder of his shift writing notes to himself regarding the purse-snatcher incident, and to the upcoming investigation of the trespassing at the manor. He did not really expect much to come of the investigation, but with Anne Hambaugh involved, *anything* could happen!

His blue eyes scrolled across the crowd as it moved in one direction, and then back in another direction. There were far more faces he did not recognize, but that was to be expected. A slender, middle-aged man standing not far away—clean-shaven, with hazel eyes and a scar on his left cheek—smiled and nodded at the youth. Harvey returned the congenial nod and continued his scanning. He could not help but wonder if one of those faces belonged to the purse-snatcher. He admitted to himself that he would be surprised if the thief returned to the scene of the crime so soon. *But then,* he told himself, *if the guy didn't get anything the first time, he just might try again.*

He found himself looking at the vehicles parked along the boundaries of the Common but did not see the lime-green Gremlin. That was a car he could not miss! He found himself wondering why someone—anyone—would use such a car as a means of escape. Or, for that matter, why anyone would have one in the first place. It was not an inconspicuous vehicle by any stretch of the imagination. A thought occurred to him just then, that the thief used such a vehicle to draw attention to it, and away from something else. *But what?* he asked himself.

"Hey," a baritone voice to his right spoke.

Harvey jumped involuntarily, turning to face the speaker and ready for a fight. He found himself facing Mitch Cavanaugh, the son of the purse-snatcher's victim. "You just scared the stuffing out of me!" he admitted, lowering his hands.

The easy-going eighteen-year-old grinned. "Sorry about that. I just wanted to say 'thanks' for helping my mom."

"Not much help," sighed Harvey. "The guy got away."

Mitch shrugged. "It happens, man. Sorry I wasn't here to help," the six-foot football player added. "I was working over at the Senator's place; his irrigation system wasn't working right." The part-time gardener-landscaper glanced around the crowd. "We could've done the guy some serious damage."

Harvey chuckled. "Not too serious, though."

Mitch laughed, but there was something in that laugh that told the cadet his fellow teen that he was not entirely amused. "No, not *too* serious, but enough to make him find another town."

"Or another line of work."

"That, too." Mitch looked through the crowd of happy faces, and asked, "No idea what he looked like?"

"Nope."

"That's a shame."

"Now, Mitch, none of this vigilante stuff!" cautioned Harvey.

"With my step-dad being a cop?" Mitch responded, feigning a hurt expression. "Besides, I have complete confidence that you—or someone—will catch the thief and do the right thing."

"You really want to pound the guy," said Harvey.

"Oh, yeah!" nodded Mitch. "But," he added with a sigh, "in the meantime, I'll focus on work and my hobby."

"What hobby is that?" inquired Harvey, almost dreading the answer.

"I want to be an illustrator," was the surprising response. "Book covers, kid's books, stuff like that."

Harvey looked at the beefy six-foot football player in amazement. "You know, Mitch, I never would have guessed that in a million years!"

"Yeah, well, I don't let many people know," admitted Mitch with a sheepish grin. "It's not what people expect from me."

Putting a hand on Mitch's solid shoulder, Harvey said, "Well, buddy, your secret is safe with me. And all I can say is, follow your dream!"

"Hey, boy!" bellowed a voice from behind the two youths. They turned to see Abner Newby approaching, swaying just slightly. His face was flushed, and his speech was slurred. "You messed that one up, didn't you, boy!"

Harvey Freeman stiffened. "You, sir, are drunk."

"No, I ain't," snarled the owner/operator of Ordinary Bait & Tackle Shoppe. "I haven't even started!"

"Public intoxication is a violation of town ordinance, sir," the cadet continued. "I must ask you to either go home or come with me."

"You'd have to catch me first!" laughed Newby. The man turned quickly, tripped over his feet, and fell on his face, knocking his breath from him.

Mitch Cavanaugh picked up the gasping man. "I'll take him home," he said. "My civic duty, and all that."

"I appreciate it."

"Hey, when are you guys going up to the manor?"

"Tomorrow morning, I guess," sighed Harvey. "Anne's calling the shots as far as the whole ghost and treasure thing is concerned; I'll be there to investigate the trespassing."

"Well, I just might stop by, if that's okay."

"Sure. The more the merrier."

With that, Mitch assisted the staggering Abner Newby away from the Common and all the happy revelers. Harvey watched them go for a moment, and then turned back to the undulating crowd. His blue eyes scanned the mass for a minute before drifting up to the wooded bluff where the decaying MacLeod Manor stood.

❧❧❧❧❧❧❧❧❧❧❧❧

That evening, after the sun had settled beyond the western tree line, Ralph Hale pulled a flat barge out to the middle of the lake. It was nicknamed The Rocket Ship from which the town of Ordinary launched its bi-annual fireworks displays: New Years and Independence Day. The townsfolk gathered around the gazebo on the Common and crowded onto the boardwalk along the lake's edge. Vendors sold snacks and sparklers, and everyone had a good time. Old friends chatted and reminisced and told wide-eyed children how it was done "back in the day."

Anne and her friends gathered at her house, standing on the edge of the lake and chatting quietly. She was lost in thought as she pondered what they had learned earlier that day about the manor and its owner. She was confident that the next day's foray up to the abandoned structure would result in more questions than answers, but she was looking forward to it. Eventually, those questions would be answered, and the mysteries involving the treasure, Macleod, and the trespassers would be revealed. A part of her did not want to find answers that would solve the mysteries around the old manor, but, at the same time, part of her was nosy and wanted to know what happened to Captain Macleod and his young wife.

When the fireworks began, launched from The Rocket Ship, all thought of the legend and mysteries ceased. The gatherings around Ordinary thrilled at the colorful display that went on for well over thirty minutes. It started with a single rocket, and then a couple, and then a few, and then several. With each launching, there were more and more until, at the end, there were a multitude of rockets soaring skyward. The night sky was filled with bombs bursting in air, and colors reflecting off the lake's calm surface.

And then it was quiet.

The sounds faded.

The moon and stars returned to dominate the night sky.

THREE

Monday, July 5th.

Anne Hambaugh was up before the grandfather clock's six morning chimes. She had had a restless night. What she had learned the previous day had gone beyond what she had expected. The background material she had gathered now resulted in a possible—and she emphasized 'possible'—connection to a centuries' old treasure. Rationally, she suspected that the jewel-encrusted gold statuette was nothing more than a fanciful legend, but a romantic part of her deep inside hoped it was true. *But,* she told herself, *what are the odds that Angus MacLeod* was *the seaman who committed the alleged murder and stole the alleged prize?*

Standing at the big bay window and looking out on the tranquil surface of the lake, she could not help but allow her mind to wander. Too much had happened in such a short time. Her troublesome brother and his best friend being spooked at the manor, the purse-snatching incident during the Independence Day festival, and now Elisa Rialdi's information on Angus MacLeod. In a few hours, she would go to her Aunt Andrea to learn more … assuming that there is more to learn. The teen was not entirely convinced.

Her aunt had been a teacher at Ordinary High School for almost thirty years and had amassed quite a wealth of trivial information. Whether the statuette was a part of the trivia was yet to be discovered, but Anne was certain that she would learn something new.

"You're deep in thought," said a voice from close behind, startling her.

She turned quickly to face her father. "Oh, Pater!" she sighed in relief. "Yes, I suppose I was."

"There's no 'suppose' about it, Anne," Nathan Hambaugh said as he eased himself into his recliner. "What's got you so preoccupied? George's ghost?"

She smiled faintly. "Oh, I don't believe in ghosts," she said, with a wave of her free hand.

"You may, yet," her father murmured quietly as he took a sip of his coffee.

"Excuse me?" she asked, not sure she had heard what she thought she heard.

Ignoring her query, he continued, "What have you learned thus far?"

She spent the next several minutes recounting what she and her friends had learned, and what was on the agenda for today. When she was done, she stood quietly and watched his face.

"Harvey told me about that purse-snatching incident," he said, nodding. "It's very fortunate that the thief got away with nothing of value."

"Yes," she agreed, noncommittally. "Quite."

"Interesting what you learned from Miss Rialdi," he went on between sips. "I'd never heard about that statuette, or that it might be—however remotely—connected to Angus MacLeod. That would be a fun twist!"

"Yes, quite."

"He was reputed to be a man who got what he wanted," Nathan said, "one way or another." He hesitated for a moment, and then added, reminiscently, "I used to spend a lot of time up at the old manor in my younger days, you know."

Anne stood a little straighter. An eyebrow rose ever so slightly. "No, Pater, I never knew."

"Your brother is a lot like me," he chuckled.

"It's good to know that there is hope for him yet," she quipped. "Did you make any discoveries of your own up there?"

"Well, when I went up there—usually with a buddy named Paul Harkness—it was just to mess around," he explained. Then with a chuckle, he added, "Paul used to go on about what he would do if he ever found MacLeod's treasure. Sure, we'd poke around, but mostly we went there to hang out. It's an awesome view from the high wall."

"Whatever happened to your friend?"

Nathan shrugged. "When I left Ordinary, I lost touch with everyone here. When I—we—returned I did some routine poking around ... for old time's sake. Paul left a few years after me, apparently, and pretty much disappeared." He sighed lightly. "Paul was the fat kid everyone picked on in school. No one really liked him much, but we got along. He always wanted to make it big so he could prove to the world that he was somebody."

"Did he?"

"Who knows?" Nathan shook his head. "That was all a very long time ago."

Anne took both empty cups to the kitchen to refill them. She was joined by her mother, who followed her into the family room. "Look who I found," Anne said, cheerfully.

Her parents exchanged morning kisses, and then her mother settled into her favorite corner of the sofa. "So," Emma Hambaugh said, "what have you two been plotting?"

"Just the overthrow of all the civilized world, if you must know, Miss Nosy," her husband replied.

"Oh," she sighed, "that again." She looked at her daughter. "And what are your big plans on the day before your birthday, my dear?"

"Oh, nothing particularly exciting," admitted Anne. "We're going to have a visit with Aunt Andrea, and then meet Harvey up at the manor to do some preliminary exploring."

Emma looked at her husband. "Ghosts!"

"George and Jorge," he responded defensively, "not I."

"You put the idea into Anne's head, Nathan," she went on.

"It's okay, Mum," laughed Anne. "It gives me something to write about in the next edition of the *Ordinary Outlook*."

"Well, that *is* true," Emma acquiesced. "Will you be taking George?"

"Yes," said Anne. "I want him to show me what happened that night. It could be very helpful."

"A good idea," agreed her father. "That, and it'll keep the boy out of trouble!"

It was then that fourteen-year-old George Hambaugh padded sleepily into the family room. The clock was just chiming seven. "Do you people have any idea what time it is?" he asked with mock irritability.

"Yes," responded Emma, "it's past time for you to be up and about."

"But it's summer vacation!" cried George. "It's a rite of passage here in the colonies to do nothing for the summer except sleep late and get into mischief!"

"Well then, oh brother dear," said his sister, "you've got that down to an art form!"

"Oh, ta!"

ঔঔঔঔঔঔঔঔঔঔ

The home of Raymond and Andrea Hambaugh was an easy walk in the direction of town from the Hambaugh ancestral home. The siblings, having been joined by Connie Bascomb, who lived nearby, arrived just as Tammy Coleman's white Mustang convertible turned off the blacktop and onto the gravel drive.

"Where's Jorge?" Tammy inquired as she parked her car.

"He'll meet us at the manor with Harvey," Anne explained. "Shall we?"

They walked up to the front door and, just as Anne was about to knock, the door swung open on silent hinges.

"Okay," murmured Connie, "that's creepy."

"Come in, children!" came a woman's voice from somewhere within.

The group entered, making their way to the solarium where Andrea Hambaugh was tending to her small collection of orchids. "Fussy things," she sighed. "I have a 50/50 success rate with them."

"Then why grow them?" asked her niece.

"Because I love orchids," Andrea answered, turning to face the foursome. "So! Have a seat and let's talk about the haunted manor …"

"'Haunted manor?'" choked George. "You mean, it's *really* haunted?"

"*You* saw the ghost," his aunt responded, smiling. "Didn't you?"

"Aunt Andrea," said Anne, quickly, "what can you tell us about Angus MacLeod, his manor, and his treasure?"

"To be honest, probably not much more than what you got from Maude Raynes and Elisa Rialdi," was her reply. "The mystery surrounding the disappearances of the sea captain and his wife has always been there, you know, and though people have looked into it off-and-on over the years no one has been able to discover what really happened to them. Some speculate a murder or suicide. Some speculate the builders did away with them for the treasure. But, when it gets right down to it, no one really knows anything. And, in a way, that's a good thing because it helps to keep the legend alive. After all, the MacLeod Manor is one of our tourist attractions, even if no one is supposed to be going anywhere near it."

"What do you think happened to them?" Tammy asked.

The older woman, seated now, and with her huge black cat on her lap, thought for a moment. Finally, she said, "I'm a romantic at heart. I like to think they loved each other and were done in by the greedy workers."

"We understand that at least one worker died on the reconstruction project," Anne said. "Could it have been retribution?"

"That's very possible," Andrea admitted, "but I don't know how likely."

"What about his treasure?" asked Connie.

"He amassed quite a fortune during his years at sea," Andrea acknowledged. "He was very … thrifty … being a Scotsman and all."

"Did he bring anything of great value back from—oh, say—Central America?" Tammy inquired.

Andrea looked carefully at the four. "So, you've heard about that," she sighed. "In all my years as a teacher and researcher, I've found nothing to irrefutably link the statuette of Tlaltecuhtli to Captain MacLeod."

Three of the four faces were crestfallen. The fourth face, that of young George, was confused.

"The statuette is real," she explained, "of that I have no doubt. I've come across a few fleeting references to it over the years—and it's been quite a number of years, now—but nothing that links it specifically to MacLeod."

"But, at the same time, there is nothing that says the opposite," Anne urged in a murmur.

"True," admitted Andrea. "And as for ghosts at the manor, there have been "sightings" periodically over the last almost two-hundred-years, and most were invariably found to be the work of either a treasure hunter, or some local just having fun. As for George's ghost, I'm inclined to go with either of those." She smiled as she added, "I will admit that, in my youth, I spent my fair share of time climbing over that ruin, exploring. Not necessarily seeking the hidden wealth—though I wouldn't have turned it away had I found it—but just being curious."

"Are there clocks there?" Tammy asked.

Looking at the seventeen-year-old, Andrea countered, "You're a local girl, have you never been?"

"Not inside," admitted Tammy. "And it was a lot of years ago that I climbed around there. Softball year round keeps me occupied."

"And you're quite good!" said Andrea. "But to answer your question: I think so but I'm not sure."

"There's at least one," interjected George, "in the great hall. It's not running or anything, and it looks like it's about ready to fall apart."

"Why do you ask about clocks?" Andrea inquired.

Anne explained to her aunt what all had been discussed with Elisa Rialdi the previous afternoon. "So, you see," she summarized, "there's a clue in the MacLeod family journal as to the location—or, possible location—of the family's treasure."

"Well, that's certainly exciting!" declared Andrea Hambaugh, smiling broadly. "I wish you the best of luck in your search!"

ઙઙઙઙઙઙઙઙઙઙ

The road that led through the woods to MacLeod Manor branched off the curvy two-lane blacktop that wound its way from the outside world to Ordinary. It was a narrow dirt road that meandered through dense, old growth trees for just a little over a mile before opening onto a small clearing that abutted the gray, moss-covered, stone walls of the Scottish manor house. It was an imposing structure, made more so by its location atop the bluff overlooking the lake. The walls soared almost fifty feet upward, with jutting turrets at each corner of its parapets. The west side of the edifice, the side facing the lake, showed where rebuilding had abruptly stopped almost two hundred years prior. Scattered about the grounds were great precision-cut stones that had yet to be put in their places. Mossy patchwork hid any identifying number. In many cases, the stone had been reclaimed by the encroaching woods.

Near the main entrance on the east side of the manor was a 1978 primer-gray Jeep Cherokee Chief, and beside it lounged two young men. They watched in silence as the white Mustang convertible bounced its way along the narrow, potholed track through the woods. When at last the vehicle came to a stop the two young men left the side of the Jeep.

"Nice trip?" asked Harvey Freeman, grinning.

"My suspension is not happy with me," sighed Tammy Coleman, slipping out from behind the steering wheel.

Anne Hambaugh stretched the kinks out of her back with an audible groan. "I had no idea the road was in such disrepair!"

"Are you kidding?" laughed Harvey. "You should have seen it *before* the county graded it!"

"We're here," groaned Connie Bascomb, "so, now what?"

George and Jorge stood together, talking to each other in quiet voices. After a moment under the steady gaze of the others, the two fourteen-year-olds looked at the older teens. "I suppose we walk you through what happened to us that night," George finally said.

"A good place to start, yes, but first tell us what time you guys got here that night?" Harvey asked.

"It was about one in the morning," Jorge replied. "We parked our bikes against the wall near the main entrance."

"It was ajar," said George. "It was ajar the first time we came here, too."

"Was there any sign of a vehicle nearby?" asked Harvey, jotting notes into a small notebook. "Did you pass one on your way here?"

"We saw no one," Jorge went on. "No vehicle. Nothing."

Harvey nodded. "Continue."

"So, we figured the place was all ours," explained George.

"It was very quiet," Jorge told them. "Unnaturally so, I thought."

"Spooky quiet," agreed George, nodding.

"It was a clear night," Tammy said.

"Not a full moon," added Connie, "but plenty of moonlight."

"That is true," admitted Jorge. "We went in through the open door, and into the great hall."

"My flashlight wasn't working," explained George, "so we only had the one: Jorge's."

"We couldn't have been inside more than fifteen minutes," Jorge told them as the group stepped through the open doors, "when we thought we saw something."

"Over there," George said, pointing toward a recess part way up the hall. "We were a bit further along when we thought we saw movement."

"I pointed my flashlight," Jorge enlightened, "but it wasn't a very strong beam, so it didn't reveal much of anything."

"It was pretty soon after that that we were escorted off the premises," George said. "We never heard anything, and not sure that we actually saw anything."

"It was all very strange," admitted Jorge.

The two fourteen-year-olds watched as the older teens moved curiously through the expansive foyer. The flagstone floor was littered with dirt and leaves blown in, and a layer of very old grime. The cold stone walls were damp in the shadows and covered in spots with a variety of mosses. Daylight streamed in through the old stained-glass of the windows in beams that illuminated parts of the hall and cast other parts into shadow. Even at midday, the manor had an air of dark surrealism about it.

Harvey walked to where the boys had thought they had seen something … or not. The niche was about eighteen inches deep, big enough for someone to hide in, but there was no way out except into the hall. Anyone stepping out would have been unavoidably seen by the two youths. He knelt and looked closely at the detritus-covered floor. There was nothing to indicate that anyone had been there. Standing, he turned slowly to take in the foyer from that location. "You guys were where, when you saw—or not—something here?"

"Maybe a dozen feet in from the door," George answered. He pointed to a spot not far behind them, and off to the opposite side. "Over there, more or less."

Harvey nodded. He stepped away from the niche. "Might have been a critter," he propositioned. "Might have been an owl."

"No," said Jorge firmly, shaking his head. "An owl—or any bird—would have flown out and we would have seen that."

"He's right, you know," added George. "It was no animal. It was just a momentary movement, enough to catch our attention, and then it was gone."

Anne walked slowly up the center of the long hall, her gold-flecked green eyes moving casually over the architecture. A stained-glass window with an ornate Celtic cross as its centerpiece cast a shadow on a doorless entry. A quick peek inside revealed a small, simple chapel with a simple, unadorned altar on the dais. About halfway along, on her right, was an old, massive grandfather clock that stood nine feet tall. It showed decay. The hands were gone, and the once-beautiful face was faded and coated in grime. She gazed at it for a long minute, her eyes wandering over it from top to bottom. She reached out to open the front panel; a slight tug and it came away in her hand. She made a face—displeased by that result—and set the panel down beside the clock. Leaning forward, a small flashlight in hand, she peered inside. The brass pendulum was dull, still, and swathed in webbing. Insects scattered before the light. There was nothing there. Stepping back, she looked up at the clock's face.

"Harvey," she called, "can you get the face of this behemoth open?"

He sauntered to a spot beside the teen journalist, twisting his mouth in thought. "I really don't want to break it," he said.

"Perhaps it's on hinges," suggested George. "Find the secret lever and it will swing away from the wall, revealing a secret passage."

"Wouldn't the workers who reassembled this place have known about that?" asked Tammy.

"Good point," agreed Connie.

"Ah!" declared George, stepping forward in dramatic style. "But if the sea captain was planning on doing them all in upon completion, the secret passage would still be secret!"

Anne shook her head. "Nice idea for a 1930s movie, oh brother mine, but not very likely."

"Especially since he disappeared, and the work was never completed," added Jorge. "Still …" The Hispanic youth ran his slender fingers up and down both sides of the clock, going up as high as he could reach. He was leaning into the clock when he lost his balance and *fell* into the clock. He scrambled out as quickly as he could, his face ashen. "The back moved!" he hissed.

They all converged on the clock, pressing and prodding, but there was no movement, the decaying relic silently resisted their attempts to discover its secrets.

Finally, Harvey called them away from the clock. "As much fun as this is," he said, "I'm going to poke around some more for my investigation into the trespassing, you guys—and gals—can do your own thing." After a momentary pause, he added, "Just try not to break anything."

Anne watched him walk away for a moment, and then looked about the grand hall. "If you were watching these two," she said to her friends and referring to her brother and his best friend, "where would be the best vantage point? I mean, you're here—trespassing—looking for the legendary—and probably mythical—treasure of Captain Macleod."

"Well, if you showed up just after them," said Connie, "then you'd be near the front entrance."

"But if you had shown up ahead of them," Tammy said, "you could be anywhere."

"I am inclined to think that the caller was here already," Anne murmured. "He—or she—could have been up above, on the landing, looking down. Far enough away to make a call without being heard."

She began walking toward the wide stone steps that formed the once-grand staircase and started upward. The second level of the manor had a landing that went all of the way around the foyer, and there were a dozen heavy wooden doors that led off the landing to rooms. None of the doors were locked and swung—some more easily than others—open on protesting hinges. She took a moment to look into each room. There was furniture to be seen in various stages of decay and disrepair: armoires, desks, chairs, bureaus and chests. Once beautiful curtains that hung at the tall windows were in tatters, or little more than dusty heaps on the cold stone floor. She was surprised that there was so much furniture and other artifacts, having thought that, over the years, it would have been taken by treasure seekers and ordinary trespassers. She saw candlestick holders and bed pans and tarnished drinking vessels scattered throughout. In armoires, she found an occasional tattered remnant. A small leather shoe was on the floor, beside a low chair with only three legs.

She could hear her friends drifting from room to room, murmuring about their finds. There was nothing left that was worth much of anything except of historical value. Heavy tapestries that once covered the gray walls were beyond repair, those that remained. The manor was a sad place. She found a narrow stairway that wound upward to the next level and took it. The heavy, iron-bound door at the top of the stairway hung askew and she was able to slip through the opening. This level did not look down on the foyer, but instead formed the foyer's high ceiling. It was an open floor plan, and devoid of everything.

As Anne wandered about the third floor, she found herself speculating about what could have happened to the MacLeods. Her impression of the captain was not of one who easily gave up. This was his ancestral home; he would not have just abandoned it. Particularly after the considerable expense of moving it. So, she found herself wondering what had happened to the old salt. She stopped at a window with yellowed glass that offered an expansive view of Lake Ordinary and the surrounding countryside. It was breathtaking. *He wouldn't have just walked away from this*, she told herself.

With some effort she opened the window and breathed in the warm air. She leaned forward just enough to look down from her vantage point. More than thirty feet below, between the wall of the manor and the precipice that was the edge of the bluff, was a sizable piece of overgrown land. *At one time*, she imagined, *it was meant to be a lovely garden*. She could visualize a gazebo, and rose trellis, and garden statuary. She could envisage young Eleanor walking through the garden, pausing to smell the flowers. For some reason, she saw the captain's young bride as a happy woman.

A noise from behind her reached her ears, and she quickly stepped away from the open window as she turned. Harvey Freeman was standing a dozen feet away lost in thought. "What have you learned?" she asked.

He looked at the young woman, a touch of a frown on his brow and his lips compressed. "I've learned that this old place is a lot bigger when you're trying to find something small, like a clue. I can't imagine anyone in their right mind wanting to be here at night."

"That would explain George and Jorge," said Tammy, joining the two. "It's been forever since I've been up here, and that was during the day. Kinda creepy."

"Why do you say that?" asked Anne. "Because it's big and empty?"

Tammy thought for a moment, and then said, "No, that doesn't bother me so much. It's just that … oh, I don't know … it's just creepy."

"Expecting a ghost?" Connie queried as she sauntered into the large room.

"There is no such thing," Harvey said flatly.

"Keep telling yourself that," Connie said, and wandered on to another location.

"I must admit," sighed Anne, "that there is a certain … feel … to this old place."

"Not you, too!" groaned the cadet.

Laughing softly, Anne said, "I don't mean haunted, silly. It's just that there is a … an ambiance that's hard to identify."

"Ghost," said Connie, walking by them in the opposite direction.

"So," Tammy said, "I've seen a clock of one kind or another in just about every room. Some are small mantle clocks, and others are large wall clocks. None seem to have any secret compartments in which to hide a treasure, let alone a clue. I have to wonder if that note in the journal wasn't a red herring."

"I don't think so," said Anne. "Captain MacLeod doesn't come across as a man with that kind of sense of humor."

Harvey wandered over to the window she stood near and looked out. "Nice view," he commented. "Wasn't it somewhere around here that a worker fell?"

"It would have happened higher up," Anne said. "This area is mostly complete, but the upper level is still unfinished." She glanced over at him as he turned away from the window. "Any luck with your investigation?"

He shook his head. "I can't find anything that shows anyone was here. If George and Jorge hadn't admitted being here, I'd be hard-pressed to find anything proving *they* were here." He sighed. "But someone made the anonymous phone call, and that means that someone—other than them—was here."

"No trace of a car parked nearby?" Connie asked.

"Maybe parked closer to the blacktop," he said. "Maybe tucked away in the bush. When we're finished here, I'm going to look for a hiding place big enough to hide a car."

"In the meantime," said Tammy, "let's mosey on upstairs and see what we can find."

As they started toward the narrow spiraling stairs that would take them to the upper level, Anne asked, "Has anyone seen the boys?"

ଔଔଔଔଔଔଔଔଔ

George Hambaugh and Jorge Bustamante watched as the older teens began to spread out in the foyer. It was as if the two had been forgotten about in the search for answers. They made no attempt to correct the situation, they just watched in silence until the other four were beyond earshot. Looking over at his best friend, a smile began to spread on George's freckled face. He ran a hand through the curly red mop on the top of his head.

"They're doing their exploring," said the youth from England, "so what say you and I do *our* exploring?"

Jorge looked at his friend for a silent moment before saying, with some trepidation, "What do you propose?"

"Well, as they are going up," George said, indicating his sister's ascent of the wide stairs, "I think it would behoove us to look down."

With a shrug, Jorge said, "I'm game if you are."

The two youngsters made their way toward the stairs that led upward, but instead walked around the stonework in search of stairs that led in the opposite direction. What they found first was the kitchen with its large open hearth for cooking and assorted pots and pans strewn about. In the center of the room was a large, heavy wooden table that looked like a giant cutting board. In a corner was a grime-covered brass spittoon. The boys circled the large room slowly, curiously investigating every nook and cranny. Eventually they came upon a stout, iron-bound door that opened to what would have been the lake-side garden.

"That's where the vegetables and herbs would have been grown," George explained, "within easy access for the cook."

Jorge opened a pantry door and stepped into the semi-dark recess. "George," he called out quietly. "I think I found the way down."

George shut the door to the outside and hurried to where his friend stood. In the semi-darkness they could see a trap door set into the floor's flagstones. A large, rusty iron ring was plainly visible. "Shall we?" he asked excitedly.

"Dare we?" Jorge countered cautiously.

"What could possibly go wrong?"

Standing straighter to make himself just slightly taller than his Anglo friend, Jorge said dryly, "Gee, I can't imagine."

Grabbing hold of the heavy ring with both hands, George began to pull. At first nothing moved, though there was the sound of protesting metal, and then the trapdoor began to open. It was at this point that his best friend hurried to his side to help. Between the two of them, it did not take long to expose narrow stone steps that led down into the dark. Pulling a small flashlight from a pocket, George started down.

"Is that wise?" asked Jorge. "I mean, without letting the others know what we're doing."

"Did they tell us what they were doing?" inquired George.

"We *knew* what they were doing," countered Jorge.

The grin on George's face widened. "Come on, mate! It'll be great fun!"

As the curly red mop descended, Jorge sighed, shook his head, and followed his friend into the unknown.

The narrow beam of light from George's flashlight pierced the darkness but did not illuminate a significant area. He had to constantly play the light on the stone steps and along the damp stone walls. He figured they had descended almost fifteen feet below the kitchen floor by the time they reached the bottom. The two stood side-by-side as the light was played around the spacious cellar. Empty wine racks were against one wall, and large wooden crates—each with large words in black to identify the contents—were positioned along two other walls.

"It's nicely organized," commented George.

"Very nice," agreed Jorge, "now, shall we go back up?"

It was then that the door to the cellar slammed shut, causing both boys to jump involuntarily. With the exception of the narrow light furnished by the George's small flashlight, the cellar became a pit of inky blackness.

"Maybe it just fell shut," whispered George, hopefully.

"You have the light," said his best friend, "I'll follow you."

George made a grimace. Training the light on the base of the stone steps, he moved it up to the closed entry. "Okay," he agreed in a hushed voice, "let's go."

They began their ascent as quickly as they could, reaching the closed cellar door within moments. Reaching out with his free hand, George pushed. The door did not move. Jorge maneuvered beside his friend and they both pushed. Still, the door did not move.

"Well," Jorge sighed, "this is another fine mess you've gotten us into."

"It must be just stuck," insisted George, worry in his voice. "We just need to push harder."

This they did, but the door refused to budge.

"Someone shut us in here," Jorge said. "It's too heavy a door to close on its own."

"But who?" asked George, as he played his around the cellar from the top of the stairs.

There was a silent pause, and then Jorge suggested, "Perhaps it was our ghost."

George shifted the light to fall on his friend's face, causing the other boy to turn his head and squint. "Surely, thou dost jest!"

With a shrug, Jorge said, "Kinda, but someone had to have done it. It didn't close on its own."

"Maybe there's another way out down there," George said, indicating the dark walls with a sweep of his flashlight.

"No one will hear us pounding on the door," Jorge admitted, "as they all went up, so it's worth a try."

The two returned to the cellar floor and took a moment to get their bearings. Except for the wall-encompassing wine rack and the wooden crates along two other walls, there was nothing else there. The boys started with the closest crate—which would have held potatoes—and opened the lid on protesting hinges, the shrieking echoed off the thick walls. It was empty and there was nothing that indicated any kind of exit. They moved from crate to crate, each with the same result, until finally they came to the wine rack.

"In all the best movies," explained George, "there's a secret entrance hidden behind the wine rack."

"In all the best movies," Jorge countered dryly, "the wine rack is full of bottles and one special label operates the secret door."

"Well, yes, that *is* true," admitted George as he moved the light across the floor-to-ceiling rack. "But there just *has* to be another way out!"

"This is real life, my friend, hidden passages are for the movies," sighed Jorge.

George allowed the narrow beam of light to play along the cellar floor toward the stone steps. He suddenly stopped its movement at the first step, and then, after a moment, moved it along the edge of the steps to a point where the steps met the rear wall. The dark was deeper there, as if recessed. Nudging his friend, he began to make his way in that direction. Moments later he was shining the light on a dark, iron-bound wooden door sunken into the stonework beneath the stone stairs.

They two boys stood there staring at the door, both wondering the same thing: *did it lead out*?

Reaching for the cold iron ring that was the door's handle, Jorge gave a gentle tug. The door shifted, but only slightly. Together, the boys gripped the iron ring and began to pull, gradually increasing the force necessary to open the door. And, gradually, the thick door began to open. With it open a few inches, George shined his light into what appeared to be a narrow passage. His light was not strong enough to illuminate the end of the passage.

"We can stay here," he said, "or see where this passage takes us."

"It may just take us deeper into the bowels of this ruin," murmured Jorge.

"Or it may lead us *out* of the bowels of this ruin," countered George.

"You have the light," said Jorge, "so I'll follow you."

"We can switch anytime."

"No, no, we're good. Lead on."

They pulled the door open enough to allow access, and George entered. Together the fourteen-year-olds moved along the narrow passage. It was, perhaps, three feet wide with a stone ceiling less than six feet high. It ran straight for twenty-five feet, and then abruptly turned to the right. The walls seemed to absorb the flashlight's meager output. The floor was rough, with the rock of the bluff jutting up with enough frequency to cause numerous stumbling. The boy's breathing seemed amplified within the narrow confines of the passage. They pressed on.

After another twenty-five feet there was one more sharp turn, this time to the left.

"I think we're going up," whispered Jorge.

Nodding, George agreed. "I noticed that, too. It's gradual, but noticeable."

"That's promising. Better than going down."

Every twenty-five feet there was an abrupt turn, alternating left and right. The boys had long since lost their bearings as to their relative location beneath the manor. They were not even sure that the manor was above them, or if they were moving inexorably toward the bluff's cliff face. The blackness of the passage deepened as the narrow beam of light from George's flashlight began to weaken.

"Please tell me you have extra batteries," Jorge whispered.

"I do."

"Oh, good."

"At home."

"I hate you."

ଓଓଓଓଓଓଓଓଓ

Harvey Freeman emerged from the narrow spiral stairway, stepping into a large unfurnished room. The floor was made of hardwood that was weathered and debris-strewn. Some of the windows had glass, others did not. There were areas where numbered stones were stacked, awaiting their final placement. There were the workmen's troughs that had held mortar, and an occasional tool lying where it was abandoned almost two centuries ago. While the manor's roof was in place, there were gaps in the uppermost level's ceiling that exposed access to the attic. Leaning against a wall at the opposite of the room was a wooden ladder.

"Cheerful place," commented Connie Bascomb, glancing about the room.

"Spacious," evaluated Tammy Coleman, "with lots of potential."

Anne Hambaugh said nothing. She walked to the center of the room and took her time looking around. While her friends moved casually about, she critically took in her surroundings. She was getting a strange feeling about the manor, a feeling that had started when she had first crossed its threshold an hour or more ago. She had the distinct feeling that they were not alone. *Who else is here?* she wondered. She watched her friends; if they felt it, they were not showing it.

"What do you think?" she asked.

"About?" inquired Harvey as he walked to the window with a view of the lake.

"Any of this," answered Anne.

"I think this would make an awesome apartment!" Tammy said excitedly.

Connie looked over at her friend with the wavy red hair. "What's going through your head, Anne?"

Anne tipped her head to one side as she began to move slowly about the upper level. "I don't know."

"Well, that's a newsflash," muttered Harvey, turning his back to the window.

Anne ignored him. "It's hard to explain," she continued. "There's just something about this old place …"

"There are *no* ghosts!" said Harvey firmly. "None. Nada."

"Perhaps not," acquiesced Anne, "but there is *something*."

"As in: something out of place?" asked Tammy.

"Could be."

"How about this ladder, then?" Tammy suggested, giving the wooden ladder a nudge with her booted foot. The other three looked at the seventeen-year-old. "I don't think this belonged to the workers putting this puzzle together."

Anne and Connie hurried over to where their friend stood. Anne knelt to get a closer look. She reached out and ran her hand over the weathered wood. "It *is* old," she told them, "but you're right, Tammy, it's not *that* old."

"So, it was maybe left by later workers," suggested Harvey from across the room.

"That's just it," Connie lectured, "there were no *later* workers!"

"That's right," agreed Tammy. "About the time MacLeod and his wife vanished, all work stopped."

"I wonder if it stopped *before* they vanished," murmured Anne, standing. "Was there a falling out between the workers and Macleod?"

"Well, at least one fell," Harvey reminded them. "And maybe that's what brought everything to a standstill."

"That's certainly possible," admitted Anne. "But accidents on job sites were not uncommon back then. Safety wasn't as big an issue as it is today."

"Maybe it wasn't about the accident," Connie suggested, "but rather about how Macleod *reacted* to the accident. If he dismissed it offhandedly the other workers may have been angry and could have taken their anger out on him."

"But would they have taken their anger out on his wife, as well?" Tammy asked.

"Possibly," said Anne, "if they were of the same mindset."

"But you don't think so," said Connie, looking at her best friend.

Anne sighed and shrugged. "I don't know. We don't know enough about her—or him, for that matter. He may have been a callous old salt, but she was considerably younger, so I don't know that she would be like-minded."

"Then again," said Harvey from his place near the window, "that may have been exactly *why* he married her in the first place. Because they both thought the same way about things—like his fortune."

"That is very possible," admitted Anne, "but, again, we just do not *know*."

"Well, I know this much," sighed the cadet, "I'm ready to be done with all this nonsense."

"That reminds me," said Tammy, "how's your trespassing investigation coming along?"

"It's not," he told her, a hint of disappointment in his voice. "I'm sure there were trespassers here—besides George and Jorge—but I'll be darned if I can find any physical evidence. It's all stonework and debris."

"Speaking of whom," said Anne, standing straighter. "Where are those troublesome two?"

No one spoke for a long moment as they pondered the question. One by one they shook their heads.

"This doesn't bode well," murmured Anne.

"I suppose we have to find them before we leave," Harvey said, a mischievous smile on his lips.

"I'm afraid so," Anne told him flatly.

ઌઌઌઌઌઌઌઌઌઌ

The light emanating from the small flashlight was no longer a strong beam cutting a swath through the darkness, but rather it had become feeble, barely lighting the way for their feet. The two boys had long since lost track of time and their sense of direction. The narrow passage had seemed to go on and on, with sharp turns every two dozen feet. The only thing of which they were reasonably sure was that they had been moving steadily—and though gently—upward. At some point they expected to emerge in daylight—and they fervently hoped it would happen *before* the flashlight went dark.

"Surely, we're nearing the end of this maze!" growled George Hambaugh, frustrated.

"You'd think so," agreed Jorge Bustamante.

Moments later George came to an abrupt stop, so much so that his friend ran into him. "Correct me if I'm wrong," murmured the former, "but is the ceiling getting … lower?"

Jorge reached above his head to feel the rough passage ceiling. "I think you may be on to something, my friend."

"So maybe, just maybe, there's an exit coming?"

"Oh, I do hope so."

The fading light showed them the end of the passage, and then it went out. In complete darkness, the boys stumbled forward until their hands reached the solid wall. They felt around; there was no turn. They had finally come to the end of the road. They became more anxious as their hands felt for an exit, a door, an iron ring, anything, but there was nothing. After several intense minutes, the two teens sank to the rough floor, their backs pressed against the cool stone walls.

"I'm refusing to accept that we came all this way only to find no way out," Jorge said, though there was a hint of disappointment in his voice.

"You know," murmured George, "there is one place we didn't look."

There was a pause, and then Jorge said, "We didn't look *up*!"

They quickly scrambled to their feet and began to run their sore hands along the rough ceiling. In a corner their hands found smooth wood about eighteen inches square. They took turns pushing upward. At first the square refused to budge, but the boys were adamant in wanting to get out of the darkness and so, bit by bit, the square began to move. Slowly it moved upward. Loose dirt showered down on the pair until, at last, the wooden square came free of the surrounding earth. Sunlight streamed in, painfully blinding the boys temporarily, but the warmth of the light drew them out.

George boosted his best friend out of the passage, and then Jorge hauled his *compadre* out. They lay on the cool ground breathing deeply the fresh air. The sunlight filtered through the leafy canopy of the woods to warm their faces. For several minutes neither boy said anything, they quietly enjoyed their freedom.

Finally, propped up on one elbow, Jorge turned to his friend and asked, "Shall we look for the others?"

"I suppose we should," sighed George. "Keeping them out of trouble is becoming a full-time job!"

As they got to their feet, they heard a car's engine start, and then idle. Curious, they made their way through the underbrush to a spot not far from what passed as the road to the manor. Not sure what they would find, they moved as quietly as they could until they had reached a place that offered them a concealed view of the vehicle.

Tucked away in a copse was the lime-green AMC Gremlin.

"Do you see what I see?" hissed George as he sank to the ground.

"You can't help but see it!" replied Jorge, following his friend down.

They inched forward along the leaf-strewn ground on their stomachs until they had reached a spot from which they could observe undetected. A brown-haired woman in jeans and a floral blouse climbed out from behind the steering wheel, leaned against the car, and looked in the direction of the manor. She was tall and willowy, and her face had prominent cheek bones. Frequently she would glance in the boys' direction, but she never indicated that she was aware of their presence. They wondered who she was waiting for.

After several minutes a man approached. He was lean, clean-shaven, with graying brown hair. He had an ugly scar on his left cheek. As he walked toward the car, he smiled broadly. His voice was hoarse, unpleasant, as he greeted the woman. "Have you seen anyone?" he asked.

The woman shook her head. "Not since those meddlesome kids went into the old dump," she replied, her own voice gritty.

"Well, two of them are locked in the cellar," laughed the man, "and it'll be a while before they're found!"

"I'd as soon they were found quickly and the whole bunch of them left," said the woman unhappily. "Time's a-wasting!"

"Relax, Hortense," the man said reassuringly. "We'll find the loot, and once we do, we'll be on easy street! You just have to have a little patience!"

"I don't like this place," she grumbled. "And I don't like that town!"

"How can you not like Ordinary?" he laughed. "It's so … quaint!"

"Maybe so, Paul," she responded gruffly, "but I don't do quaint!"

"Relax, it won't be much longer," he told her. "What we need to do is get hold of someone who could tell us where to look, or, at least, point us in the right direction."

"Sure, let's involve someone else!" she snorted. "We don't need witnesses! That's the *last* thing I want!"

An unpleasant smile formed on his lips. As he patted his left side he said, "There *won't* be any witnesses."

"Right, like there weren't any witnesses to your little stunt yesterday," she guffawed bitterly.

"I want the local yokels to be looking for a purse-snatcher, not paying attention to a little trespassing up here," he explained to her. "That clueless cadet in there," he went on, gesturing toward the manor, "couldn't find his head if it weren't attached! And as for those other teenagers, their attention will be elsewhere by the end of the day. Kids nowadays have zero attention span!"

Hortense looked at the man. She was slightly taller than he. "I hope you're right, Paul. I hope you're right."

The pair climbed into the lime-green Gremlin and drove away.

The two teen boys stood up after the strange couple had left. In silence they looked at one another, and then to the manor.

"Well, we know how we ended up locked in the cellar," George said. "And it wasn't any ghost."

"True," agreed Jorge. "And we know who the trespassers were who probably called the law on us."

"They're after the treasure," said George.

"We need to get to the others and tell them what we've learned," Jorge said as he started toward the manor.

"I think my dad will be impressed by what we've learned!" declared George happily.

With a laugh, Jorge added, "We've all but solved this mystery single-handedly!"

As they approached the manor, they both looked up at the same time. It appeared that someone was teetering out of a top floor window.

"What do you suppose is going on up there?" asked George, picking up his pace.

"I don't know," said Jorge, "but I suppose we'd best get up there to straighten out those crazy kids!"

ᴓᴓᴓᴓᴓᴓᴓᴓᴓᴓ

Tammy Coleman knelt beside the old wooden ladder and looked closely at it. "You know," she said, "as old as it is, it's in really good shape." She looked up at the ceiling. "And there just happens to be a hole in the ceiling above it."

"Someone used it to get up there?" Connie Bascomb asked as she approached.

"Why not?" replied Tammy. "And I'm thinking, because it's such a heavy ladder, that it would take at least two people to get it into place."

"Good thinking," Anne Hambaugh agreed. She peered up into the dark hole. "Shall we?"

The three girls struggled to get the long, heavy ladder upright, leaning against the wall with a few feet of it up inside the irregular hole. With the ladder in place, the trio looked over at the cadet, still standing by the window. He was leaning out of it now.

"Thanks for the help," they said in unison.

Harvey Freeman turned without straightening, caught his feet in antique debris, and began to pitch forward. A yelp escaped him as he grabbed for anything that would prevent his falling out of the window to the ground far below. Seeing his predicament, the three younger teens ran to his aid. Tammy reached him first, in time to grab him by his belt. His forward momentum, however, pulled her along, too. He was teetering out of the window, and pulling Tammy with him, when Connie and Anne reached the imperiled pair. Connie wrapped her arms around Tammy's waist and dug in her heels. Anne grabbed Harvey's belt, even though he was most of the way out the window and pulled hard. Tammy regained her traction on the stone floor and the three were able to bring Harvey inside.

The four collapsed onto the floor, among the debris, breathing heavily.

"What happened?" asked Anne, having caught her breath.

Harvey shook his head as he willed his heart to stop racing. "I don't know," he finally answered. "I was just looking out the window. When I turned, I lost my balance." He paused for a moment, and then added, "If I didn't know any better, I'd think I was pushed!"

"Don't be silly," said Tammy, standing up and brushing herself off. "There's only us up here, and we weren't anywhere near you."

"I know," he murmured as he slowly got to his feet and stepped away from the window. "Weird."

"Are you all right?" asked Anne as she stepped toward him.

"Thanks to all of you," he responded gratefully. "That was definitely too close for comfort!"

"Not to sound unsympathetic," Tammy said as she started toward the ladder, "but shall we poke our heads up into that hole before we go?"

The foursome met at the ladder and looked up into the darkness.

"I'll go up," said Harvey, taking hold of the ladder.

"Not a chance!" declared Tammy. "You've had your fun for today, give someone else a chance!"

Connie took hold, placing her foot on the lowest rung. "I'll go up," she told them, and started to ascend.

It took her a little time as she tested each rung before putting all her weight on it. No one pushed her to pick up the pace, but rather, they patiently watched her as they steadied the ladder. Eventually, she reached the hole in the ceiling and craned her neck.

"It's really dark up here," she said. "Anyone got a flashlight?"

Fishing a small penlight from his pocket, Harvey tossed it up to her. Deftly she caught it, turned it on, and looked again into the hole.

"What do you see?" asked Anne.

After a moment, her best friend said, "Not much. It's hard to tell, but it looks like a bunch of junk."

"One man's junk is another man's treasure," said Tammy.

"Especially to a rag-and-bone man," added Anne.

Connie inched further into the opening, playing the narrow beam about the attic. "It's a sizable room," she told them. "But I'm not seeing anything that would contain any kind of treasure, or whatever."

"Any kind of a timepiece?" asked Tammy.

"No," was the disappointed reply. "No timepiece of any kind. Mostly it's old boards and stuff, like flooring."

"Well, come on down," sighed Anne. "It was worth a look."

As Connie descended, she remarked, "This old place is kind of neat. I wish I'd explored it before now."

"You would've been trespassing, then," Harvey told her as he accepted the return of his penlight.

"People have been trespassing here forever," Tammy reminded the cadet, chuckling. "And not just us locals, either. A couple of years ago—I remember—there were some hobos camped out here for quite some time until some kids stumbled across their camp. Scared the kids and the hobos!"

"Oh, I'm not saying it doesn't happen, that it hasn't happened, and that it won't continue to happen," Harvey said, "I'm just saying that it's trespassing."

"Speaking of trespassing," Connie said, "where are our youthful trespassers?"

"Right here!" declared two voices from the stairs across the room.

As the six teens came together in the middle of the room, Jorge asked, "Who was hanging out the window?"

"I was," admitted Harvey.

"You shouldn't do that," George reprimanded the older teen. "That's dangerous."

"What have you two been up to?" asked Anne.

"Solving your mystery," Jorge replied, grinning.

The two boys quickly told of their experience in the cellar and their eventual escape. It was the part about Paul and Hortense that grabbed the attention of the others, to which there were several questions.

"Well," said Harvey, "at least now we know who's driving that Gremlin, and who spooked these two the other night."

"We have first names," corrected Anne, "but we don't know *who* they are."

"Yet," said George.

ଓଓଓଓଓଓଓଓଓଓ

Nathan Hambaugh sat patiently as he listened to the teenagers tell him of their morning adventures. He jotted down notes onto a yellow legal pad. It was when the two people with the Gremlin were mentioned by their first names that he finally spoke. He asked for a description of each, writing the information down as the two fourteen-year-old boys told what they remembered.

"That's promising, thank you, boys," he said as he put down his pen. "Well," he continued, addressing the group as a whole, "you've had quite the morning! Interesting about the ladder, though it could very well have been there for years. And, Harvey, what were you looking for by hanging out that window?"

The nineteen-year-old shrugged his shoulders. "I'm not so sure, now," he confessed. "But it was the weirdest thing. As I was turning my feet got caught up in some debris, but I was working them free when—the next thing I knew—I was pitching headlong out that window! If I didn't know any better, I'd say I was pushed!"

"But there was no one near you," Tammy reminded him. "And I just barely reached you in time."

"For which I am eternally grateful, believe you me!" he responded. "It's just … oh, I don't know … weird."

"What are your thoughts on all this, Anne?" her father asked.

"Well, I think the mystery of who reported George and Jorge is solved," she replied, "or will be when you catch Paul and Hortense. They were the other trespassers, and they're obviously hunting the treasure. As for our part, while we found several clocks of different types, we found nothing that could be construed as a clue. We're missing something."

"What do you make of Paul's comment about finding someone who could point them in the right direction?" Nathan asked. "Who do you think he has in mind?"

"If they aren't from here," Connie said, "they wouldn't really know who to ask. And they couldn't very well walk the streets asking random people what they knew of the legend of the manor and its treasure."

"That's very true," admitted the interim police chief.

"Unless," murmured Jorge, "at least one of them *is* from here."

All eyes settled on the young Hispanic boy.

"Why do you say that?" asked Nathan, interested.

"Well, the woman made the comment that she doesn't do quaint towns," explained the youth, "so she is probably not from here. He, on the other hand, mentioned Ordinary as being a quaint town, and finding someone who might answer their questions. That doesn't prove anything, I admit, but it got me to wondering if—just maybe—he was from here or had spent time here before."

"I was wondering that as well," nodded Nathan Hambaugh. "What I need is an artist's rendering of these two characters …"

"I know a really good illustrator who might fit that bill," Tammy said excitedly. "Mitch Cavenaugh! He wants to be a professional illustrator, and he is *good*!"

"Can you call him?" asked the interim chief.

"You bet!" she said and hurried out of his office.

"That will be a big help," he said with satisfaction. "As for the rest of you, you've done very well. Keep an eye out for our 'visitors' but don't confront them. This Paul fellow sounds like an unpleasant sort."

"We will," they all responded.

"So, what's on the agenda for the rest of the day?" asked Nathan. "Besides staying out of trouble."

"You take all the fun out of being a kid, Pater!" laughed his daughter. "But, seriously, I need to do some more research into the manor, MacLeod, and the legend. The clue was written for a reason, I just need to figure out what it means."

"And I have no doubt that you will," he said with a nod. "All right, out with you lot! I've work to do!"

The five teenagers filed out of the office, coming to a stop at Maude Raynes' nearby coffee bar to partake of the remaining donuts and pastries.

Sixty-seven-year-old Maude Raynes growled at the game of solitaire on her desk, scooped up the playing cards, and put them in a drawer. She then turned her chair so that she was facing them. "How goes the investigation?" she asked. They gave her a quick recap to which she let out a long whistle. "Good heavens! You children need to be more careful! Harvey, your mother will *not* be happy hearing how you almost took a dive!"

"I expect not," he sighed. "I just hope she doesn't make me quit!"

Tammy returned just then with a broad smile. "I talked to Mitch," she told them, "and he is absolutely *thrilled*! As soon as he finishes the job he's doing, he'll be right over."

"Where is he?" asked Connie.

"He's taking care of some yard work for Miss Rialdi," Tammy replied. "I'll let the Chief know."

"What do you suppose the bits about the key to the treasure and time means?" asked Maude.

"Well," said Anne, "we thought that it had something to do with a clock, or some other timepiece, at the manor. And, while we found several old, non-functioning clocks of various sizes and types, we found no key, or clue, or anything. So, we're at a bit of a standstill there."

"Does it have to be a clock?" the police department's secretary/records clerk/dispatcher inquired.

"What else could it be?" inquired Connie, finishing her cinnamon roll with a satisfied sigh.

"Consider the time at which the entry was written," suggested Maude, "and who the author was."

"True," murmured Anne, her gold-flecked green eyes lighting up. "What else involves time?"

"That's a tough one, oh sister mine," said George. "I mean, when one thinks time, one typically thinks clocks, or watches, and such."

"He was a sea captain," murmured Jorge. "Perhaps there's something in *that*."

"Perhaps," admitted Anne thoughtfully.

"There is one place we haven't been," said Tammy.

"Where's that?" asked Harvey.

"The museum."

Everyone was quiet for a moment as they pondered this. Several heads slowly nodded.

"There are things from the manor on display," Maude Raynes finally said to the group of youths. "I don't recall what, off hand, but I do remember that a display had been put together some years back."

"It's certainly worth a try!" declared Connie excitedly.

"And there is still plenty of daylight," added Harvey.

"Tally-ho!" exclaimed George gleefully. "It's off to the museum we go!"

ഗഗഗഗഗഗഗഗഗഗ

The six teens took two cars to the museum: the three boys went in Harvey's 1978 primer-gray Jeep Cherokee Chief, and the three girls went in Tammy's 1967 white Mustang convertible.

The Ordinary Museum was located east of town, just before the winding road that took travelers to 'civilization.' It was in an old two-story farmhouse dating back well over one hundred years and made from locally quarried stone. The slate roof was colored by mossy lichen, and from its chimney curled wisps of whitish-gray smoke. The heavy wooden front door was ajar, but there were no vehicles in the small parking lot.

Anne was the first to reach the door, followed closely by Harvey. He stopped her from rushing inside with a touch to her shoulder and a shake of his head. He indicated to her to call for help. She nodded, stepped back, and allowed him to go first as she pulled her phone from a pocket. He opened the door with a gentle push, but he was wound like a spring ready to pounce. There was no sound at first, then they heard the low moan. Harvey stepped inside followed by the rest. He instructed the younger boys to stay at the door: *no one in or out* he had told them. The others split into pairs and circled around opposite sides of the interior.

There were numerous artifacts mounted on the walls with small plaques that explained what they were and from where they had originated. There were glass display cases that contained smaller items that dated back to the early days of the town when it was fewer than fifty people. Paintings depicting life at various periods in Ordinary's timeline were strategically placed with artifacts specific to those periods in time helped tell the town's story.

In a corner of the museum's ground floor, behind a display case containing household items of a bygone era, they found the curator. John Rosendale was the sixty-year-old curator of the Ordinary Museum. He lay on his back, his brown hair matted with blood, and his brown eyes unfocused. His brown bushy mustache and eyebrows seemed to move independently of each other as he tried to remain conscious. When he saw the youths approaching him, he gestured weakly toward the second floor, and then passed out.

Approaching sirens could be heard in the distance.

It was a sudden noise on the second floor that drew the attention of the teens. Harvey indicated to Tammy and Connie that they should stay with the unconscious curator. He and Anne moved stealthily to the stairs. As with the floors throughout the building, the stairs were worn smooth from many decades of use. Gripping the handrail, Harvey gestured to Anne to wait while he investigated. One step at a time, he moved upward.

On the second floor were several stained-glass windows, one of which depicted an hourglass and a sailing ship. The layout on the second floor was very similar to the one on the first floor with strategically positioned display cases and artwork. There were also creaky boards. One such board protested beneath Harvey's weight, and the noise from the second floor suddenly stopped.

The wailing of the approaching sirens was much louder now, with the arrival of Ordinary's law enforcement officers only moments away.

There came a vehement expletive from among the artifacts and the pounding of feet toward stairs at the back of the old farmhouse. Harvey rushed onto the second floor and took up the pursuit. The fleeing figure was wearing a black hoodie and carrying an aged hickory ax handle. *Deja vue*! thought Harvey as he bolted after the person. As he reached the top of the stairs only seconds behind the escaping runner, he was hit in the shins by the hard-wooden ax handle. With a yelp of pain, the cadet went down, and the escapee vanished out the back door.

Harvey stumbled down the back stairs and out the diminutive back door in time to see the lime-green 1975 AMC Gremlin careen around the side of the old farmhouse and speed off down a narrow strip of paved country road. He stood in the doorway gently rubbing his tender shins and glowering after the ugly little car. A sound behind him caused him to straighten and turn.

Interim Chief of Police Nathan Hambaugh came down the stairs, stopping beside the unhappy cadet. "Got away, eh?"

"Again," sighed Harvey. "He had to whack my shins with an ax handle to do it, though."

"Are you okay? Maybe you should go to the hospital and have them looked at," suggested Nathan.

With a shake of his head, Harvey said, "I'll be all right. Nothing a cold pack and aspirin—and time—won't cure."

"You said 'again,' so I'm to assume it was your purse snatcher?"

Harvey nodded.

"Did he find what he was looking for?"

"I don't know. The only thing in his hands was the ax handle. I'm guessing that was to smash his way into the display cabinets."

"Well, what say you and I mosey on back upstairs and see what's what?" proposed Nathan as he turned to go up the stairs.

They found Anne and the others already milling about the upper floor of the museum when they got there. She looked at the limping nineteen-year-old with concern in her eyes. Before she could speak, he shook his head. She nodded slightly, understanding.

"How is our curator?" asked her father.

"The ambulance crew have taken him to the emergency room," she explained. "It looks like he took quite a blow to the head—"

"From an ax handle," interjected a desolate Harvey.

"—and he may have a concussion," she continued, "but they're pretty sure he'll be all right."

Nathan Hambaugh nodded. "Thank God for that." He glanced about the museum's upper floor. "Any idea what our troublemaker was after?"

"Well, Pater," answered Anne thoughtfully, "if he—or, rather, they—are the same who were up at the manor and called in the local constabulary on George and Jorge, and are the same two who locked the boys in said manor's cellar, then I think it's safe to assume that they are after Captain MacLeod's treasure, specifically, the bejeweled golden statuette of Tlaltecuhtli."

"If it exists," Tammy added.

"True," admitted the young investigative journalist.

"I'm curious," said Nathan. "How big is this thing?"

"From what I could find on the internet," Connie pitched in, "it's about eleven inches long and four inches high and wide."

"So," said the interim chief of police, "not particularly big."

"Which means easier to hide," George said.

"If it's solid gold, though," Jorge added, "it would still be quite heavy."

"My understanding," Connie went on, "is that it's a very detailed stone carving sheathed in a thick layer of gold, and the jewels are inserted in that sheathing."

"All right," Nathan murmured, nodding his head slightly, "so, what we're looking for is something about the size of a shoebox."

They walked about the second floor but saw nothing that was out of place.

"I just can't figure out what they were looking for," Connie finally said disappointedly.

Anne was standing beside a display case that contained artifacts from the MacLeod manor, her eyes casually drifting from item to item. Mostly, it was household items: crockery, silverware, and such. There were some finely embossed silver goblets and intricately etched glasses. A brass sexton—showing years of use—and a still-functioning hourglass completed the display. Her eyes settled on the hourglass.

"I'm not so sure they *know* what they're looking for," she said, tilting her head slightly. "And I'm not so sure we were looking for the *right* timepiece, either."

"Whatever do you mean, oh sister mine?" inquired her brother as he moved toward her.

"Well," she explained, "we were thinking clocks. Grandfather-type clocks, wall clocks and such. Right?"

"Yes," he agreed. "And?"

She gestured the hourglass that was built into a stout wooden frame.

By now everyone was standing around the display case to see to what she was referring. The hourglass was nothing particularly amazing. It was simple, made of wood and glass, and showing decades of wear at sea.

"You know," Tammy said, "that never crossed my mind!"

"It never crossed *any* of our minds," laughed Anne. "It's just not something one thinks about when one thinks about time."

"The clue in the journal mentioned 'time,'" said Connie, "nothing about a time*piece*."

"Quite so," agreed Anne, smiling.

George leaned over and looked closely at the artifact under glass. "I don't see anything on it," he said. "What sort of key are we looking for?"

"I expect it's hidden within the hourglass," his sister answered. "Probably not in the sand, but somewhere in the wooden frame."

"I'll go downstairs to the curator's office and look for a key to open the display case," said her father, and he hurried away.

The six teens stood around the case looking at the contents.

"It just occurred to me," said Harvey, "that this hourglass is probably not much bigger than the thing we're looking for—if it even exists."

"Your deduction is spot on," admitted Anne. "Somewhere in it, I suspect, is another key—or clue—to the treasure's location."

"Or a clue to another clue," murmured Jorge.

"Oh, great!" exclaimed Tammy. "We're going to be following a string of clues to find something that may or may not even exist!"

"Exciting, isn't it?" laughed George.

"I am inclined to think," said Anne, "that, as there *are* clues, there also exists … something."

The Chief of Police was not gone long when he returned with a clutch of keys on a ring. Small bits of tape on each key had a number and a letter written on them. "I'm going to have a wild guess and say that the number is for the floor—as it's either a one or a two—and the letter identifies which display cabinet it goes to."

"This cabinet has a Q," said his son, pointing to a small brass plaque on the front left corner of the lid and which bore the letter he mentioned.

"So, 2Q?" inquired Connie.

Nathan Hambaugh sorted through the keys until he found one with a matching alpha-numeric identifier. "This should be the one," he said, approaching the display of MacLeod paraphernalia. The key fit, and turned, and there was heard an audible 'click' as the locking mechanism disengaged. "So far, so good," he said as he took hold of the glass top and carefully opened it. A stick on the inner left side of the case was used to prop the lid open. He reached in and took hold of the hourglass. "Heavier than it looks," he commented.

"Probably the sand," suggested his daughter.

With the utmost care the police chief examined the artifact from top to bottom. Finally, he told those gathered around him, "There is a screw in the base, which is probably where the sand is added. I'm willing to bet George's allowance that there's a cavity in there for the next clue."

His son looked at him. "I get an allowance?"

"It's been going into your college fund," responded the boy's father with a grin and wink.

"I'd rather have a car fund," George said.

"I'm sure you would," chuckled Nathan. "All right, who has a standard screwdriver on their person?"

"I've one on my multi-tool," said Tammy, pulling the tool from its leather holder on her hip and handing it over. "Careful of the knife blade," she added, "it's sharp!"

Minutes later Nathan had the base removed and set aside. Inside was a small cavity, and in the cavity was a folded piece of paper, and inside that folded piece of paper was a brass key. "'The key to the treasure is in the time,'" he murmured, the key lying in the palm of his hand.

"Now what?" asked Harvey.

"Now we figure out what that key opens," replied Anne.

"It could go to anything," Connie sighed gloomily.

"True," admitted her best friend, nodding, "but it goes to something specific."

"Such as?" inquired Tammy.

"I don't know," confessed Anne. "Yet."

Replacing the base to the hourglass, Nathan Hambaugh returned the artifact to its place in the display case, and then closed and locked the lid. "It's getting late," he told the ensemble, "so I suggest we call it a day. We can think on what the key goes to on our own tonight, and then discuss it tomorrow."

The others nodded in agreement as they began to file toward the stairs that would take them to the first floor.

Anne was the last, lingering among the display cases and casting a casual eye over the collection of artifacts from the town's past. Her eyes finally settled on the stained-glass window that depicted a sailing ship and an hourglass. It did not escape her that the hourglass depicted was almost identical to the one on the display case. A small plaque beneath the colorful window identified it as having come from the sea captain's manor, from a place on the second floor facing west. She studied the window, biting her lower lip in thought.

She assumed that the ship was Captain MacLeod's, perhaps commemorating his final voyage. She stopped biting her lip and stood just a little straighter. She moved closer to the piece of art—for that is what it was, as well as a window—and began to look at it more closely. The hourglass was in the upper left corner, and the ship took up most of the lower two-thirds. Considering the medium, the detail was quite impressive. She could make out two small figures on the quarterdeck. She could not help but wonder if those minuscule figures were supposed to represent Angus and Eleanor.

"Are you coming?" boomed a voice from below.

"Yes, Pater," she replied. "I was just looking at this stained-glass window from the manor."

"Oh?" Moments later her father was standing by her side. "I sent everyone else on," he said. "So, what about this window has captured your inquisitive attention?"

She was quiet for a moment, and then she replied, "Well, I'm not really sure."

"But there *is* something," he encouraged gently.

"You see the hourglass in the upper left corner," she said, pointing to the small image, "and you see the sailing ship with two tiny figures," she went on, "so I just began to wonder if there was something here that may give us a clue as to what that brass key goes into."

"Makes sense," he admitted with a nod. He moved closer to the window and began to look it over. "Is there anything in particular that you're looking for?"

"Honestly, Pater," she sighed, "I have no idea. I just thought that perhaps there would be a clue somewhere in it."

"Well, it almost looks like the manor there in the background," said her father, pointing to a minuscule structure beyond the ship, barely discernible through the billowing sails.

She peered more closely. "You're right!" she declared. "I hadn't seen that!"

"Could this body of water be Lake Ordinary?" hypothesized her father.

"I don't see how," she replied. "While it *is* a good-sized lake, there is no way an ocean-going merchantman could sail to it. The river feeding the lake just isn't that deep, and it comes down from the mountains."

"True," admitted her father, adding, "but it feeds out the other side, and that eventually leads to the ocean."

"Yes, but—"

"And, while I'm not a sailor, I'm guessing that the vessel depicted is more like a ketch, or a yawl, which would mean a shallower draft." He paused for the briefest moment before adding, "It's definitely not an ocean-going merchantman."

"And if the draft is shallower," she murmured, "and if the vessel was empty …"

"… it could navigate up the river to the lake," her father finished. "He was a man of the sea, so I'd be surprised if he *didn't* have a boat of some kind."

"I suspect that you are right, Pater," she said, nodding.

"Come along," said Nathan Hambaugh. "It's time we got home for dinner. We can talk about the possibilities on the way"

"Very well," she sighed, and, as she turned away from the stained-glass window, she murmured, "I wonder what happened to his boat."

FOUR

Tuesday, July 6th.

Anne Hambaugh's gold-flecked green eyes opened with the chiming of the clock in the family room. Today was a special day for her. Today was her seventeenth birthday. She was less of a child and more of a woman, and still one hundred percent investigative journalist with the *Ordinary Outlook*. She smiled as she stretched, which was followed immediately by a sizable yawn. Surprisingly, she had slept quite well. With all the activity of the previous two days, her mind had been alive with the goings-on, yet she had slept soundly.

She swung her feet out from beneath her warm blankets and into her pink fuzzy bunny slippers. She pulled on her daisy-print robe as she followed her freckled nose to the brewing coffee pot. Pouring two cups of the piping hot morning elixir, she added cream and sugar to hers. She turned and handed one cup—untainted black—to her father as he entered the kitchen.

"Good morning, my little birthday girl," said Nathan Hambaugh, kissing her forehead. "And thank you for my cuppa."

"You are quite welcome," she responded, and the two walked into the family room.

Her father went to his leather recliner and settled into it, sipping his coffee as he did. She went to the big bay window that allowed an unobstructed view of the lake. As the day warmed, a mist formed on the water's surface.

"How does it feel to be a year older?" he asked.

"Oh, much the same as yesterday," she admitted, "but different as well."

He nodded, chuckling, "Yes, that's about it." After a moment, he added, "So, what are your big plans for today?"

"More research," she told him. "I want to find out what the key goes to, and whatever I can about his boat. You are right, being a seaman all his life, he would have had a boat of some kind to use here on the lake. And the stained-glass window depicted a boat that was—as you said—obviously *not* a merchantman, so I have to assume that it depicts the boat he had here."

"Makes sense," nodded her father.

"I'm going to speak with Miss Rialdi again," Anne went on, "and with Mr. Rosendale, if he's up to visitors."

"Well, he took a good wallop," said her father, finishing his coffee and holding out the cup. "Refill, please, my dear. I'd call the hospital before making the trip out there."

"Oh, I shall," she said, taking the cup and walking into the kitchen. There she topped up her cup, filled his, and poured up a fresh cup as her mother entered. "Good morning, Mum."

"Good morning, my dear." Emma Hambaugh kissed her daughter's forehead. "There is a rumor going around that today is your birthday."

"You're the second person to have mentioned it, so it must be true!" laughed Anne, returning the kiss.

"And, if my hearing serves me correctly, rather than spending the day frolicking, you intend to spend it investigating your mystery."

"You are," Anne said, smiling broadly, "beautiful with exceptional hearing!"

"True," admitted her mother, winking.

"I have a couple of mysteries going on," Anne said. "We have solved—to a point—who reported George and Jorge the other night; trespassers reporting trespassers. I suspect that the 'ghost' they think they saw was one of them. We're still investigating the alleged treasure. The statuette existed, and there is mention of it being stolen, but whether it was Angus Macleod who pinched it is still up for debate. There is something, however, that people have been looking for—off and on—for well over one hundred years, and the clue in the old Macleod journal has led us to a key in an hourglass. So, right now, that is the mystery we're working on."

"I see," said Emma as she settled into her comfy corner of the sofa. "No one is being shot at this time?"

"Oh my, no!" laughed her daughter. "Just because there is supposed to be some kind of curse following the statuette of Tlaltecuhtli—the one who gives and devours life and requires many human sacrifices to sustain her—doesn't mean there is any *substance* to it."

Her mother looked at her. The green eyes beneath the unruly red hair blinked only once. Turning her head to face her husband, Emma asked, "Is this wise, Nathan?"

"What could possibly go wrong?" was his reply.

"You are *not* being helpful."

"Emma, my love," he said, "Anne is quite capable of taking care of herself. In addition to that, she will be doing this investigating with the others; she won't be alone." He looked over at his daughter. "That's right, isn't it?"

"Oh, Pater!" Anne laughed. "Of course, I won't be alone!" She finished her coffee and smiled at both her parents as she headed out of the family room. "Off to shower before my dearly beloved brother awakens!"

After their daughter had bounced happily from the room, Nathan turned to his wife and said, "It's funny, you know, to think that—not too long ago—she was miserable and angry."

"Yes," agreed Emma, sipping her coffee, "funny that."

ଓଓଓଓଓଓଓଓଓଓ

Harvey Freeman was parked outside the Hambaugh ancestral home when Anne emerged. Connie Bascomb was seated up front, so her best friend scrambled into the backseat of the 1978 primer-gray Jeep Cherokee Chief. She greeted the two effusively, her eyes bright and full of optimism.

"How's the birthday girl?" asked Connie, grinning.

"I am *marvelous*!" was the happy response.

"Birthday?" inquired Harvey as he started the Jeep.

"The big 1-7 today!" laughed Connie. "You need to pay more attention!"

"Ah. Well, happy birthday, Anne," he said as he pulled onto the blacktop and headed for town.

"Thank you, the both of you," she said happily. "I feel good about today. I'm hoping that Miss Rialdi will be able to tell us a little more about Angus Macleod, and about the boat he had."

"Boat?" the two in the front of the vehicle asked in unison.

"Yes," Anne told them. "There is a stained-glass window at the museum that is from the manor depicting an hourglass—"

"Ah!" declared Harvey.

"—and a sailing vessel that was definitely not a merchantman, and through the sails of which one could make out the manor in the background."

"Very clever," said Connie. "Do you think the boat is significant?"

"Probably not," admitted Anne. "Mostly, I'm just curious about what happened to it. I'll also go through the old newspapers in the basement of City Hall once I have an idea of when it was around, and when it stopped being around."

"I can poke around on the internet," offered Connie, "though I'm not too optimistic about digging anything up on that."

"That's okay," said Anne. "I just want to satisfy my own curiosity. It may or may not be something I can use in my story."

They chatted about where they were in their respective investigations and before they knew it the Jeep was rolling to a stop outside the quaint cottage of Elisa Rialdi. As usual, on the front porch was seated the substantial Maremmano-Abruzzese Sheepdog, Amico. The teen trio walked up the cobblestone path and through the gate of the white picket fence. The white dog did not move as it watched them approach. It was only as they came up to the porch that a low, rumbling growl was offered as a warning.

Before any of the teens could say or do anything, the door to the cottage opened and Elisa Rialdi emerged. "Hello!" she declared happily. "I thought I heard Amico making noise. Do come in and join me; I'm about to sit down to a cup of hot cocoa and cinnamon buns."

The teens followed the older woman into her museum-like sitting room and sat where she indicated. They waited patiently as the retired librarian gathered together cups of hot cocoa and warmed buns on a silver salver. As she passed the tray around, each took a cup and a bun.

This done, everyone enjoyed a sip and a bite before getting down to the business at hand.

Anne filled in Elisa as to what had transpired since their last visit. "So, while we're closer to solving this little mystery," she said, "we're not much closer to solving this little mystery."

"Isn't that the way of things?" laughed the older woman. "I'm trying to remember if there was any mention of Captain Macleod's last vessel." She thought for a moment. "There is a book," she finally told them, "in the library about the boats and their captains of Lake Ordinary. It was locally published for the author by a vanity press. There may very well be something in that book to help further your investigation."

"Definitely!" declared Anne, excitedly. "At this point, any information would help!"

"Miss Rialdi," said Harvey around the last bite of his cinnamon bun, "what do you think happened to MacLeod and his wife?"

"I think they are still here," was the quiet reply.

An uncomfortable stillness enveloped those in the room.

"Come again?" he asked after an uneasy moment.

Elisa Rialdi smiled just a bit as she looked at the young cadet. "I think they are still here," she reiterated. "Or rather," she qualified as she gestured in the direction of the manor, "up there."

"Why do you think that?" asked Anne.

"Oh, I don't know, really," replied Elisa. "It's just a … feeling."

"You don't mean … like … you know … ghosts …?" Connie asked nervously.

"I can't explain it," chuckled the former librarian. "I just don't think they ever left." After a moment, she added, "There are those who believe Angus and his wife were driven away by those who first settled here."

"Why?" asked Harvey.

"Because, in the very early days of this settlement, the people were very … cliquish," Elisa explained. "They had traveled a long distance and settled here together. They had built Ordinary together. They had established themselves here together. Angus and Eleanor were outsiders. They had come along later. And, I suspect, the locals were not very happy when the manor started going up, although it was some distance from the town."

"But the MacLeods employed local labor for the reconstruction, didn't they?" insisted Connie.

"Some, perhaps," responded Elisa. "Remember, Ordinary was much smaller than it is today."

"Which isn't saying much," quipped Harvey, grinning.

"True," admitted Elisa, who then continued, "Many of—indeed, most of—the laborers would have been brought in from elsewhere. It is a very distinct probability they were brought in from Scotland with the disassembled manor, having been the ones who did the disassembly."

"More outsiders," murmured Anne.

"Yes," agreed Elisa, "more outsiders."

"But the manor was nearing completion before trouble started," pointed out Connie.

"Well, we don't know when trouble started," said the older woman, sipping her hot cocoa. "There may very well have been instances of trouble all along. There is nothing in the good sea captain's journal that indicates much of anything other than his occasional jabs at the workers. No names. No specifics. He did not put much to paper."

"Workers from Scotland would have known of the treasure," murmured Anne. "I suppose it's possible that, as work progressed and they weren't finding it, they could have revolted."

"That is one possibility," agreed Elisa, watching their faces.

"Here's a silly question," said Harvey, setting down his empty cup. "The manor is being reassembled. The workers are being paid—I'm guessing—weekly. Where did MacLeod keep his loot? You know, the funds he used to pay them, and to live off while the work was being done."

"That, my dear Harvey," said Anne, sitting slightly straighter, "is a very *good* question!"

There was silence for a minute as they each pondered the question.

"On his boat, perhaps?" inquired Elisa, a helpful lilt in her voice.

Three sets of eyes focused on her. She smiled knowingly.

"That would make sense," Anne said. "If Angus had a boat on the lake, he and Eleanor would have lived on it while the manor was being built."

"Why *pay* for a place to live when you already *have* a place to live," agreed Connie, smiling.

"Exactly," said Elisa, nodding.

"So, we need to find out what happened to that boat," Harvey said as his eyes shifted to the large window and the lake beyond.

"And the place to start is the library," added Connie.

"You two find out what you can there," Anne instructed them. "I'm going to see what I can find in the back copies of the *Outlook*. The last time I went through them I wasn't looking for anything specific; I was just familiarizing myself with this strange little backwater. But now..."

ଓଓଓଓଓଓଓଓଓଓ

Anne Hambaugh stepped out of the Jeep Cherokee Chief and bade her two companions a cheerful *arrivederci*. As they drove off for the library, she turned and went up the front steps of City Hall. She could hear indistinguishable voices coming from the council chambers which told her that the town council was in session. She walked past the main hall a short distance to the desk of Maude Raynes, who was focused on a game of solitaire spread out before her.

"Good morning, Miss Hambaugh," said the sixty-seven-year-old police department secretary/records clerk/dispatcher.

"Good morning, Mrs. Raynes," Anne responded cheerily. "Are we winning?"

"This game is out to get me," sighed Maude as she sat back in her chair. "And what brings you to these hallowed halls?"

"The archives of the *Ordinary Outlook* in the basement," replied Anne. Glancing toward the closed doors of the council chambers, she asked, "You're a member of the town council, why are you not in with the others?"

"Believe it or not," the older woman responded with a small smile, "it isn't a regular council meeting going on in there. Just a handful discussing what to do with Captain Ezekiel Cartwright's remains. I saw no point in putting in my two cents. Besides, your father knows where I stand on that."

"Ah!" said Anne, nodding. "A next of kin was not found, as I recall."

"Well, kin were found, but none responded," explained Maude. "For whatever reason."

"Well, it will be nice to finally put him—and his illegal escapades—to rest," the seventeen-year-old journalist said.

"How are things progressing on your new investigation?" asked Maude, her hazel eyes watching the younger woman's freckled face.

"Oh, it's progressing!" laughed Anne, and she told what had transpired over the last few days. "I want to ask you: did you ever hear about Captain MacLeod's boat? I believe he had one here on the lake."

The woman behind the desk thought for a moment, and then answered, "You know, Anne, I vaguely recall some passing mention—oh, ages ago in my youth—about his boat … a ketch, I believe it was. I don't really know that much about boats."

"Me, neither, truth be told. Do you know what became of it?" the teen asked.

With a slow, thoughtful shake of her head, Maude replied, "I don't really … Wait. If memory serves me, it sank, I think, during a particularly bad storm. Why do you ask?"

"All part of the mystery!" Anne laughed. "Anyway, thank you. I'll leave you to your cards and browse through local history in the archives."

"Enjoy," said Maude, bidding the younger woman farewell as she returned to her unfinished game.

Anne took the stairs down to the basement where the offices of the *Ordinary Outlook* were, and where copies of the weekly journal were archived. She entered the former-jail-cell-now-archive-room at the far end of the basement and walked slowly along the bank of battered old filing cabinets until she found a date-range she thought would be a good start. Carefully pulling copies from the drawers, she began to diligently examine them.

It was noon when she heard the cell phone in her cross-body bag suddenly come alive. She jumped involuntarily, and then laughed at herself. Seeing who the call was from, she said, "Talk to me." A minute later she told the caller that she would meet them at the malt shop for lunch, and then hung up.

Satisfied with what she had found among the timeless words, she returned the aging copies to their rightful place, tidied up, and left the basement in darkness. Upstairs she found that Maude Raynes had left—probably for lunch—and that the building was very quiet. For a moment, she felt unsettled. Shaking the feeling, she hurried out the building's front doors, down the steps, and made her away to the Common. There were people milling about, enjoying the warm, midday sunshine. She made her way across the Common, reaching the Ordinary Malt Shoppe as her friends emerged from the Jeep.

"Perfect timing!" laughed Connie.

"Tammy's here," Harvey said. "She's holding a booth for us."

The trio went in, saw their friend waving at them, and made their way through the busy establishment to the booth. Seated, with orders quickly placed, the foursome began to share what had been learned.

ଔଔଔଔଔଔଔଔଔ

"The book which Miss Rialdi mentioned was there," Connie Bascomb told them. "There was a pen-and-ink drawing of Captain MacLeod's boat."

"A ketch," added Harvey Freeman. "Sleek."

"He called it '*Banrigh na Locha*,'" Connie continued. "'Queen of the Lake.'"

"Very regal," commented Tammy Coleman.

"The book made mention that the boat sank during a storm," Harvey went on, "—apparently the storm of the century—and that there were no survivors."

"Implying that there were people on board," murmured Anne. "The captain and his bride, perchance?"

Both Connie and Harvey shrugged. "It didn't say," she answered for them.

"Could have been just his crew," suggested Tammy.

"If he had a crew," said Harvey. "If he used the boat as his go-to bank, he probably didn't have a crew."

"He wasn't always on the boat," Anne said. "I rather doubt he would leave his wealth unguarded. I suspect he had one or two trusted associates who kept an eye on things."

"Good point," admitted Harvey.

"Hey!" exclaimed Tammy in a hushed voice. "What if his trusted associates did him in and took all his loot?"

The other three looked at her.

"They wouldn't have been very trusted," replied Connie.

"True," agreed Tammy, "but it's a possibility."

Anne was thoughtful. "It's certainly worth considering."

"What were you able to learn in the bowels of City Hall?" asked Harvey.

"Ah! Well, not much, actually," responded Anne. "Apparently, Angus did bring in quite a few workers from Scotland, men who had been part of the disassembly."

"Makes sense," said Connie.

"Yes. And, as Miss Rialdi said, the locals were none too keen on that," continued Anne. "But these were mostly agricultural folk, and this was mostly a farming community. They helped build each other's homes, certainly, but work on City Hall and other buildings came later, and with outside help."

"So, the locals tried to stop the reconstruction?" asked Tammy.

"It wasn't stated in so many words," answered Anne, "but the short answer would be 'yes.' They didn't storm the place with torches and pitchforks, but there was mention of things coming up missing, or damaged."

"Sabotage," said Harvey with a nod.

"For the most part," agreed Anne. "Interestingly, I found some mention—indeed, almost bragging—in the journal of Malachi Somerfield, Esq."

"He was the fellow not keen on your ancestors?" inquired the young cadet.

"The same," replied Anne with a nod.

"What did he do?" asked Tammy. "Or did he not say?"

"He never confessed outright," Anne told her friends. "It would seem, however, that he was—at the very least—involved with the death of a worker at the manor."

"And Macleod was blamed," Connie said.

Anne nodded again. "It looks that way."

Their lunches were brought which put a pause in the conversation. Customers came and went without notice as they thoroughly enjoyed the respite. With empty plates cleared away, they paid the bill and stepped outside. On the sidewalk, they looked casually around at the mid-week activity. The sidewalk was rather busy with curious visitors, so the quartet crossed the street to the Common.

"What are your big birthday plans?" Tammy asked as she settled onto a park bench.

"This is it," laughed Anne. "Spending time with friends."

"And working on a mystery," added Connie, smiling.

"Yes, well, that, too," agreed Anne.

"Speaking of which," Harvey said, "did you find anywhere in your reading *where* the boat went down?"

"Not latitude and longitude, if that's what you mean," Anne replied, shaking her head.

"I wonder of Ralph Hale could find it," mused Tammy.

"It's an awfully big lake to look for one sunken boat," Connie murmured.

"Especially one that is well over one hundred years old and probably in pieces," added Harvey.

"He found that downed fighter plane," Tammy reminded them.

"He also had an idea of where to look," interjected Connie, glancing in the direction of Lake Ordinary. "That boat could be anywhere out there."

"Tammy is right, though," said Anne. "We need to find Captain MacLeod's ketch. We need to know if—just maybe—the statuette of Tlaltecuhtli is there."

"So, how do we figure out where to start looking for this shipwreck?" asked Connie. "Start in the middle of the lake and work our way outwards? A hunt like that could take weeks!"

"I think we should present our problem to Mr. Hale," Anne replied. "He knows the lake; he just might have an idea how best to conduct such an exploration."

"That would wrap up that part of the mystery," admitted Harvey. "Then we'd be able to focus on what happened to Angus and Eleanor."

"That's true," agreed Anne.

"If we find that treasure," Tammy suggested, "we could use it as bait to reel in those two in that ugly Gremlin."

Harvey visibly brightened. "Yes!"

"In the meantime," said Anne, "we have an old brass key that goes to a lock ... somewhere."

There was a pause in the conversation, and then Connie murmured, "We could always ask a locksmith." Three heads turned to the young African American. "What?" she asked.

A broad smile appeared on Anne's face. "You are a genius!" declared the seventeen-year-old. "That never occurred to me!"

"Me, neither," confessed Harvey. "Well done, Connie."

"It's an old key," Tammy said, "but Mr. Bernbaum might be able to answer some questions about it."

"It's certainly worth a try," agreed Anne. "He may be able to tell us what *type* of lock it goes to, which would narrow down our search."

"Let's go, then!" Tammy declared.

"I'll drive," added Harvey quickly.

ઌઌઌઌઌઌઌઌઌ

Theo Bernbaum was the owner of the Ordinary Lock & Key. A short and portly man, with a receding blond hairline, he enjoyed breaking up his rather mundane day with visits by inquisitive youths. When the little bell on his shop door tinkled, he stepped out of his backroom to greet his customers. In this case, there were four eager-faced teens who filed inside.

"Well, quite the honor!" he declared effusively. "I've enjoyed your articles very much, Anne!"

Happy with the review but just slightly embarrassed at the same time, the young journalist responded, "Thank you, Mr. Bernbaum. That's very kind."

"I expect you're here on yet another mystery," he continued in a knowing tone.

"As a matter of fact," she laughed lightly, "you are quite right!"

"Excellent! Excellent! How may I help?"

Anne produced the old brass key that had been recovered from the weather-beaten hourglass and presented it to the locksmith. "What can you tell us about this?"

He turned it over in his small hands for a long minute, as he examined it closely. "Hmm," he grunted softly, and started toward his backroom. "Come along!" he called.

The four teens followed him through the curtained entry to the man's inner sanctum. On a workbench along one wall were locks in various stages of assembly—or disassembly. There was a cluttered desk nearby with a bookshelf attached to the wall above it. Theo Bernbaum went to the bookshelf and looked at the bindings of several dog-eared books. At last, he pulled out a very worn edition and began to go through the pages. Several minutes later he turned to the youths, a smile on his face.

"This is quite a key you've brought here," he said with a broad smile. "And quite an old key to boot."

"We know that much," said Tammy before realizing how she had said it. "Sorry."

"No, no, it's fine," the locksmith said with a slight shake of his head. "This key, if my sources are correct, goes to a specific type of chest that was made only in Scotland almost three hundred years ago. I doubt there are any left in the world."

"There's at least one," muttered Harvey under his breath.

"The chest," continued Bernbaum, "is made of hornbeam."

"What's that?" asked Connie.

"It's a white hardwood," explained the shop owner. "The name actually comes from its use in oxen yokes—the beam between the horns, specifically—which were subjected to significant wear, as you can well imagine. Hornbeam was used for anything that required a high resistance to wear."

"A chest doesn't fall into that category, though," pointed out Tammy.

"Typically, that is true," admitted Theo, "but for a chest that was—oh, let us say—going to sea where weather conditions often were quite adverse, such a hardwood would stand up nicely."

"Yes," said Anne softly as she eyed the locksmith. "Yes, it would."

Handing the key back to her, a broad smile on his face, he said, "I hope I've been able to help somewhat."

"Yes, sir, you have," she told him, returning his smile. "It certainly narrows down the field of locked things."

On the sidewalk outside the Ordinary Lock & Key the four teens took a moment to talk among themselves. Theo Bernbaum, having mentioned a sea chest, had raised a red flag with Anne, and the others had noticed. While it could have been a coincidence, Tammy had pointed out, it did seem odd timing. Connie mentioned that, being a small town, news traveled fast … and rumors even faster. Harvey did not say much as he looked from the direction of the lake to the direction of the manor.

"There has to be a way," he finally said, "to figure out about where the ketch went down. Or, at least, the general area."

"Let's go talk with Ralph Hale," said Anne.

The foursome climbed into the Jeep, and moments later were on their way to the boardwalk on the lakefront. It took a little longer than anticipated because of the heavy visitor traffic—the increase, in part, to Anne's articles which were picked up by outlying newspapers—to reach their destination. Along the lakefront were a number of shops, one of which was the Ordinary Guided Tours and Fishing Expeditions owned and operated by sixty-three-year-old Ralph Hale. Harvey parked his Jeep in an available spot at the far end of the parking lot and the teens sauntered to their destination.

"Quite the crowd," commented Connie as they sidestepped inattentive tourists.

"I know they bring dollars into our economy," sighed Tammy, "but sometimes I wish there weren't so many."

"Maybe you should tone down your articles, Anne," suggested Harvey with a grin.

"I only print the truth!" declared the investigative journalist defensively.

The door to the Hale business was open, but there appeared to be no one inside. They stepped in with some apprehension; Harvey called out. There was no response.

"Why would the door be open and no one here?" asked Connie.

Looking about the spartan room, Tammy replied, "It's not like there's anything to steal."

"Hey," came a voice from behind them, and as one the teens turned. Marty Hale, the elder of the proprietor's sons, was standing in the entry. "If you're looking for my dad, he's out there." He gestured with his head toward the lake.

"We were, actually," said Anne. "We wanted to ask him about Angus MacLeod's boat."

"He ain't here," Marty said.

"Yes, we know that now," she continued. "Do you know when he'll be back?"

"Later."

"I see."

"You want a charter?" Marty asked. "I can set you up with a charter."

"No," she sighed, "not just yet, anyway. Really, we just wanted to talk to him."

"He ain't here. He's out there."

"Could you let him know we'd like a chat at his earliest convenience?" asked Anne, leading her friends around Marty and out the door.

"Sure."

They walked out onto the pier and stared out across the calm lake.

"Hard to believe," Connie said, "that there was ever a storm so bad that it sank a boat."

"Unless it had help," Tammy added unexpectedly.

Anne looked at the older seventeen-year-old. "What do you mean?"

"I don't know," was the reply. "It just, you know, came out."

"It *is* a thought," said Harvey.

"Scuttled, you think?" Anne pressed.

"It wouldn't be the first time," admitted Connie.

"For the insurance," added Tammy with a mischievous smile.

Anne was quiet, leaning against the weathered wooden rail and staring thoughtfully out across the lake. *Somewhere out there,* she contemplated, *was the Banrigh na Locha*. "I wonder," she said to no one in particular, "if our Scottish sea captain left a clue somewhere …"

"What?" asked Connie. "Another clue? We don't have enough as it is?"

"I mean a clue to the whereabouts of his boat," Anne clarified.

"Maybe he left a map with 'X' marking the spot," quipped Tammy.

"He could have drawn a *picture*," added Harvey with a chuckle.

"Isn't that the same as a map?" countered Tammy with a wink and a grin.

"A picture," murmured Anne, a thoughtful frown touching her brow. "A picture …"

"Uh oh," said Connie, "she's thinking again."

It was then that Anne's cell phone sounded the first handful of notes from Tchaikovsky's *1812 Overture*. "My father," she said as she pulled it out of her bag. "Hello, Pater!" she added, speaking cheerily into the device. "We're on our way." Returning the phone to her bag, she looked at her friends. "Our presence has been requested," she told them, "for an early dinner and birthday cake."

"I'd forgotten it was your birthday!" laughed Tammy.

"What with how this day has been," added Connie, "it's easy to do."

ଓଓଓଓଓଓଓଓଓଓ

Nathan Hambaugh, a glass of iced tea in hand, was seated in his leather recliner when the four teens entered the family room of the Hambaugh's ancestral home. In the comfortable room with him were his wife, and his brother and sister-in-law. On the lakefront deck outside the large bay window were George Hambaugh—who sported a stained grilling apron and held a spatula—and his best friend, Jorge Bustamante. Hamburgers and hotdogs were cooking on the built-in wood-burning grill. The delicious aroma of cooking meat and the sizzling of fat dripping into the flames were filling the air.

"George is cooking?" asked Anne, a hint of trepidation in her voice.

"And he is doing a fine job," Emma Hambaugh replied firmly.

"He's actually doing very well," chuckled Raymond Hambaugh. "He was a bit unsure when your father handed him the apron and spatula, but he took on the job like a champ."

"So," said Nathan to the four teens, "tell me about your day."

Anne gave those in attendance a recap of what they had accomplished, and finished by saying, "I've yet to speak with Mr. Rosendale about his experience at the museum."

"I figured you'd be busy," admitted her father, "so I went and had a quiet word with him. I took his statement as part of my investigation."

"How is he doing?" his daughter inquired.

"Considering he got knocked about with an ax handle," sighed the police chief, "he's doing remarkably well." After a pause, he added, "He was able to give me a description of his assailant."

"Excellent!" exclaimed Harvey.

"He described the man was being around five-feet-nine, and slightly built—perhaps around one hundred fifty pounds," Nathan continued. "He went on to say he had graying brown hair—apparently the hood of his hoodie was back a bit—and was clean-shaven, and he's pretty sure the guy has hazel eyes."

"That's pretty good," said Tammy.

"Oh, and he has a scar on his left cheek," finished Nathan, which he followed by a swallow of his tea.

Anne looked at her father's face. There was something in his eyes that troubled her. "What else, Pater?" she asked gently.

He looked at her and smiled. "What else, indeed," he murmured. "John Rosendale is of the humble opinion that his assailant resembled a thinned-down version of a former resident he remembered from our school days—Paul Harkness."

After a momentary pause, his daughter said, "Wasn't he …"

"My childhood friend," finished her father with a nod. "My partner in youthful crime, as it were. *If* this guy is that Paul, then we got into a lot trouble as kids. Nothing serious, mind you, but we were a mischievous pair."

"He certainly would have known the story of MacLeod's treasure," Andrea Hambaugh said. "Perhaps he decided that now was as good a time as any to find it."

"And he isn't aware that his former best friend is now Ordinary's Chief of Police," added her husband.

Quiet settled on the room as everyone was lost in their own thoughts.

"Is he dangerous?" asked Emma hesitantly.

Nathan looked over at where she sat in her corner of the sofa. "He had a bit of a mean streak as a kid," he admitted, "but he was never violent."

"Until now," his wife said.

It was then that George and Jorge entered the home with platters of hamburgers, hot dogs, and toasted buns. Everyone converged on the kitchen to prepare their individual plates, and to enjoy the delicious meal accompanied by light conversation. An hour later, with all dishes and silverware put in the dishwasher and the kitchen tidied up, it was time for the birthday girl to open her gifts.

Her aunt and uncle gave her a quill pen-and-inkwell set, and her brother gave her a very nice two-blade pocket knife. The gift from her parents, however, was neither wrapped nor in the house. Anne looked suspiciously at the smiling pair. "You two remind me of the Cheshire Cat," she said, a smile tugging at the corners of her mouth. "What are you up to?"

"Did you hear that, Nathan?" Emma asked, a mock expression of hurt on her face.

"I did, Emma, I did," he replied in a sad tone.

"One would think she did not trust us," went on his wife sadly.

"The youth of today," he sighed. "So suspicious. So distrustful. So … oh, I don't know."

"I apologize for my suspicions and distrust," said Anne, still eyeing the pair dubiously.

Nathan Hambaugh came out of his chair in one fluid motion. "Come along, then, out behind the woodshed."

"That's usually a bad sign," murmured Andrea Hambaugh.

"It certainly was back when I was a youngster," admitted Ray. "Though Nathan spent more time there than I did."

"You were the good child," his wife said.

"Naturally," he admitted with false modesty.

"Oh, you lot!" declared Anne with a laugh as she followed her father.

Everyone else fell in behind and filed through the kitchen and out the house's side door. They crossed the short bit of open ground, past the detached garage, and to the weathered old woodshed filled with a cord of seasoned firewood. When Nathan suddenly stopped at the house-side of the shed, everyone else came to a bumping, laughing stop. He turned to face his followers.

"This is a solemn occasion," he began in a deep, serious voice. "I think it best that Anne go first."

There was silence.

Anne took a tentative step forward, glanced at her parents, then straightened to her full five-feet-three and marched around to the back of the shed. Moments later there came a joyful squeal and the wide-eyed teen came back to face the gathering. "It's a car!" she declared happily.

"Mind you," said her mother, "it's not new."

"But … it's a car!" Anne reiterated elatedly.

"You're spoiling the child," said her uncle to her father in mock-condescension.

Nathan laughed. "She's earned it!"

Everyone hurried around the woodshed to find a green subcompact 1997 Mercury Lynx 5-door station wagon. Anne walked around it several times, speechless, and then she stopped and looked at her parents.

"It's beautiful!" she declared, a huge smile on her freckled face.

"Looks like a little green jellybean," her brother quipped.

"That may be," she admitted, "but it's *my* little green jellybean!" She rushed to her parents and gave each a hard hug.

"Next year you get the keys," said Uncle Raymond, with a wink.

"Always the comedian," responded his younger brother, pulling a set of keys from his pocket. Handing them over to Anne, he said, "Now all you need is your license."

"I can teach her everything she needs to know," volunteered Tammy.

"Ha!" guffawed Harvey.

ଓଓଓଓଓଓଓଓଓଓ

That night, after everyone had gone and it was just the immediate family relaxing in the family room, Anne thanked her parents and brother again for their thoughtful gifts. She was happy, content. Her life in Ordinary had not started out very happily, but that had changed quickly with new friends and a purpose—investigative journalism with the *Ordinary Outlook*. She had quickly come to love the quirky little town and, especially, her family's ancestral home. There were still times when she felt that there was more to the old house, that there was something—or someone—who made it more than a home, but a sanctuary from the craziness of the world ... which included Ordinary.

FIVE

Wednesday, July 7th.

Anne Hambaugh found her father—coffee cup in hand—already up and in the family room. He was standing at the big bay window looking out at the lake. With her own steaming cup, she walked up beside him and bumped him slightly. "What are you thinking, Pater?"

He kissed her forehead and replied, "I'm thinking my cup's empty."

She rolled her gold-flecked green eyes, laughing lightly at the same time. Handing him her cup, she took his and filled it. Upon her return, they swapped cups. She asked, again, "What are you thinking, Pater?"

"Well," Nathan Hambaugh said quietly, "I've been thinking about this whole … investigation. Starting out as a look into a 'ghost' sighting at the manor, and now we have a treasure hunt happening. Harvey almost fell out of a window at the manor, George and Jorge were locked in the manor's cellar, John Rosendale got knocked about pretty roughly, and Harvey had his shins whacked …"

"And the purse snatching," his daughter added.

"Yes, and that," he sighed. "And now there's a chance that the person behind all that—or at least some of that—could be a childhood chum of mine." He was quiet for a moment, and then added, "This may be getting too dangerous."

"Pater," Anne said, "I—we—have been involved in more dangerous investigations; this is mild in comparison."

"Up to this point."

"Yes, up to this point," she acquiesced. "But I feel as if we're getting close to not only finding the treasure, but to solving the mystery about what happened to Angus and Eleanor Macleod. Please, let us continue. If it becomes too dangerous, we'll stop."

"If what becomes too dangerous?" asked a voice from behind. Emma Hambaugh watched the two figures turn to face her. "Well?"

Nathan kissed his wife. "Good morning, my dear," he said affectionately.

"Good morning," she responded, returning his kiss. "Now, one of you answer my question."

"Pater is worried that this case may be getting dangerous," her daughter explained after giving her mother a hug and kiss.

"Is it?" Emma asked.

"Well, no one's been killed," her husband admitted. "Yet."

"Pater is worried about the involvement of a possible-childhood chum with a mean streak," Anne elucidated.

Emma looked at her husband, her green eyes focused on his face. "Is there danger?"

He sipped his coffee as he thought. Finally, he said, "There is always a chance of danger when it comes to treasure hunting. If the other person seeking that treasure is Paul Harkness … well, he can be a bit of a loose cannon."

"Meaning … what?" she pressed.

"I'm basing all this on when we were kids getting into trouble," he clarified cautiously. "I have no idea what he's like now … if it is Paul."

"How certain was John Rosendale?" Emma inquired.

Again, Nathan took a moment to ponder the question. "He was pretty certain," he admitted.

"Then it seems to me," his wife went on, "that you need to find him before things get out-of-hand."

"I've already started," Nathan said. "After I spoke with John, I put out inquiries as to Paul's whereabouts, criminal history, and so on. I'll be getting results back today."

"And, in the meantime," said Anne, "we continue with our investigation."

Her parents looked at the young woman with her wavy red hair. For a long moment, neither spoke. This made Anne a little nervous.

Her red eyebrows rose up slowly in pleading inquiry. Her parents looked from her to one another, and then back at the silent teen.

"For now," her father nodded.

With a gleeful little squeal, Anne hugged her parents in a group hug. "Oh, thank you!" she said effusively.

"Take your brother," her mother added, suppressing a small smile.

"Of course!" Anne declared. "My dear, dear brother!" With that, she scampered off to her room to prepare for the day.

Emma turned her attention to her husband. "They will be all right?"

Nathan nodded. "They will be all right," he reassured her. It was then that the telephone rang, interrupting them. "Who can that be at this time of morning?" he muttered as he started toward the kitchen to answer the insistent device.

"Your brother enjoys early morning chats," suggested Emma, going to her corner of the sofa and curling up.

ଔଔଔଔଔଔଔଔ

Nathan Hambaugh had left the house by the time Anne, George, and Connie Bascomb biked into town. It was mid-morning and traffic on the Old Mill Road—which was the only road between their north-of-town homes and Ordinary—was virtually nonexistent. Even so, they kept in single file and on the edge of the right shoulder of the two-lane blacktop. They brought their bikes to coasting stops at the back of City Hall and parked them in the bicycle rack. Entering through the back door, they walked to the front of the building where Maude Raynes was busy typing the previous night's reports into her computer.

"Good morning!" the three teens greeted her.

The older woman stopped her data entry, sat back in her chair, and turned to face the trio. "Good morning, Miss Hambaugh and Miss Bascomb," she responded, "and young Master Hambaugh."

"Busy night?" asked Anne, peering unsuccessfully at the computer screen.

"You could say that," replied Maude. "The library was broken into in the wee hours of the morning."

"Who breaks *into* a library?" laughed a skeptical George Hambaugh.

"I would," replied Anne. Addressing the police department's secretary/records clerk/dispatcher, she said, "My father said nothing of this earlier this morning."

"We didn't know about it until Mr. Carmichael showed up to open the doors," Maude answered, referring to James Carmichael, the librarian. "Your father is there now."

"Was anything damaged or taken?" Connie asked.

"Interestingly enough," Maude said, "from early reports, there is no indication of anything missing ..."

"But ..." added Anne gently.

"Yes, 'but,'" Maude continued. "There was a book sitting out when there shouldn't have been. Mr. Carmichael has a standing policy that all books are put in their rightful place before he locks up for the night."

"And ..."

"It was a book on boats that once cut through the waters of Lake Ordinary." Maude Raynes looked at the trio and nodded. "It was open to the page concerning Angus MacLeod's ketch. Someone decided to get in some late-night reading."

"Paul Harkness, perhaps?" asked Anne.

Maude, with a curious expression on her face, looked at the teen investigative journalist. "Why do you mention him?"

"Pater thinks he may be the one behind the recent hauntings at the manor," Anne explained.

"And the purse snatching on the Fourth," added Connie.

"And the to-do at the museum," George supplemented.

"Really," murmured Maude thoughtfully.

"Did you know him?" Anne inquired.

"It's been a very long time since I've heard that name," confessed Maude, "but I found a report—a response to something your father sent out late yesterday, I presume—in our fax tray."

"Are we permitted to know what it said?" asked Anne hopefully.

"Technically ... no," answered a voice from the building's front entrance. Harvey Freeman walked up to them. The police cadet was clad in an immaculately cleaned-and-pressed tan uniform complete with shiny gold-colored badge.

"That is true," agreed Maude with a nod to the young man, "but if your father wants to tell you, that's his call."

"And he's at the library now?" Connie inquired excitedly.

"With Sergeant Nielson, yes," Maude told them.

"Care for a lift?" offered Harvey.

ଔଔଔଔଔଔଔଔଔଔ

Chief of Police Nathan Hambaugh walked slowly around the Ordinary Library, the leather soles of his shoes slapping lightly on the marble floor. Beside him walked the forty-six-year-old librarian, James Carmichael. The two men spoke softly; their voices still echoed—albeit faintly—within the cavernous edifice. They finally came to a stop at the front doors where Sergeant Bradley Nielson stood in silence.

"If I didn't know the backstory," said Nathan, "I'd think someone breaking *into* the library a hoax."

The librarian nodded. "It's just bizarre to me."

"Well, if my suspicion is right," continued the interim police chief, "Paul Harkness is the man we want to talk to." Looking to his sergeant, he asked, "No latent prints?"

"Well, I didn't dust the entire building," was the response, "but the point of entry showed a lot of smudges and partial obliterations."

"Gloves?"

"That's what I'm thinking."

Nathan nodded. "All right, Brad, you can go about your day. Thanks for your help here."

It was then that the library doors opened, and four teens entered as the police sergeant exited. They stopped just inside the building and glanced around inquisitively. The Chief of Police, seeing who had entered, waved them to where he stood with the librarian.

"I was wondering how much longer it would be before you lot showed up," he commented.

"We didn't want to seem overly curious," his daughter responded with a grin.

"Well," he went on, "there isn't much to see here. The trespasser jimmied the lock and came in through the front doors, found what he was looking for, and then left. He was probably in here for less than an hour."

"I wonder what put him on the track of the boat," said Connie.

With a shrug, Harvey said, "He could have overheard us—or someone else—mention it."

"I doubt it," Anne countered, shaking her head.

"He has a girlfriend," pointed out George.

There was a moment of silence as the others pondered this simple statement, then Anne said, "I'd forgotten about her." Looking at her brother, she asked, "You saw her, what does she look like?"

George thought for a moment, and then answered, "She was tall, with brown hair and prominent cheek bones. Maybe middle-aged?"

"Fat?" asked Harvey. "Skinny?"

"I think … willowy … would best describe her."

"Did we see anyone like that?" Connie asked, unconvinced.

Anne shook her head. "If we did, I certainly don't remember. We were so many places, and there were so many people, she could have been anywhere."

"Like in the booth behind us as we discussed the case yesterday and talked about our dear Angus's boat," Harvey muttered.

Everyone looked at him.

"You think so?" Connie asked.

He shrugged. "It's the only logical place," he answered.

"So, we have to assume that they know—more or less—what we know," Anne said unhappily.

"But *they* don't know that *we* know who *they* are," her father interjected.

"*Do* we know, Pater?" Anne asked.

"I got some reports back this morning," he explained, "that lead me to believe that the man is, indeed, Paul Harkness. His partner is believed to be one Hortense Grimes, a small-time grifter."

"Not exactly her line of work, then" pointed out Harvey.

"True."

"And him?" asked Anne. "What do we know about him?"

Nathan Hambaugh sighed; his expression revealed the sorrow he clearly felt. "My childhood chum … is a petty thief and swindler who has been in and out of lock-ups all over the country."

"I'm sorry, Pater," whispered Anne.

Nathan forced a smile. “It is what it is, right? He could have been anything he wanted to be …”

“Maybe he is,” James Carmichael said.

ᏧᏧᏧᏧᏧᏧᏧᏧᏧᏧ

“What do we do now?” queried Connie as they left the library.

“I still want to speak with Ralph Hale,” Anne said firmly. “His knowledge of the lake could help us find the *Banrigh na Locha*.”

“Do you think that’s where the treasure is?” asked George.

“Well, yes, I do,” his sister replied. “The fact that no one has found it at the manor over the last however-long-it’s-been makes me think that it is elsewhere. The most likely ‘elsewhere’ would be on Angus MacLeod’s boat.”

“Which, if recent memory serves me, is somewhere at the bottom of the lake,” pointed out Harvey.

“Exactly,” agreed Anne. “Hence, Captain Ralph Hale, owner-and-operator of Lake Ordinary Guided Tours and Fishing Expeditions and unquestioning expert regarding anything and everything pertaining to said lake.”

With a slight nod of his blond head, Harvey acquiesced, “I’ll buy that.”

“And here comes Tammy,” added Connie, pointing to the white 1967 Mustang convertible that came to a stop behind the cadet’s patrol car.

Tammy Coleman stood up on the tan leather driver seat and waved to the small group. “Hey!” she called out. “Guess what?”

As the four approached her, Connie asked, “What?”

“I was talking with Mitch earlier about our mystery,” she explained, grinning broadly, “and he thinks the old pirate’s loot went down with his boat, as well!”

“‘Old pirate?’” laughed Anne.

“Well, you know what I mean,” Tammy said, laughing as well. “He’s supposed to have stolen that statuette—”

“Allegedly,” corrected Harvey. “There’s no proof of that.”

“True,” admitted Tammy, sighing.

“Which brings us back to what we were talking about,” said Anne.

"Which was?" asked Connie.

"Talking to Ralph Hale," answered her best friend.

"The Old Man of the Lake," George said, trying his best to sound serious.

"He hasn't called since our visit to his—er—office?" Harvey inquired.

"I've heard nothing," admitted Anne, "so I suppose another trip to see him is called for."

"Not to sound paranoid," said Connie softly, after a brief silence, "but if we keep talking to people about this, isn't there a chance they—or others—might start their own treasure hunt?"

Anne looked at her for a moment, and then said, "You have a point, I must admit, but we need to speak with people to get information."

"It's tricky," admitted Tammy. "Talk of treasure tends to make people go crazy."

"We shan't speak of treasure unless absolutely necessary," Anne told the small group. "What we want to know right now is the whereabouts of Angus Macleod's boat … for the purpose of a story I'm writing for the *Ordinary Outlook*. We can call it … historical research."

"Well," murmured Harvey, "I'm man enough to admit that this whole thing's making me nervous."

"Because you almost fell out of the manor, and you got your shins knocked about a bit?" asked George with a mischievous smirk.

"And getting run over by a purse-snatcher," added Tammy, smiling.

"Yeah, well," he grunted defensively, "I've just got a feeling that bigger trouble is coming … for one of us."

Anne gave him a concerned sidelong look. She felt that, too. "We will all have to be extra careful," she said. "I think we're getting closer to solving this mystery …"

"Which one?" asked George.

"I think," his sister answered, "that when we find the lost treasure—"

"Provided it actually exists," interjected Connie.

"—then we will learn what happened to Angus and Eleanor."

"All right, then!" declared Tammy. "Let's go do this!"

"You go ahead," said Harvey. "I have patrolling to do today. Let me know what you find out, though."

After the cadet had gone, George looked to his sister. "If it's all right with you, Jorge and I were going to do some work on the old Studebaker."

With a nod, she replied, "That should be all right. We can give you a lift."

"No need," he told her. "My bike is behind City Hall, and it won't take me but fifteen minutes to bike to his house."

"Very well," she agreed. "Do stay out of trouble."

"*Moi*?" he laughed, and off he went in the direction of City Hall.

"And then there were three," said Tammy. "Shall we?" she added, ushering her friends toward her convertible.

"Wait," said Anne as she saw her father emerge from the library.

"What sort of trouble are you young ladies up to?" he asked with a smile as he approached.

"Oh, you know, the usual," replied Tammy, grinning.

"Well, as long as it's just the usual," the Chief of Police chuckled. Looking to Anne, he asked, "Where's your brother?"

"He is off to Jorge's," she replied. "They're going to work on the Anja's car."

"Good," said her father with a nod. "That project ought to keep him out of trouble ... at least, for a little while."

"Pater," said Anne, "would it be possible to get back into the museum?"

Nathan Hambaugh looked at his daughter for a silent moment, and then asked, "Why?"

"It's the stained-glass window on the second floor," she told him, her brow furrowing slightly.

"What about it?" asked Connie eagerly.

With a frustrated sigh, she said, "I'm not sure. Yesterday I had the strangest ... thought. We had been speaking among ourselves about clues and maps—"

"I remember that!" declared Tammy. "I made a comment about 'X' marking the spot!"

"Yes."

"And Harvey said something like 'He could have drawn a picture,'" Tammy continued with a chuckle. "And then I said something like 'Isn't that the same as a map?'"

"And I said: 'A picture,'" Anne added. "A picture …"

"Uh oh," said Connie, "she's thinking again."

Anne's father narrowed his eyes. "You think there's a clue in the stained-glass window?"

"I … I'm not positive," his daughter admitted, "but there is something about it … something I just cannot explain."

"Well," he said, "it *is* open. His wife is there."

"By herself?" asked Connie aghast. "After what happened to her husband?"

The Chief of Police smiled. "Their son is there as well, so no need to worry."

"Eskil 'Sure-Shot' Rosendale is back in town?" asked Tammy, surprised.

Anne looked to the other seventeen-year-old. "I have the distinct impression that I am missing something here."

Her father chuckled. "Eskil Rosendale is an Air Force Special Operations—Special Ops—veteran," he explained.

"A curious name," she said.

"Apparently, it means 'Vessel of God,'" he explained, adding with a smile, "I thought it was *so* unusual that I had to ask."

"He was a sniper," Tammy told them, "hence the nickname: Sure-Shot."

"Ah! One to be taken seriously, then," said Anne with a nod.

"He came back last night after what happened to his father," Nathan told the trio, "and may the Lord have mercy on the perpetrator's soul—"

"—because Sure-Shot sure won't," finished Tammy with a tone of finality in her voice.

The teenagers took their seats in Tammy's Mustang and followed the police chief to the museum, parking beside his patrol car in the parking lot. There were several vehicles already there—curiosity-seekers brought by the recent happenings in Ordinary—so they took two spots at the far end of the graveled lot, beside a large black 2000 Harley-

Davidson Road King motorcycle. They walked in silence to the two-story building and stepped inside.

Not far off was a man who could only be described as a beefy biker, sporting a short, blond flat-top and a very full, blond walrus mustache. He stood fix-feet-four and filled out his t-shirt to the point of nearly bursting its seams. The back of his worn leather vest proclaimed his motorcycle club allegiance, a veteran's group. His blue eyes settled quickly on the newcomers. "Chief," he said in a sonorous gravelly voice.

"Good Morning, Eskil," the Chief of Police replied, shaking the big man's massive hand. "The curiosity-seekers are behaving?"

"Of course," came the rumbling response. The weathered face of the thirty-two-year-old broke into a grin.

"Good. We're going up to look at the stained-glass window from the Macleod Manor," Nathan said.

"Enjoy," said Eskil, and he began casually wandering about the ground floor of the museum.

"A man of few words," Anne commented quietly, watching as he moved away.

"A man like that doesn't *need* many words," Connie pointed out.

There were a handful of young visitors on the second floor milling about. They wandered among the display cases and commented among themselves in quiet voices. When they saw the police uniform, they wandered back downstairs. This suited Nathan Hambaugh and the teens just fine, as it allowed them to do what they needed to do without an audience of gawkers.

Anne went straight to the stained-glass window, light streaming through it, and studied it in silence.

"What, exactly, are you looking for?" her father finally asked.

She let out a short sigh. "When you look at this window, what do you see?"

"A boat," answered Tammy.

"The manor," added Connie.

"And, of course, the hourglass," her father said.

"The manor is in the distance," Anne went on, "creating the image that the boat is at a certain point on the lake."

"Ah ha! And if we could find that point …" said Tammy, becoming excited.

"… from that angle …" added Connie, her smile growing.

"… there lies the boat?" Nathan queried.

"X marks the spot," Anne grinned.

"Theoretically," her father qualified, "but it's as good a theory as any. And, on that boat, you believe is Angus MacLeod's wealth?"

"It's the only thing that makes sense, Pater," Anne said. "He had to keep his money—gold, silver, whatever he used to pay the laborers—somewhere. He didn't keep it in Ordinary's bank—even if the townsfolk would allow him—and the manor has been gone over—off and on—for well over a century."

"And the mysterious statuette, as well?" he pressed gently.

"We don't know that he's actually the one who stole it," his daughter replied. "That's all legend … or myth. Mind you, it makes for good copy, but there's no proof. He certainly never mentioned it in his family journal, according to Miss Rialdi. For all we know, someone started that rumor back in the mists of time, and it's just hung on."

"Well," her father said with a nod, "I suppose the only way to find out is to find the sunken wreck, then."

"We went to pick Ralph Hale's brain yesterday, but he was out with a charter," she explained.

"I think, perhaps, I should handle that inquiry in my official capacity," the Chief of Police told the trio. "Your Uncle Ray, though, has a nice boat …"

"Now, there's an idea!" Tammy declared enthusiastically.

As the four arrived on the ground floor, they were approached by a stout woman of sixty. Her auburn hair was brushed back from her cherubic face, and her hazel eyes shone bright. Joan Rosendale was Ordinary's premier horticulturalist by education and trade and was the town's coordinator for the annual flower show. "Hello, Chief," she said in a sing-song voice, "and ladies."

"Afternoon, Joan," he responded, smiling kindly. "How is John doing today?"

"Much better, thank you," she said with a sigh of gratefulness. "He'll be coming home today, so we've been told."

"That *is* good news. None the worse for wear?"

"He just needs to rest," she explained, "and then he'll be back here on Monday."

"Good for him."

"Has there been any … progress … on who attacked him?" she asked hesitantly.

"There has been, actually," Nathan told her. "We think we know *who* did it—thanks to John, actually—so now it's just a matter of finding the culprit, and I expect that to happen in the very near future."

She nodded, said her thanks, and returned to the curator's desk.

Her son, who had been hovering within earshot, approached. His face was set, and his blue eyes were hard. "For his sake," growled Eskil in a low, rumbling voice, "*you'd* better find him before *I* do." Without waiting for a response, the veteran turned on his heel and walked away.

"Oh, dear," murmured Anne.

"Oh, dear, indeed," agreed her father.

Outside they paused in the warm sunshine to discuss their next moves. The police chief was off to the town's boardwalk to speak with Ralph Hale. The trio of teens were off to find Anne's uncle to discuss a boat ride. After the lawman left, the teens stood around the convertible Mustang talking about the case thus far. It was Connie Bascomb who brought up the manor.

"What do you think about what Miss Rialdi said?" she asked.

"About?" Tammy Coleman queried.

"About Angus and Eleanor still being there," the younger teen replied.

"I don't know," admitted Anne, her brow creasing slightly with a frown. "She may very well be right."

"I don't know," mused Tammy. "Seems to me that they'd have been found by now."

"Not necessarily," Anne countered. "Even back in England they're still looking for Richard the Third; it's just a matter of time before his remains are found."

"You really think they'll find him?" Connie asked, interested.

"Oh, yes, eventually," said Anne definitively. "Probably under a carpark."

"A what?" Tammy inquired, looking at her English-American friend.

"A carpark. What you in the colonies would call a parking lot."

The other two teens laughed.

"So, back to the manor and its missing owners," said Connie, "what are our options?"

"They *may* have gone down with the boat," suggested Tammy.

"But, why, then, the stained-glass window?" countered Anne thoughtfully. "I'm inclined to believe that it was made after the sinking, and before they disappeared. No, they survived whatever happened out there on the lake." She hesitated for a moment, and then added, "That window is a treasure map, I'm sure of it."

"So, you think they're still in the manor somewhere?" asked Connie.

"Or on the property …" was the quiet response.

"But where?" persisted Tammy. "The grounds—including the manor—have been scoured for ages. What's left to search?"

"No one knew of the hidden tunnel George and Jorge got themselves stuck inside," Anne pointed out. "What is to say there isn't another hidden passage, or secret room?"

"Okay, okay," sighed the older seventeen-year-old. "Maybe there is, but where? Where do we look for it? There's nothing in the journal. There's nothing in the library. We've no blueprints to consult. If there's a secret *anything*, where do we look?"

"Aye," admitted Anne, exaggerating her accent, "therein lies the rub!"

ꕥꕥꕥꕥꕥꕥꕥꕥꕥꕥ

George Hambaugh left his sister and her friends standing outside the library. He walked quickly to the nearest corner and crossed the street at the crosswalk. He waved at Harvey Freeman as the cadet drove by on his duly appointed rounds. He hurried across the Common to City Hall and went around to the back where his bicycle was parked with the others. He jumped on the bike and wheeled it around, pointing the front wheel at the entrance/exit. Minutes later, he was happily pedaling toward his best friend's house. From there, they would bike to the Ordinary Car Care Center where the 1934 Studebaker was sitting on a hydraulic lift in a cordoned-off bay.

He was only a few blocks from the Bustamante residence when he became aware of the car following him. With a quick glance over his shoulder he saw that it was the lime-green 1975 AMC Gremlin. His heart skipped a beat as he rose from the saddle and began pumping the pedals for all he was worth. He knew, though, that he could not outdistance the ugly little car and that, barring a miracle, he was in very deep trouble.

He made sharp turns and sped down alleys, always with the Bustamante house as his final destination. He decided that, if he did it right, he could reach the back fence of his friend's house and jump over it. This spurred him on, but the car continued to draw closer. He was getting tired. His legs began to ache. No matter how evasive he was, he knew that his chances of escaping were rapidly dwindling. When his front wheel caught the side of a sizable stone and twisted the handlebars from his hands, he knew he was doomed. Down he went into the shallow gutter in the middle of the alley. He tucked, he rolled, and he came to a rest in a sitting position shaking his throbbing head. He could see the back fence of his sanctuary. As he scrambled to his feet, a pair of strong hands grabbed him and forced him into the cramped backseat of the Gremlin.

"Relax, kid," growled an entirely unpleasant voice as a black hood was pulled down over the boy's head. "You're not going anywhere … except with us!" He was roughly gagged and pushed to the hard floorboard.

The lime-green car quickly pulled away from the scene of the crime and wound its way along backstreets and alleys until reaching the northeast edge of town. Just outside the town limit, there was a narrow dirt road that was invisible unless one knew where to look. The driver took that dirt road, slowing to spare the suspension. George had lost all track of time and direction and relegated himself to that of being a very frightened and unhappy prisoner. He was certain that no one had seen what happened, which meant that no one knew he was missing, and wouldn't know until much later.

After what seemed like an eternity to the fourteen-year-old, the vehicle came to a stop. There was no sound that clued him into where he might be. He tried to swallow, but his mouth was dry. He wanted to shout, but knew that, even if he was able, no one would hear. As far as the rest of the world was concerned, George Hambaugh had ceased to exist.

He was pulled roughly from the car and brought to his feet. His captor turned him a quarter turn and gave him a push to start him walking. He staggered at first, almost falling, but caught himself and proceeded to walk hesitantly in the unknown direction. He could make out two sets of footsteps following him. A dozen or so steps into his blind walk, he was coarsely brought to a stop by a hand on his collar. He stood, wavering, waiting for what was to happen next. He heard what sounded like a door being opened … or not. Perhaps it was more like a wooden barrier being shifted aside. He was guided inside whatever-it-was and again brought to a jarring stop. In silence, he waited.

George heard angry muttering from the man—he had heard nothing from the driver of the car, but suspected it was the second person from the manor cellar incident, Hortense—and sounds that seemed to indicate physical exertion. Finally, the man—Paul, the boy assumed—took the youngster's arm and led him down a dozen uneven steps. George was shoved to the ground. It was damp, musty, and entirely unpleasant.

"This ought to hold you," growled the man.

"There's some water and food," said a female voice, trying to be kind. "We'll be back to check on you."

"Or not!" laughed the man.

"Paul!" she exclaimed.

"Why not tell him who we are, Hortense?" the man exclaimed angrily. "Oh, blast!"

The gag was removed none too gently. The teen listened as the two kidnappers went up the steps and closed—what he assumed was—a trapdoor. He was alone, and afraid. No one knew where he was, let alone that he was missing, and the thought brought him near to panic. He focused on getting his breathing under control. They were gone, he was alone, now was the time to figure out how to escape. *The first step,* he decided, *is to get this hood off!*

His hands had been tied behind his back. Being a limber teen, he was able to pass his hands beneath his feet, thereby bringing them in front of him. He quickly removed the hood and found that his surroundings were just as dark without it as with it. But he saw narrow bits of light coming between the slats of the trapdoor and that made him feel a little better. He peered closely at the bonds around his wrists as best he could, and chiefly at the knot. *A granny knot*, he thought, *and not a particularly good one.*

Using his teeth, he began to work the knot loose. It took longer than he expected. This he knew by the waning light coming through the trapdoor slats. But he continued, and, bit by bit, the knot loosened. He was in complete darkness when the bonds finally fell away from his wrists. He rubbed first one aching wrist, and then the other, for several minutes. Even though the knot had not been very well tied, the bonds had been tight and painful. He sat for several more minutes pondering his predicament, and decided that, as bad as it was, it could be worse. He crawled in the direction of where he believed the food and water to be and eventually found a full disposable water bottle and a zip-lock bag containing a peanut butter sandwich. Hungrily, he wolfed down the sandwich and drained the bottle.

His hunger satiated, he began to plan his escape. While he did not know where he was exactly, he knew that he was probably not all that far from Ordinary. He figured that, as quiet as his surroundings were, that he was somewhere in the woods, which put him either northeast or southeast of town. He was certain that, once outside, he would know—generally—where he was and how to get to safety. *And*, he thought grimly, *I'll be able to tell Dad where to find these two hoodlums*!

***

Nathan Hambaugh picked up his cell phone from where it was vibrating across his desk. "Hello, my love," he said seductively to his wife, a smile on his face. A moment later, the smile was gone. "He's not with Jorge?" he asked, just slightly stunned by her news. "No, I don't know where he is," he told her, "but you can bet I'll find him!" He bid her a distracted farewell as he sat back in his chair to think. After a minute's thought, he took up the receiver of the old-but-still-functioning rotary telephone on his desk and dialed his brother's home number. "Ray," he asked, "is George there?"

Raymond Hambaugh was clearly taken aback by the query, and his face showed it. "No, he's not. Anne and her friends are here. She said that George was going over to Jorge's to work on the old Studebaker."

"He never got that far," sighed the younger brother. "Jorge called the house just a few minutes ago looking for George."

"That's not good," murmured Ray. "No idea where he is?"

"None. If it were both boys, I'd suspect them of returning to the manor to do a little illegal snooping," Nathan replied. "But George on his own? Not likely."

Anne Hambaugh watched her uncle's face and listened to his side of the conversation. At last, no longer able to contain herself, she asked, "What's going on, Uncle Ray?"

"I'll talk to Anne," Ray said into the mouthpiece, "and figure out something from our end. Not to worry, brother, we'll find him." He hung up the telephone, hesitated thoughtfully for a moment, and looked at the three teenage girls. "George is missing."

"That much I gathered," said Anne with a nod.

Connie Bascomb said, "He left us and went to City Hall for his bike."

Nodding, Tammy Coleman added, "So, that's where we begin our search."

Anne smiled at her friends. "Brilliant minds think alike!"

Raymond looked upon the trio with pride. "You three follow up that lead," he told them, "and I'll see what I can do from here."

Minutes later the teen trio was heading toward town in Tammy's convertible, the wind whipping their hair. Traffic was light on the old Mill Road north of town and, as such, the drive was reasonably quick. Tammy pulled into a spot reserved for a police vehicle. All three looked at the bike rack and saw that only two were there: Anne's and Connie's bikes.

"Well," said Tammy, "we know he got this far."

"He would have taken the most direct route to Jorge's house," Anne told them.

"Unless he was being followed," added Connie softly. The other two teens looked at her. "I mean, since he didn't make it to where he was headed, he might have been followed and nabbed."

"Oh, Connie!" gasped Anne, horrified.

"She's got a point," admitted Tammy unhappily. "And it makes sense. If George had been in any kind of accident, your folks would've been contacted."

Anne nodded, having gotten over her initial shock. "You are both right, of course," she murmured. "He could have taken any route, but he still would have gone to Jorge's for safety. We need to go there!"

Tammy put her car into reverse, backed out of the reserved parking spot, and started for the Bustamante residence. Rather than approach the front of the pleasant, single-story ranch-style house, she—with input from her passengers—approached from the alley. They saw the bicycle lying in the gutter that ran down the middle of the alley.

Anne was out of the car before it stopped. She ran to the bike and looked it over quickly. "There's no damage!" she declared, relief in her voice. "That is a good thing as it means he wasn't run down."

"Judging by the sizable stone near the front tire," pointed out Connie, "I'll bet he hit that and went down …"

"… allowing the kidnappers time to scoop him up and make good their getaway," finished Tammy.

"We need to talk to Jorge," said Anne firmly, "to find out if he knows anything. Maybe he saw or heard something."

"I'll bet your dad's already spoken with him," said Connie.

It was then that the Chief of Police arrived in the alley, stopping behind the Mustang. Nathan Hambaugh emerged from the police cruiser and walked up to the teens. His face was grim. As if reading their minds, he told them, "Jorge didn't see or hear anything. He was in his room, listening to music, waiting for George."

"Mr. and Mrs. Bustamante?" asked his daughter hopefully.

Her father shook his head. "They were both out." They all searched the area for clues that might help put them on the missing boy's trail but found nothing. Nathan opened the trunk of his vehicle and put the bike in it. "For now," he sighed, "this is evidence, so I'll take it back to City Hall and lock it up in the evidence-and-property room."

Anne, on impulse, gave her father a tight hug. "We'll keep looking, Pater," she told him determinedly.

"Just be careful," the Chief of Police told them. "By no means do I want any of you to take any risks. If you learn *anything*, I want you to call me immediately." After a momentary pause, "I think I'd better get Harvey to accompany you."

"I think, Pater," said his daughter gently, "that perhaps he should be assigned to look for the Gremlin. I've his cell phone number. We'll rendezvous in an hour or so to discuss what we've found … if anything."

Nathan Hambaugh looked down at the freckled face of his daughter and smiled. "Very well," he acknowledged with a nod, "but I am serious about not taking any chances."

"Taken as read, Pater," she replied with a smile. After her father had left the alley, she turned to her two friends. "So," she said, her brow creased in thought, "if you were a kidnapper, where would you take your kidnapped prize?"

It was then that Jorge Bustamante emerged through the gate in the property wall of his family's home. "*Hola*," he greeted the trio. "I'm really sorry about George. I should have been out here waiting for him. It's all my fault."

"Rubbish!" declared Anne affectionately. "There was no way for you to know what evil lurked in the kidnapper's mind, so think nothing of it. However, you are welcome to join us in our search for my wayward brother."

"He does get himself into messes," acknowledged the fourteen-year-old. "What can I do to help?"

"We need to put our heads together and think," she told the group. "I think it's safe to assume that George *has* been kidnapped, and most probably by Paul Harkness and his companion."

"But why?" asked Connie.

"To learn what we know," answered Tammy firmly.

"I would have to agree," sighed Anne. "To learn what we know about the treasure …"

"Which may or may not exist," interjected Jorge.

"… either from him, or to use him as leverage to get the information from us," Anne concluded.

"They wouldn't take him up to the manor, would they?" Connie inquired.

"No," replied Anne with a slow shake of her wavy red-haired head. "No, it would be someplace … unknown … to us. A secret hideout."

"They definitely wouldn't be staying in a hotel," said Tammy. "They've got a hideout close to town. Someplace that no one ever goes to. Someplace that's been forgotten."

"The old mill, maybe?" asked Jorge.

"Not with Bruno Gorchek and his shotgun on the prowl!" declared Connie, remembering their encounter with Senator (retired) Aaron Mathering's property caretaker just a few weeks earlier.

"No, the mill is out," agreed Anne. "It has to be a place that is accessible by car yet is out of the way. Hidden …" Her voice softened as her gold-flecked green eyes roamed the skyline to the northeast. "As you said, Tammy, someplace that's been forgotten …"

Connie watched her best friend's freckled face, her own soft brown eyes trying to peer into the older girl's mind. "I can tell by the steam coming out of your ears that you're thinking," she said.

"It would have to be a place known to Paul Harkness," Anne explained. "He grew up here so he would know of places that were abandoned, forgotten … lost."

"Well, I grew up here," said Tammy, "and I have no idea where you might be thinking."

Connie visibly straightened, and her face seemed to brighten with an epiphany. "Anne," she murmured, "are you thinking that abandoned homestead way back in the woods? That one you stumbled across last month on the day I first met you?"

A smile appeared on Anne's face. "It *did* cross my mind."

"Wait," said Tammy, her brow creased slightly in thought, "you mean the old log cabin outside of town? But there's no road going to it! How would they *drive* to it if there's no road?"

"Especially in a Gremlin," added Jorge, who had been listening to the trio intently.

"It would not have to be much of a road," explained Anne. "A track just wide enough to allow the car access …"

Tammy bit her lower lip in thought. "Well, maybe …"

"We need to get back to the police department and talk to my father," Anne said. "Unless there is another—similar—place, it's our best bet."

ଓଓଓଓଓଓଓଓଓଓ

Nathan Hambaugh walked into his office and sat heavily in the chair behind his desk. His son's bicycle was downstairs … in the basement … in the evidence/property room. His son … drawing in a deep breath, he released it slowly. He felt as though he was in a fog. It all seemed so … illusory. When the rotary telephone on his desk jangled to life, he was startled almost out of his chair. After a moment's hesitation, in part to regain control of himself, and in part due to trepidation, he lifted the heavy receiver.

"Chief Hambaugh," he said in what he hoped was a strong, worry-free voice.

There was a pause on the other end of the line, and then a voice asked, "*Chief* Hambaugh?"

"Yes," Nathan replied. There was something about the voice …

"Well, Hambaugh, I got your kid," said the voice gruffly, "and if you want him back, you'll cooperate."

"Go on," said the interim police chief, anger growing inside him.

"All I want is Macleod's treasure," the voice went on. "I know you're looking for it; I want it. A simple trade."

"I see."

"I'll call you same time tomorrow," said the voice. "For your kid's sake let's hope you've found it!"

The line went dead.

Nathan looked at the receiver in his hand. *So, George* has *been kidnapped,* he thought as he returned the receiver to its cradle. He was not sure how long he had been lost in elusive thought when there came a knock at his door and a head of wavy red hair poked into view. He waved his daughter to enter and was not surprised when he found her not to be alone.

"I just had a call," he told them quietly.

"Paul Harkness?" his daughter asked.

"I think so."

"He has George?"

"Yes."

"We may know where."

Nathan Hambaugh sat in stunned silence, staring at his daughter.

"There's this old, abandoned log cabin in the woods," Tammy said.

"It's near where Anne and I first met," added Connie.

"Do you know anything about it?" Anne asked.

"East of here," her father murmured. "North of the road into town…"

"Yes," she acknowledged. "I stumbled across it some weeks ago. I got the strangest feeling from it."

Flipping a switch on the intercom that was connected to the desk of Maude Raynes, the Chief of Police said, "Maude, could you step in here for a minute?"

The sixty-seven-year-old secretary/records clerk/dispatcher appeared a moment later. "Yes?"

"Maude," began Nathan, his elbows on the desktop and his fingers steepled before him, "you know more about Ordinary than anyone I know."

"It helps to be nosy," she explained.

A smile touched his lips. "There is an abandoned old log cabin in the woods northeast of town," he told her, "and I—we—were wondering if you knew anything about it."

She looked at each of the five expectant faces in turn as the wheels in her mind delved into her memory. At last, she said, "If it's the one I think you mean, Chief, it was built by a family that arrived about ten years after Ordinary was settled." She hesitated, and then continued, "The family's name—if memory serves me—was Webster. He was a farmer, as most folks hereabouts were. There was the mister and missus, and three or four children—all girls. The girls grew up, married, and moved away … except one. She married a local fellow—Johnson, I think—and they lived here in town as he was a shop owner. After her parents passed on, the cabin fell into ruin."

"You are amazing," Nathan Hambaugh said in awe.

"Yes, that's true," replied Maude with a smile and a wink. "Now, they—the Johnson's—had only one child, a girl, who grew up and eventually married a newcomer to the area." She paused, her brow creasing as she brushed away the cobwebs in her memory. The creases suddenly cleared as the new information surfaced. Her expression was one of concern. "His name was Harkness."

The silence that befell them was almost terrifying.

"Paul never mentioned it," Nathan murmured.

"He wouldn't," said Maude. "That man turned out to be an unscrupulous boor who left his young family."

"Why?" asked Tammy.

"There are a number of plausible explanations," the older woman answered with a shrug. "One—and the most likely—was that he was caught stealing and run out of town. She was permitted to remain with their infant son as she was not involved with whatever he had done." She sighed. "At least, that's the story as best I can recall."

Five sets of eyes were focused on the quiet woman.

"So," Nathan Hambaugh finally said, "the abandoned log cabin in the woods is his family's old homestead. He was my boyhood chum, and I never knew that."

"*He* would have known that," Anne said.

"And what better place to hide out?" supplemented Connie.

Reaching for the telephone, the police chief said in a firm voice, "It's a place to start. We will need reinforcements!"

ଔଔଔଔଔଔଔଔଔଔ

George Hambaugh cautiously stood up to avoid banging his head on the root cellar's ceiling. At five-feet-six-inches, he found that he was able to stand mostly erect. He estimated the floor-to-ceiling height of the cellar to be about five-and-a-half-feet. He made his way to where the stairs were, at which point he stopped and listened. He heard movement. He heard quiet conversation. He was not alone, which would make escape impossible. *Unless this hole has a back door*, he thought wryly.

It occurred to him then that, while studying history at some point in his distant past, it was not uncommon for escape tunnels to be built into root cellars to allow the owners/occupants a way out in case of attack. *But what are the odds*? His thought process was suddenly interrupted when the trap door was opened.

Standing at the top of the decrepit stairs was a man with graying brown hair, hazel eyes, and a scar on his left cheek. "Got yourself loose, did you?" growled the man as he started down.

George could only retreat into the semi-darkness of the cellar. "Stay away from me!" the youth warned. "My dad is coming for me, so, if you know what's best, you'll get while the getting is good!"

The man laughed cruelly. "Your old man has no clue where you are, kid!" With a sneer, he added, "He was never very bright!"

"You're wrong!" countered George bravely. "You'll see! You'll get what's coming to you!"

"Speaking of which," the man said, "why don't you tell me what you brats have been able to find out about my treasure?"

"Treasure? What treasure?" the teen stalled, his hazel eyes darting about in search of a way out.

The man stood as best he could in the height-restricted confines of the cellar. "Don't you play stupid with me, boy! I know you kids have been snooping around for it, but it's mine! Now, tell me what you know, or I'll beat it out of you!"

"Paul," came a woman's voice from above. "Stop terrorizing the boy. He's not likely to know where it's at."

"Mind your own business, Hortense!" Paul snapped back at her.

"I'm just saying," she went on, "that, if the kids knew where the thing was, they would've dug it up already, that's all."

"They know," he growled in a low voice, "or they've a good idea …"

"Actually," said George, "we don't."

"You're lying, kid!"

"I would *never*!" exclaimed the youth in a shocked tone of voice.

"Why were you brats at the museum?" pressed Paul Harkness.

"Why were you?" countered George.

The man looked carefully at the boy. The youth's very curly red mop, freckled face, and wide hazel eyes gave him an air of innocence. "You kids found something …" he began to say.

"No, we didn't," responded George just a little too quickly. In that moment, he knew he had erred.

The smile that spread across the kidnapper's face was not a pleasant one. "So …" he said slowly, "you *do* know something!"

"No, I don't!" exclaimed George as fear of the approaching man gripped him. "I don't know anything! It's my sister! She knows everything! She knows where the treasure is buried!"

Harkness stopped his advance and stared hard at the boy. "Why should I believe you?" he growled.

The fourteen-year-old was silent.

Harkness turned back toward the stairs, saying to his companion above, "Looks like we got the wrong kid. We'll have to get rid of him someplace—"

George bowled the man over as he bolted for the freedom the stairs offered. The man howled in rage as he went down but the youth continued. He scrambled up the stairs and directly into the waiting arms of the other kidnapper. "Let me go!" he screamed, twisting in her surprisingly firm grip.

"Not a chance, kid," Hortense Grimes said, tightening her hold. "You okay down there?" she called out, a smirk on her face.

"I'm going to kill that kid!" bellowed the man in rage.

"Just tie him up … again," she told her furious partner, "and leave him down there. We'll be long gone by the time he's found … *if* he's found. We need to be gone from this place now, Paul, it's getting too hot."

"I'm not leaving without my treasure!" he snarled as he emerged from the cellar, rope in hand. "We'll get the girl tomorrow."

"How are you going to work that?" Hortense sneered. "Knock on her front door and say, 'come with us, honey?'"

"No," he growled as he tied the boy's hands behind his back—making certain to cause the boy pain. "There's an annual music festival at the Common tomorrow—an all-day thing—we'll nab her there."

"With all those people?" she laughed derisively. "You're nuts!"

"We'll create a diversion, dummy," he snarled, finishing the knot on the boy's bindings. "It'll be a piece of cake!" And then he chuckled unpleasantly. "You want to hear something funny? The police chief here is an old friend of mine."

"What?" the woman gasped.

"Yeah. My old boyhood pal," continued Harkness. "And this is his kid."

"Are you insane?" she exclaimed. "Kidnapping the police chief's kid? Are you out of your ever-loving mind?"

Pushing the bound-and-gagged boy down the age-worn stairs, Harkness slammed the trapdoor shut. "It doesn't matter," he said as he shifted rotting lumber over the trapdoor, concealing it to some degree. "We'll find that treasure and be out of here by this time tomorrow."

Hortense Grimes looked at her partner in crime. With a slow shake of her head, she said to him, "You *are* nuts!"

Going to the door that hung askew on a single ancient hinge, he said, "It's getting dark; time to go."

George lay on the hard-packed dirt floor fighting back tears of pain. The tumble down the stairs had been frightening as he could not use his hands and arms to break the fall and impacting the cellar floor had knocked the breath from him. He was not sure how long he had lain there, slowly regaining his senses, but he was certain that it could not have been more than a few minutes. It had been plenty of time for his captors to depart d. He struggled into a sitting position, his back against the hard, earthen wall. The cellar was cool and damp.

His hands were too tightly tied, and this time Harkness had passed the rope through his belt. There was no chance of stepping through his bound hands this time. All he could do was wait in the dark to be rescued … and to pray for that rescue to come soon.

ઌઌઌઌઌઌઌઌઌઌ

It took longer than he liked to get his posse together, but when everyone was assembled Chief of Police Nathan Hambaugh addressed them. "Most—if not all of you—know what this is about. George was nabbed earlier today, and we think—thanks to Anne and her friends—that he's being held at an old cabin in the woods that belongs to Paul Harkness."

His posse was a small one, consisting of two Ordinary police officers—Sergeant Bradley Nielson and Officer Carl Newberry—and its cadet, his older brother, and his daughter. The other teens had vociferously complained. He patiently explained to them that he could not, in good conscience, allow them to accompany the others for risk of putting them in harm's way. As it was getting late, he suggested they go home and wait for a call from Anne when George was found. They were not happy as they left.

As the posse went down the front steps of City Hall, they were confronted by a very stern Eskil Rosendale. "Word gets 'round," he said in his sonorous gravelly voice.

The Chief of Police paused for only a moment as he took in the big man in black leather. "I was hoping it would," he finally said. "Glad to have you aboard."

The posse, now numbering seven, split up among three police cruisers: Nathan and Ray Hambaugh; Bradley Nielson and Carl Newberry; Harvey, Anne, and Eskil. There were last-minute instructions: no lights, no sirens, and no one does anything unless instructed to do so by the Chief of Police. They made the circuit of the Common via the Circus Maximus and headed northeast out of Ordinary. The first two cars missed the nearly-invisible narrow dirt road that led to the log cabin, but the Air Force Special Ops veteran saw it and told Harvey Freeman.

As Harvey turned onto the almost nonexistent road, he radioed the other cars. Now he was in the lead, which would probably not please his chief. He turned off the headlights and moved slowly forward, on more than one occasion side-swiping a tree. He had only gone a hundred feet, or so, when he parked his patrol car and shut off the engine. The trio emerged and waited for the others. It was not a long wait.

"We'll go on from here on foot," Nathan told the gathered. "Ray and I will take the left flank. Brad and Carl, the right flank. Harvey, Eskil, and Anne, move *carefully* up this … road. Keep your eyes peeled. Don't take any chances."

With everyone in agreement, the seven set out.

As soon as the dark form of the cabin came into view, Eskil Rosendale instructed his two young companions to find a safe place to hide and observe. He was going to approach alone. Though the teens protested, the Air Force Special Ops veteran silenced them with a guttural hiss. Resigned, the pair slipped into the thicket that allowed them a concealed observation post. They never heard the man slip away into the darkening night.

"Do you think they're in there?" asked Harvey in a hushed voice.

"I sincerely hope so," Anne replied in a cold tone.

"If he finds them first," sighed the cadet, "it won't be pretty."

"Good!"

The nineteen-year-old looked in the younger teen's direction. This was not a side of her that he recalled having experienced. She was vengeful. *But, then,* he admitted to himself, *it is her baby brother we're talking about here.*

"I think he's there!" she hissed excitedly, pointing toward the cabin.

As Anne began to move forward, Harvey gripped her shoulder to restrain her. "He told us to stay put."

"That's my brother in there!" she snapped at him.

"I understand that," he answered sympathetically, "but if we go blundering up there, it could tip off the bad guys, and things could get nasty. Best that we wait until we hear from either Eskil or your father."

She glared at him in the darkness but knew, in her heart, that he was right. "You are so annoying sometimes," she muttered.

"It's a gift," he responded with an unseen smile.

They did not have long to wait. Though the woods were dark, there was just enough ambient light for the teens to watch the drama unfold. From the left and right sides of the cabin they saw shadowy figures approach the derelict structure. From near the entrance they watched as a figure suddenly materialized—seemingly from nowhere—and burst through the skewed door. From the left and right, the other four figures came running, surprise now immaterial.

Anne and Harvey erupted from their hiding place and ran as fast they dared toward the cabin. By the time they reached it—which was but moments—any action there might have been was over.

"No one's here," Nathan Hambaugh said, disappointedly.

"Maybe they were never here," suggested his older brother.

"Someone was here," growled Eskil, moving about the cluttered interior with flashlight in hand, "and recently."

"Could they have known we were coming?" asked Sergeant Nielson.

"I don't see how," replied the police chief as he glanced around. "*We* didn't know until just a little while ago. No, I suspect it's just bad timing."

"Where is George?" inquired Harvey, as he too took in their surroundings.

Officer Carl Newberry shook his head. "Not here."

"Yes, he is," insisted Anne adamantly, moving slowly around the chaotic interior.

"Here!" bellowed Eskil as he began moving rotting wood. "A trapdoor! And I thought I heard something from below!"

It took only moments for the seven to clear away the debris that covered and surrounded the trapdoor. Eskil grabbed the rusted iron ring and heaved, inadvertently removing the cover from its hinges.

Nathan Hambaugh, his flashlight in hand, went down part of the way and swept the bright beam around the dark interior. "He's here!" came a whoop of joy and relief. As he stumbled downward, he called up to the others, "Mind the stairs! They're in pretty bad shape!"

It was not long before the fourteen-year-old was out of his prison and unbound. He hugged his father hard enough to make the man gasp for breath.

"Easy does it there, George," chuckled his Uncle Raymond, "we want him to be able to run for police chief next month!"

With a sheepish grin, he released his father. "Sorry about that, Dad, but I'm awfully glad to see you!"

"It's okay," wheezed Nathan Hambaugh, tousling the boy's red mop. "Actually, your sister and her friends figured out your whereabouts."

"*Possible* whereabouts, Pater," clarified his daughter, who was obviously very happy with the outcome. "So, brother mine, you've had quite an adventure!"

"It was horrible!" declared George. "Just horrible! And that man ... he's just horrible!"

"Well, you're safe enough now," said Sergeant Nielson. "Carl and I will snoop around here, Chief, if you and the others want to head on out."

George suddenly went pale. "Oh, no!" he gasped, his hazel eyes falling on his sister.

"What is it?" his father asked.

"They think Anne knows where the treasure is!" the boy continued anxiously. "They're going to nab her at the music festival tomorrow and make her talk!"

For a long moment, there was quiet in the ruin, and then the chief of police murmured, "Are they, now?"

"You're plotting something," his older brother said, the hint of a smile tugging at the corners of his mouth. "You may have been gone for decades, but I know that look!"

Nathan glanced slyly around the debris-strewn remains of the cabin at those who stood with him. "I think, just maybe, we ought to set a trap ..."

"Said the spider to the fly?" Ray paraphrased.

Chief of Police Hambaugh smiled in silence, and it was not a friendly smile.

SIX

Thursday, July 8th.

Anne Hambaugh lay in bed staring at the ceiling of her room. She went over in her mind the plan her father had devised to capture Paul Harkness and his companion, Hortense Grimes. It was actually rather simple: let them grab her, and then her father—et al—would grab them. She knew, though, that things were rarely so simple when it came to executing a plan. She found herself to be anxious which—she told herself—was perfectly normal. She was bait.

As the grandfather clock in the family room began to chime the six-a.m. hour, she swung her feet out from beneath her sheet and blanket and into her fuzzy bunny slippers. She pulled on her daisy-print robe as she made her way to the kitchen where the automatic coffee maker was brewing the morning elixir. She knew that everyone would be getting up—if not already—so she poured three cups of coffee and one cup of hot cocoa. Taking her cup, complete with cream and sugar, she went to her usual place at the big bay window. She looked out over the calm surface of Lake Ordinary and thought *What a silly name for a town*!

"Good morning," came a masculine voice from behind.

She turned to greet her father. "Good morning, Pater."

As he stood beside her, he asked, "How did you sleep?"

"Restlessly," she sighed.

"I think we all did," Nathan Hambaugh agreed. "Except for, maybe, your brother."

"He does take his bedtime seriously, that one," she admitted with a small smile.

"In his defense," came a woman's voice from behind them, "he had rather a traumatic experience. I expect he was quite exhausted."

"I expect you're right, my dear," Nathan said as he kissed his wife. "Good morning, my sweet."

"And I'll have you know that I am not too keen on what you have planned for today," Emma Hambaugh continued firmly.

"None of us are keen on it," he admitted, "but we need to catch these two before someone gets hurt." He paused for a moment, and then added, "They're expecting her to be at the music festival with the rest of the town, and it just wouldn't be very friendly to disappoint them. There will be people everywhere, so it will be easier for us to mingle, to watch, and to grab them when they try!"

"I'll be all right, Mum," Anne told her mother reassuringly as she accepted a kiss on the forehead. "There will be so many watching out for me that nothing could possibly go wrong."

Emma looked at her daughter's face. What she saw was a mix of emotions. She knew that—at the back of her mind—the teen feared the worst. "Well then," the woman said upliftingly, "we will hope for the best and plan for the worst."

"Benbow could accompany me today," Anne suggested, referring to the family's stocky brindle rescue mutt.

Nathan shook his head. "Benbow would probably scare Harkness off. Best he stays home."

"So," sighed Emma, "what happens first?"

"Breakfast?" suggested a sleepy voice from kitchen. "Ta for the cocoa, oh sister mine."

ଓଓଓଓଓଓଓଓଓଓ

Nineteen-year-old Harvey Freeman, clad in civilian attire, was inwardly nervous.

"Relax," said Tammy Coleman, "what could possibly go wrong?"

The six-feet-six-inch police cadet looked down at the five-feet-nine-inch seventeen-year-old seated in her white 1967 Mustang convertible. "We're talking Anne here," he countered. "*Anything* that could possibly go wrong probably will!"

Connie Bascomb, seated in the Mustang's passenger seat, interjected, "With half the town keeping an eye on her?"

Harvey shook his blond head slowly. "I don't know …"

"Look," sighed Tammy, "George heard the baddies say that they were going to get Anne in order to get the treasure, right?"

"Right."

"So, Anne being bait to draw them out only makes sense," finished the auburn-haired teen.

"Well … maybe …"

"You just need to have more faith in Anne," Connie told the older teen as she used a pick-comb on her kinky black hair.

"Oh, I have faith in Anne," he told both girls, "it's this Harkness fellow I don't trust. How can we be so sure he'll do what we think he'll do?"

"We can't," admitted Tammy.

Glancing at his watch, Harvey said—with a determined edge to his voice— "It's showtime."

He walked across the street from the Ordinary Malt Shoppe to the Common and mingled with the townsfolk and visitors who were coming together at the Victorian-style gazebo for a day of good music and good food. It was easy enough for him to wander among the people, and he was tall enough to see over most heads. He picked out Mitch Cavenaugh—the six-feet-tall eighteen-year-old football player and part-time landscaper/gardener—in the crowd. The step-son of Sergeant Bradley Nielson, Mitch had willingly joined the posse. Moments later, his blue eyes focused on Eskil Rosendale; the youth felt better knowing the Air Force Special Ops veteran was close at hand.

The entire police force—such as it was—would be on the scene, along with a select few non-law enforcement types. He watched as the crowd grew. He was still uneasy. He had a bad feeling that things could go horribly wrong. *But how?* he asked himself. Glancing at his watch again, he muttered, "Let the festivities begin."

From the gazebo came the clanging of an iron triangle to get the growing throng's attention. At the microphone stood this year's mayor—the position was rotated among the permanent members of the town's council—who cleared his throat into the mike. Senator (retired) Aaron Mathering—who was also the town's judge—was seventy-five-years-old, very fit, and had a full head of snow-white hair. "Ladies and gentlemen!" his baritone voice bellowed into the microphone, "welcome to the … I don't remember which … annual music festival! We've been doing this for so long," he laughed, "that I'll be darned if I can … wait, one of my colleagues is whispering … ninety-ninth annual music festival! Well, next year will have to be an extra special one, then! And so, without further ado, let the music begin!"

The band gathered behind the mayor struck up a rousing tune as he stepped down and the air was filled with pitch-perfect sounds. Clapping and cheering could not drown out the music. It was beautiful.

ઝઝઝઝઝઝઝઝઝ

Anne Hambaugh bounced off one person after another as she made her way—in no particular direction—through the mass of happy humanity. As she smiled and laughed, her gold-flecked green eyes kept a wary watch for her would-be kidnappers. Being five-feet-three-inches, that was no easy feat. Occasionally she would espy one of her protectors, which made her feel a little better about things, but not entirely. Things could still go very wrong. No matter how much planning was involved, there was always the human factor with which to contend. Still, she pressed on.

An hour had passed, and she was beginning to wonder if—just perhaps—Harkness had said what he had said for George's benefit and that there was no plan to kidnap her. In a way, she felt disappointed. She admitted to herself that part of her had looked forward to the adventure, while another part told the previous part to get a grip. That thought brought a smile and a chuckle.

It was nearing noon, and the music festival was in full swing. The fourth band was in the gazebo churning out big band music. The air was filled with smells of delicious grilled foods that kept everyone hungry. All the food and beverage booths were staying busy as the crowd moved from one end of the Common to the other in waves. Laughter and singing—some of it in key—joined with the music. It was a beautiful day, a perfect day …

… then the shooting started.

The merry-makers were unsure and confused when the first sharp sounds of gunfire shattered the happy event. It was difficult for anyone to tell from which direction they had originated. The ebb and flow of the crowd increased in pace. The shooting continued, and then the panic started. As no one knew the origin of the gunfire, the people just broke and ran in every direction. Those not fast enough were pushed out of the way, or to the ground. The joyous sounds that had wafted up from the Common were now replaced by screams and shouts of terror.

Anne felt a hard hand cover her mouth and a sinewy arm encircle her, pinning her own arms to her sides. She was lifted off her feet and carried roughly through the panic-stricken mob to an awaiting older-model, faded red, four-door Chevy Blazer. She was thrown onto the back seat—banging her head on the door in the process—and as the door slammed shut the vehicle pulled away. A hood was quickly pulled over the dazed girl's head and a gag was tied tightly to squash any potential screams. She was flipped onto her face and her hands were quickly bound at the wrists, painfully. A kick from her was rewarded by a fist to the side of her head that returned her to her dazed condition.

They had taken her in broad daylight with almost a thousand people crowding the Common; Anne knew she was in trouble.

Getting out of downtown Ordinary was a challenge with panicky people flooding the streets and vehicles in various stages of movement—though the majority managed only to block traffic and any hope for escape. The driver of the Blazer took the sidewalk at one point and managed to find a narrow, one-way unoccupied side street. Driving the wrong way, the woman behind the wheel effectively exited the scene of mass hysteria and terror.

Within minutes, the Chevy Blazer was headed out of town with its frightened prisoner.

ଓଓଓଓଓଓଓଓଓଓ

Nathan Hambaugh felt hemmed in, and he did not like it. There were just too many people, certainly more than he had expected. He did not remember the annual music festival being so popular. *But then,* he had admitted, *I have missed the last forty-four.*

He strained to keep an eye on his daughter, and to watch for anyone fitting the description of Paul Harkness or Hortense Grimes. What he found was that all that straining was giving him a pain in his neck. At times he was able to slip through the crowd with some ease, and at other times he had to force—with apologies—his way through. The dirty looks he got were predominantly from out-of-towners, of that he was certain. With a hand casually on the pistol he wore under a loose-fitting shirt, he made his way as unconcernedly as he could through the throng. On occasion he would link up with another member of the posse and briefly exchange information. As the morning wore on, the surveillance became more unnerving.

He jumped at an unexpected touch on his arm and spun around to face the person. "Ray!" he declared. "You scared the blazes out of me!"

Grinning, the older of the Hambaugh brothers responded, "It's been a long time since I've done that."

"Well, don't do it again! I don't think the old ticker could handle it!"

"I'll try to be good," chuckled Raymond Hambaugh. Then, on a more serious note, he asked, "Anything yet?"

"No," grumbled the police chief unhappily. "This waiting is getting to me. What if I got this all wrong? What if I'm putting everyone through this for no reason?"

Shaking his head, Ray told him, "I don't think you've got this wrong, Nathan. I think that guy's here ... somewhere ... and he's just biding his time. We've just got to be patient."

"I know you're right," sighed the younger brother, "but it's driving me nuts!"

"Oh, good," grinned Ray. "I was afraid I was the only one feeling that way." Giving his brother a reassuring pat on the shoulder, he added, "I'm going to meander over to the northern end, I think, and get a cold one."

"Drinking on duty?" asked Nathan with a frown touching his brow.

With a wink, Ray responded, "Iced tea, little bro. I'll see you around."

Once again alone in the crowd, Nathan Hambaugh continued his haphazard patrol. Twice he saw his daughter's head of wavy red hair. He saw Harvey Freeman weaving through the mass, towering over most. He noticed that the mob parted like the Red Sea for Eskil Rosendale, the beefy biker with his full blond walrus mustache; that brought a heartening smile. One by one, the police chief accounted for each member of his posse. Now all he needed to do was account for those they hunted.

It was completely unexpected.

There came the sudden sound of gunfire.

He quickly looked around as he tried to home in on from where it was coming. The noise from the band and the crowd made it difficult. When the screaming and shouting started, the task became impossible. The panicking mass of humanity first moved in one direction—pulling him along—and then in another direction—pushing him along. The shooting continued, and the crowd broke. A thousand—give or take a couple of hundred—people were suddenly running, pushing and shoving, in every direction to escape. Twice Nathan found himself on the ground. The second time, however, he felt strong hands lift him to his feet.

"You okay, Chief?" asked Eskil Rosendale in his sonorous gravelly voice.

"Yes!" answered Nathan with a grateful nod. "Where's the shooting coming from?"

Three inches taller than the police chief, Eskil had a slightly better view over the heads of the panicking mob. "It's not gunfire!" was the big biker's definite response. "Probably fireworks!"

"A diversion!" exclaimed Nathan angrily.

"Coming from the northwest end, as best I can tell," agreed Eskil, as he began pushing aggressively through the people.

"Where's Anne?" shouted Nathan, trying to be heard over the cacophony.

Pausing a moment, Eskil looked quickly above the fleeing public. "There!" he bellowed, pointing toward the south end of the Common. "They've got her!" He was off with a terrifying roar that parted those in his way.

As the two men began to move in earnest, Nathan Hambaugh used his walkie-talkie to summon the rest of his posse. He tried to determine the locations of the others while staying focused on his daughter. He knew that his brother was coming in from the northern end of the Common, but he was not certain as to the whereabouts of the others. He began to feel panic grip him at the thought of not only putting his daughter in danger but also at the chance of losing her.

ଔଔଔଔଔଔଔଔଔଔ

Harvey Freeman and Mitch Cavenaugh rendezvoused by chance at the southern end of the Common. The two teens, their expressions set on the seriousness of their mission, spoke in low tones as they watched the revelers. Both admitted to one another that they had not seen anyone acting suspicious. The cadet lamented not being able to escort a very inebriated and boisterous Abner Newby from the festival because of the stakeout. Mitch assured him that there will be plenty of future opportunities.

"All this waiting is driving me up the wall," sighed Harvey as he took a bite of a foot-long corndog. "A little action is all I ask for."

"Careful what you ask for," warned Mitch, his brown eyes constantly on the move.

"Is it too much to ask for a little action?" went on Harvey with a mouthful of battered lunch.

"I'm just saying ..."

The sound of gunfire shut both their mouths as they wheeled about to find from what direction it came. They began to move toward the center of the Common as best they could as the revelers began to move quickly, first in one direction, and then in another. They were forcibly bumped and jostled, and on more than one occasion completely turned around. Harvey tried to listen to what was coming across his walkie-talkie, but the din of the masses had grown too great. The only word he thought he had heard was 'west.' Grabbing his partner's shoulder, he pointed toward the west end of the Common.

Mitch, being an Ordinary High School football player, began to aggressively push through the terrified merrymakers—though cautious enough not to cause anyone harm. Harvey, a substantial youth in his own right, joined in the splitting of the sea of people. Within a matter of minutes, they were nearing the location of the stoic Chief of Police and a furious Eskil Rosendale when Raymond Hambaugh joined them from the north. Sergeant Nielson and Officer Newberry appeared only moments later.

"They have her," said Nathan Hambaugh in a cold, angry voice. "They have my Anne."

"We'll get her back, Chief," the police sergeant assured his boss. "We'll get her back."

Eskil looked at the distraught face of the girl's father, and then, without a word, he hurried as fast as he could run to where his Harley-Davidson was parked. Within a minute he was weaving through bottle-necked traffic in the direction of the getaway Blazer.

"More's the pity if *he* catches them before *we* do," said Raymond, a hint of satisfaction in his voice.

"Yes," agreed Nathan through clenched teeth, "more's the pity …"

ꕤꕤꕤꕤꕤꕤꕤꕤꕤꕤ

The Chevy Blazer sped through the near-empty streets of Ordinary's outlying area. Everyone—mostly—was at the music festival and waiting until the festival was in full swing meant even fewer people on the roads. It had been a brilliant plan, and the use of fireworks to simulate gunfire had worked better than either perpetrator had expected. The panicked crowd had delayed any pursuit, allowing the girl to be grabbed and hauled away with no one paying attention; everyone was focused on their own safety, or that of loved ones. Anne Hambaugh had been whisked away in broad daylight in a sea of people.

Hortense Grimes, by her own admission, was not much of a getaway driver. She did not like driving fast and having someone yelling at her to go faster did not help. She gripped the steering wheel so tightly that her knuckles were white, and her hands hurt. She tucked her head into her shoulders every time her backseat driver bellowed. "I'm doing my best!" she hollered back as she jerked the steering wheel to avoid a black cat crossing the road. "Oh, no!" she cried out.

"What now?" Paul Harkness bawled.

"A black cat just crossed us!"

"Just drive, woman!"

At the outskirts of the town limits she was able to speed up. It was a winding two-lane blacktop that paralleled the road closer to the lake on which the aerodrome was located. There were about three miles between the two roads. There were several farms that occupied this real estate from which the good folks of Ordinary received the bulk of their fresh produce and meat and had since its founding. The countryside was lush, beautiful, and relaxing … except for the speeding older-model four-door Blazer.

Far ahead, she could see the deer that stepped out of the woods to the side of road. Her chest tightened as she willed the deer to go *back* into the woods. But the deer merely stood where it was and watched the oncoming vehicle with indifference in its big, brown eyes.

"Why are you slowing?" yelled Harkness.

"There's a deer!"

"So what? Speed up! It'll run the other way!"

"Are you sure?"

"I grew up here!" he growled angrily. "I *know* deer!"

Though not convinced, she did as she was told. Her eyes stayed on the animal on the side of the road. It did not move as she rapidly drew closer and she began to believe that her partner-in-crime may have truly known what he was talking about.

Without any forewarning, the deer sprang from its place to the middle of the road.

With a scream of surprise, Hortense Grimes stomped on the brakes. The wheels locked. The back end lifted. The front end swerved. Anne rolled painfully to the floorboard. Paul Harkness slammed into the back of the front seats.

And the deer pranced regally away to the other side of the road completely unscathed.

The Chevy Blazer was stopped in the middle of the road at a diagonal, blocking would-be traffic in both directions. The driver, having put the transmission into 'park,' quickly debarked and leaned against the vehicle, breathing deeply. "You," she gasped as her partner also emerged, "are an *idiot*!"

"Watch it, Hortense," he said threateningly, rubbing his head, shoulders, and back. "You get in the back with the girl. *I'll* drive from here on out!"

"Be my guest!" she spat as she clambered into the back of the SUV, ignoring their captive's plight.

Grumbling under his breath, Paul Harkness took over the driver's seat. The vehicle was idling a little roughly, but he ignored that. Putting the transmission into gear, he stepped down on the accelerator, but not before observing a fast-approaching motorcycle in the distance. "Great!" he grumbled.

"What is it?" asked Hortense, the tone of his voice alerting her to a change in his demeanor.

"We may have company," he told her as they sped away.

It was only a minute later that he turned off onto a wide dirt driveway that wound through aging oak trees to a quaint two-story farmhouse. He parked the Blazer behind the white-with-blue-trim structure and stepped out of it. He stood there and listened as the motorcycle sped past their location, and he smiled as the guttural roar of the powerful machine faded to the south.

He gestured that his partner should wait in the vehicle as he walked up to the back door. Opening the screen door, he rapped on the backdoor's glass. There was no answer; nor was he expecting there to be one. Turning the knob, he pushed the door inward and stepped inside. He called out; no reply. Smiling smugly, he gestured Hortense join him, and to bring their prisoner.

The kitchen through which they had entered was spotless, with a wood-burning stove and well-maintained copper cookware. The living room was immaculately clean, and the furniture was covered with white cloths to keep off any dust. Along one wall, above an old upright piano, were clustered paintings and black-and-white photographs of the owner's ancestors—presumably some being the original settlers of the farm. It was a comfortable room, and a comfortable home.

"Now what?" Hortense asked, clearly exhausted by the day's activities.

"Now," Harkness said, turning his attention to the gagged and hooded teenager, "we find out what we need to know!" None too gently he removed the black hood and glared at the frightened youth. "You heard?"

The kidnapped teen nodded. No longer blind, her fear was quickly replaced by anger.

"You gonna tell us what we want to know?" he pressed arrogantly.

Looking him in the eyes, Anne Hambaugh shook her head defiantly.

Harkness grunted. "You will if you know what's good for you!" he said threateningly.

"Well, she's not going to say much with that gag in her mouth," quipped Hortense acerbically.

He looked at his colleague for a moment, and then back at the insubordinate teen. "You know, Hortense," he said, "you may just have something there." He laughed harshly as he removed the gag. "Now, what have you to say?"

"Ta," was Anne's dry response.

Paul Harkness looked hard at her. "You think you're pretty tough, uh?"

"If you had any sense at all," she continued in a quiet, even voice, "you would make good your escape and pray that my father never catches you."

With that, Harkness laughed out loud. "Your old man? Catch me? Fat chance! Even as a kid he could never keep up with me! Your old man is nothing more than a nobody cop in a little nowheresville town!"

A smile touched the corners of Anne's mouth.

With a sigh, Hortense said, "Can we get on with it? I really want to be elsewhere. *Any*where!"

"What makes you think I know anything?" asked Anne.

"A little birdie told me!" barked Harkness.

"Your little birdie was sadly mistaken," sighed Anne, shaking her head.

He looked at her freckled face for a long moment, wondering if she were telling him the truth or not. Finally, he said, "Look, girlie, just tell me where the treasure is, and then we'll be out of here forever."

"First," Anne replied coldly, "I am not '*girlie*' to you or anyone else. And second, even if I *did* know, I certainly wouldn't tell a churl such as you."

He blinked. "A … what?"

"Churl," she repeated. "A bumpkin," she explained. "A chaw-bacon. A hick. A clodhopper. Not grasping it yet? Shall we try: cornball, hayseed, rube … you know, a local yokel."

His face turning red with rage, Harkness grabbed the front of her blouse and jerked her off her feet. Screaming—complete with spittle—into her face, the blue veins at his temples pulsed. He shook her roughly. "You're going to tell me what I want to know, or else!"

"I think not," she said, putting on a brave face. She knew that she was playing a dangerous game, but all she could think to do was stall until help came. If help came …

ᏣᏣᏣᏣᏣᏣᏣᏣᏣᏣ

When the people learned that they had been sent into a panic over fireworks, they calmed down, the majority feeling silly and joking with each other. Many of the visitors left Ordinary to return to their homes and decompress. Many of the local folks did the same. A sizable percentage stayed as the only band not to leave struck up an upbeat chord. The Common was covered in litter from the stampede but small groups of young people—more than a few with ages in the single digits—took up large black trash bags and began picking up. In less than two hours the Common had been returned to its original beauty.

All the posse—sans Eskil Rosendale, Sergeant Nielson, and Officer Newberry—gathered in police chief's office back at City Hall. Grim-faced, Nathan Hambaugh looked at them as a whole. "I apologize," he told them.

"For what?" asked his older brother.

"For not thinking through all the possibilities," was the demoralized response.

"*Could* you have planned for *all* the possibilities?" Raymond Hambaugh pressed gently.

"No," admitted Nathan, "but that doesn't change the fact that I am responsible for this fiasco." He sighed. "All right," he said, sitting up straight in his chair, "enough of that. Anne is out there somewhere …"

They heard the rumbling arrival of the Harley-Davidson at the front of the building, and a minute later a very stern-faced, angry Air Force Special Ops veteran entered the chief's office. "I lost them," he said in his gravelly voice, "south of town. They're holed somewhere south of town."

With a nod, the Chief of Police said, "I appreciate the effort, Eskil. You may not have caught up to them, but you've narrowed down the search area."

"Did anyone recognize the getaway car?" inquired Harvey Freeman from a corner of the room. "It was pretty much gone by the time Mitch and I got there."

Nathan shook his head. "There was a time—in my youth—when I could tell you who drove what car in this town, but not now. It was an older-model Chevy Blazer, I know that much. Four-door. Probably red at one time, but the paint job was pretty faded …"

"Faded red," muttered Mitch Cavenaugh.

Everyone looked to the eighteen-year-old.

"Four-door …"

No one moved, let alone spoke.

"Older model," the part-time landscaper/gardener continued quietly as he thought. "Chevy Blazer …" He became aware of the silent stares and his face flushed slightly. "Sorry, I was just thinking."

Nathan smiled at the aspiring illustrator. "And what have you come up with?"

"Well," Mitch said, "I'm all over the place you know, being a landscaper and gardener, and all that, so I see cars all over the place, and y'all know that I like cars, especially older model cars 'cause they've got more character than the boring new ones, so I've been trying to think of where I might have seen this older model Blazer with its four doors and faded red paint …"

"And?" asked Raymond.

"Well," Mitch went on, "there's a farm south a ways belongs to the Harpers, you know …"

"Samuel Harper?" asked Nathan and Ray at the same time.

Nodding, Mitch said, "It's been in their family since they settled here more than a hundred years ago. Not the Blazer, the farm. I do some stuff around the house to help Miss Lydia from time to time when everyone else is working the fields. They're sure nice folks."

"Yes," agreed Ray, "yes, they are. Now, about the Blazer?"

"Oh, right!" Mitch chuckled. "Well, it came to me that the oldest Harper boy—"

"Samuel Junior," interjected Ray impatiently.

"—has an older model, four-door, faded red Chevy Blazer."

"What would they have to do with Paul Harkness?" Nathan asked. "Sam and Paul hated each other in school, as I recall."

"Well, they're all out of town for a spell," explained Mitch. "A wedding, or funeral, or something."

The police chief sat back in his chair. "If Paul knew they were out of town for a couple of days …" he thought out loud. "He could hotwire anything …"

"What are we waiting for?" growled Eskil, moving toward the office door.

"This is a police matter," Nathan told the biker. "I can't allow you, Mitch, or Ray to be involved."

Those named looked at Ordinary's police chief with bemused expressions.

"It's a free country …" his brother said.

"And if we just *happen* to be in the neighborhood …" added Eskil, grinning just enough to worry anyone.

"I could swing by to check on a job …" offered Mitch. "You know, get the lay of the land, as it were,"

Nathan Hambaugh suppressed his smile. "Seems I'm in a no-win situation."

"Seems that way," agreed his brother, smiling broadly.

"At the risk of repeating myself," said Eskil Rosendale, "what are we waiting for?"

"Well, for starters," explained Nathan, "I need to bring in my officers and brief them as to this new development, arm those who need to be armed, and come up with a plan. Mitch can innocently reconnoiter, and from what he learns we can finalize our rescue operation."

"A suggestion?" said Eskil.

"Yes?" responded the police chief.

"Wait until dusk," the veteran said. "They'll be more tired. Better for us to strike in the dark." His smile broadened ever so slightly. "This'll be fun!"

"I think," murmured Mitch, "that someone's in for a very rough night."

"Good!" Harvey growled.

"Then it's agreed?" queried Nathan of those gathered. Everyone nodded. "I'll bring in Brad and Carl, as well."

ЖЖЖЖЖЖЖЖЖЖ

It was just reaching that point when day and night mixed. Mitch Cavenaugh brought his metallic copper—with tan interior—1958 Chevy 3100 truck to a rolling stop in the front parking area of the Harper farmhouse. His brown eyes scanned the two-story home. There were no lights on at the front of the house, and all the curtains were drawn. With a deep breath, the six-feet tall eighteen-year-old stepped from his truck. He went up to the steps that took him to the front porch and the front door. He hesitated for only a moment, and then he rapped firmly on the solid wooden door.

He stood there for almost a minute, swaying back and forth on his heels, and whistling a toneless tune. When there was no response, he knocked again. Harder. He listened carefully. He heard movement, but no voices. Someone was home, and he was sure it wasn't the Harpers. He turned and returned to his truck and drove away, turning north on the blacktop and out of sight of the house.

Half a mile up the road he pulled over where three police cars—Ordinary Police Department's entire fleet of patrol cars—were parked with lights out. As the Chief of Police approached him, he said, "Someone's definitely in there, but no one answered."

"We didn't expect anyone would," said Nathan with a nod. "Good job, Mitch." He turned to the others as they gathered at the part-time landscaper/gardener's truck. "We'll wait here until it's full-on dark," he said. "Everyone knows what to do?" The assembled nodded. His smile was grim.

They waited in silence as the night settled in. On a country road, where there were no street lights, it got unbelievably dark. City people were always amazed—and, in some cases, terrified—by how deep the darkness was. One thing everyone agreed on, however, whether country or city, was how incredibly indescribable the night sky was without the interference of man-made light. There was a depth that drew a person in, and a calming blanket of innumerable stars that filled it.

"Eleven o'clock," Eskil Rosendale whispered in his gravelly voice.

With a curt nod, Nathan Hambaugh said, "Time, everyone."

On foot, they moved the half mile along the empty country road to the long winding driveway of the Harper farm. On either side of the dirt drive, the seven divided their force and stealthily advanced. When in sight of the darkened farmhouse, they began to spread out to encircle the structure. Raymond Hambaugh and Eskil went to the right front from where they could observe the front and right sides of the farmhouse. Harvey and Mitch went to the left rear where they could observe the rear and left side of the farmhouse. Sergeant Nielson and Officer Newberry went to the rear and hunkered down near the back door to await anyone who might emerge. The Chief of Police, taking a deep breath, walked up to the front door and rapped on it solidly.

"Police!" he declared in a very loud and authoritative voice. "I know you're in there, Paul! Open up!"

There was complete silence.

And then he thought he heard movement within.

"Come on, Paul, it's all over!" he continued, his tone and volume unchanged. "Release my daughter and come on out!"

He could definitely hear movement now as feet scrambled toward the rear. Moments later there came a loud commotion from the back of the farmhouse. A screen door slammed open, followed immediately by shouts and curses. He ran in that direction. By the time he got to the scene of the excitement, it was all over.

Hortense Grimes sat on the ground, handcuffed, between the two police officers. Paul Harkness was held in a crushing bear-hug, arms firmly pressed to his sides, by Eskil Rosendale. Whenever the kidnapper squirmed in an attempt to break the hold, the burly biker merely flexed his steel-like arm muscles, which brought a pained squeal from the captive. Ray, Harvey and Mitch emerged from the farmhouse moments later with a disheveled Anne.

Hugging his daughter tightly, he asked, "Are you all right?"

Wordlessly, she nodded into her father's chest.

Releasing his daughter into the comforting arms of her uncle, Nathan turned his attention to the two prisoners. He walked up to the resigned woman seated on the ground. "You made a huge mistake taking up with him," he said.

"You're telling me," she mumbled, her eyes downward.

He looked at Harkness. "You never were particularly bright, Paul," he said in an even voice. There was no gloating in his tone, there was no sadness, there was no inflection at all.

Paul Harkness glared hatefully at his childhood chum but said nothing.

Anne stepped away from her uncle and approached the now-handcuffed prisoner. "I believe," she addressed the angry man in a calm voice, "that you said something about my father being 'nothing more than a nobody cop in a little nowheresville town.'" And then she turned her back to him. "Good-bye, Mr. Harkness … for a very long time!"

ଓଓଓଓଓଓଓଓଓଓ

Paul Harkness, looking just a little worse for wear after being manhandled by the Air Force Special Ops veteran, sat on the uncomfortable bed in the cell in the basement of City Hall. He was leaned back against the wall, still-throbbing arms crossed against his chest, and a sour expression on his face. He was doing his best to ignore the police officer who stood at the locked cell door.

Officer Newberry glanced toward the stairs that led down from the ground floor as the sound of footfalls reached his ears. "Hey, Chief," he said.

It was well after midnight and Nathan Hambaugh was exhausted, both physically and emotionally. "Hey, Carl," he replied. "How are our prisoners?"

"Well, the gal is … resigned … I think the word is. This fellow here, though, is not a happy camper."

"No, I expect not," admitted Nathan as he stopped at the cell door. "Go ahead and get you some coffee, Carl, I'd like a word with this … fellow."

"Right, Chief," said Newberry with a nod, and he went upstairs.

Only then did Harkness turn his head. "So," he spat contemptuously, "you're the big chief."

"Interim, actually," Nathan corrected gently. "There's a special election next month." After a momentary pause, he asked, "What happened to you, Paul?"

"I got caught," snarled the prisoner. "You were there, remember?"

"That's not what I mean, and you know it. Why this life of crime?"

"Beats working a boring nine-to-five job," he laughed bitterly.

"I see," nodded Nathan. "Small-time stuff mostly, I noticed. But two counts of kidnapping, that's the big-time, Paul. That's serious prison-time."

"What do you care!"

Nathan cocked his head just slightly as he looked upon the man who had been his childhood friend. This was the fellow with whom he had got into all sorts of mischief. This was the fellow with whom … "Shouldn't I care?"

Harkness came off the bed and walked up to the cell door. Only the bars separated them. "No," he snarled.

"You came back here for the MacLeod treasure," said the police chief, "which you know probably doesn't exist."

"Doesn't it? Then why was your kid looking for it?"

"George? For the same reason you and I—and every other kid—looked for it: the adventure."

"Him, yeah," agreed Harkness, his hazel eyes narrowing, "but your daughter was on to something. She'd learned something about it."

"She was doing research for an article about Angus MacLeod to write up in the *Ordinary Outlook*," explained Nathan. "And it all started with your playing ghost at the manor and calling us into cart off George and Jorge."

Harkness blinked. "Playing ghost? What ghost? I admit I called—well, Hortense did—to get those brats out of our way, but I don't know what you're talking about ghosts."

"Hmm," nodded Nathan. "Probably an owl, then." He looked into the other man's eyes. He was telling the truth as far as that went. "No matter. The purse snatching wasn't very bright; that just drew attention to you."

"Told you so!" Hortense Grimes exclaimed angrily from the other cell.

"Oh, shut up!"

"*You* shut up, Mister Bigshot!"

"Both of you knock it off," sighed Nathan.

The two went quiet, but their resentment for one another smoldered.

Officer Newberry returned with a thermos of hot coffee and took a seat near the foot of the stairs. He was discreetly quiet.

"Well," Nathan said to the man behind the steel bars, "I'm sorry it's come to this, Paul. We had a lot of fun as kids, and those memories I'll always cherish."

"Whatever!" snapped Harkness as he returned to his cot.

With a slow, sad shake of his head, Nathan Hambaugh turned and walked away.

SEVEN

Friday, July 9th.

Really? thought Anne Hambaugh, opening one eye and glaring at the pewter clock on her bedroom wall. *Really? After what I just went through, and how late I got to bed, I'm not allowed* one *morning to have a bit of a lie-in?*

She sat up and looked at the family's gently snoring stocky brindle rescue mutt at the foot of her bed. Benbow, sensing that he was being watched, raised his head and returned her gaze. If she didn't know any better, she would think he was smiling at her. *He very well might be!* she thought with a little laugh.

She swung her feet from under her sheets and into her fuzzy bunny slippers, and then toddled into the kitchen while donning her daisy-print robe. The coffee maker was just finishing its important task as she produced three coffee cups from the nearby cupboard. She poured her father's first—black with no sugar—and then her own, with generous amounts of cream and sugar. Nathan Hambaugh strolled into the kitchen just as she finished. Handing him his cup, she said, "Good morning, Pater."

He kissed her forehead. "Good morning, Anne, and thank you for this." He raised his cup in a salute.

They went into the family room where he settled into his leather recliner and sipped the hot, steaming elixir. "I really don't want a repeat of yesterday," he sighed. "First, George gets himself kidnapped, and then you get yourself kidnapped."

"Well, if you recall," she said, "I wasn't *supposed* to get kidnapped."

"True," he admitted with a nod. "I think yesterday took ten years off my life."

"I think it added your ten to mine," said Anne whimsically. "I'm just glad it's over."

"I'll drink to that!" declared a crisp English voice. Emma walked into the family room with her own cup steaming. "And if either of you pull a stunt like that again, I'll box your ear holes!" She leaned over and gave her smiling husband a kiss. "And I'll give you *two* just for good measure!"

"Yes, dear," he said affectionately. "Anyway, it's not likely to, is it. My old childhood friend is behind bars. His ... companion has said that she would tell all." He paused for a moment, a sigh escaping him. "Paul Harkness ... life is funny sometimes."

As Emma settled herself into her corner of the sofa she asked, "So, what happens now?"

Anne was looking out across the lake. "Out there somewhere," she murmured softly, "beneath the waves lies a vessel that very well may hold some answers." She turned to her parents. "I must admit that part of me really wants to find the statuette of the goddess Tlaltecuhtli—if it exists—but, at the same time, part of me doesn't. The legend, generations of children hunting for the elusive lost treasure ... it would be a shame in some respects to take that away. After all, it *is* one of Ordinary's appeals."

"Quite the dilemma," admitted Nathan.

"Well, I suppose we'll just see how this treasure hunt plays out," she murmured. "Oh!" she added with renewed vigor, "I meant to ask: did you find their car?"

The police chief smiled. "Their lime-green Gremlin?" He chuckled. "Yes, Sergeant Nielson found it tucked away in the Harper's barn under an old tarp. It was impounded last night."

"Well, I, for one," said Emma from her comfy spot, "am glad this entire thing is over and done with!"

"And without any shooting," added Nathan as he drained his cup.

"That's always a plus," agreed Anne with a smile. Reaching for his empty cup, she asked, "Top up, Pater?"

"Oh, ta," he responded with a nod. After she had disappeared into the kitchen, he turned to look at his wife. "She's handled herself very well these last several weeks, wrapping up three dangerous mysteries."

"Yes, that's true," admitted Emma, "but I hope this is the last dangerous one. I think I'd rather she stays with nice, pleasant news stories."

"Now," said Anne, returning to the family room, "where is the fun in that?"

"*I* am more interested in *safe* than in *fun* where my children are involved," responded her mother.

"Your mother's right," the teen's father said. "Anyway, let's talk about today!"

A sleepy voice wafted into the family room. "A chap can't get any sleep around here with you lot."

"Now, there's a little ray of sunshine," laughed Anne.

Three inches taller than his older sister, George Hambaugh grunted an unintelligible response and reversed course for the kitchen.

Nathan Hambaugh drained his second cup of coffee and set down his empty cup on the side table. "I want to get with Ralph Hale this morning to get his input into your theory, Anne," he said. "Finding MacLeod's boat on the bottom of the lake may, or may not, answer some questions. I must admit, growing up here, I never gave much thought as to what happened to Angus and Eleanor; I don't think anyone did … or does to this day. But this investigation of yours has brought to light what could be Ordinary's oldest missing persons cold case file."

His daughter looked at him. "I *am* curious as to what became of them," she admitted. "It isn't likely that they up and moved away, and had they expired in some kind of accident there would have been some mention in the *Ordinary Outlook*, but there was nothing to indicate that." After a momentary pause, she added, "I fear the worst."

"Well, we'll do our best to solve that mystery," said her father firmly.

George wandered back into the family room, this time with a steaming cup of hot cocoa, and sat on the sofa with his mother. Everyone was quiet for a minute, and then he spoke. "So, let me get this straight … did they go down with the boat, or not?"

"I would be inclined to say 'not,'" Anne told him.

"Why is that, pray tell, oh sister mine?" he muttered between sips of his hot beverage.

"Because, oh brother mine," she replied, "if Angus went down with his boat, why would there be a stained-glass window made showing the position of the boat on the lake in relation to the unfinished manor?"

"Maybe his wife wasn't on the boat," the younger teen suggested with a shrug, "and she had it done to mark his final resting place."

The room became very quiet as three sets of eyes rested on the fourteen-year-old clutching his warm cup. Slowly, he looked at each of the observers, very much feeling the center of their attention. "What?" he asked.

"I had never thought of that possibility," Anne said.

"Nor I," admitted Nathan.

"Nor I," chimed in Emma, adding, "Anyone for breakfast?"

ଓଓଓଓଓଓଓଓଓ

Ralph Hale, owner/operator of Lake Ordinary Guided Tours and Fishing Expeditions, watched as the group of eight moved toward his 'office' on the boardwalk. They were a mixed group of young people and adults, civilian attire and uniforms. He knew that they were coming to see him—his oldest son, Marty, had made mention of it the other day—so he calmly waited for them. He figured they wanted to ask him something having to do with the lake. Perhaps another diving job like the one he handled to find the World War Two fighter plane that had been missing for sixty-seven years. He leaned back in his chair, letting it rest against the faded boards at the front of his shop.

"Good morning, Ralph," said Nathan Hambaugh.

"Morning, all," was the fisherman's response. "What brings you down to the water?"

"We have a mystery that you might help solve," the police chief told him.

"Might'n you? Let's hear it."

"We are looking for the *Banrigh na Locha*," Anne said, doing her best to control her excitement.

"Are you, now?" went on Hale, still leaning back in his chair.

"Angus MacLeod's ketch," explained her father.

"Is it, now?"

"Do you know where it might be, Ralph?" inquired Raymond Hambaugh, becoming just a little annoyed with the fisherman.

Hale nodded. "Yep."

There was a pause, and then an exasperated Tammy Coleman blurted, "Where?"

With a vague gesture toward the lake, Hale replied, "Out there. Sunk."

"If I were to show you a stain-glass window that depicted the boat on the lake," Nathan said evenly, "do you think you might be able to narrow down its location?"

Hale thought for a moment, and then said, "I suppose it can't hurt none to try."

The three older men went in the chief's patrol car; Harvey took George and Jorge; and the three girls went in Tammy's convertible. The three vehicles went to the museum at the edge of town, parking at the far end of the empty lot near an immaculate Harley-Davidson Road King motorcycle. They walked as a group to the building and went inside. They were met at the door by the beefy six-feet-four biker.

"Morning," said Eskil Rosendale in his gravelly voice. "How are your … guests, Chief?"

Nathan smiled. "Good morning, Eskil. They weren't happy with each other when I spoke with Brad Nielson this morning."

"Good," said the biker with a definite nod. "Come to look at that window upstairs?"

"Yes," replied Nathan. "Hoping Ralph here can glean a clue from it."

"Go right on up; the place is yours," said Eskil. "Visitors usually start showing up later in the morning. If you need anything, just holler."

The party of nine filed up the narrow stairs to the second level and wound their way through the displays until they reached their destination. They stood among the glass display cases facing the stained-glass window. Sunlight streamed in enveloping them in color.

Ralph Hale stood between Raymond and Nathan Hambaugh; the others stood back. He examined it in silence for several minutes. "So," he finally asked, "you're of the mind that this shows where the ketch sank?"

"We believe so," Nathan answered. "Is it a certainty? No. It's really nothing more than a best guess."

Ralph nodded thoughtfully. "Well," he muttered, "if that's the manor … and the ketch is out near the middle of the lake … no … no, it's not that far out …" He went quiet for a minute. "What we can do," he finally said, "is go on out on the water and visualize the size and angle of the manor in reference to where we are on the water … be the best way … My fish finder might help locate the wreck on the bottom … if there's anything left of it. As big a storm as you tell me, it might have broke that boat all to pieces."

"That's very possible," admitted Ray. "But there's only one way to know for certain, and that's to see what we can find."

"Yep," nodded Ralph. "I don't have any charters this afternoon so we can go after lunch."

"Sounds like a plan," nodded Nathan.

"Take me back to the boardwalk so I can get everything ready," Ralph said as he turned toward the stairs. "I'll get my boys and their dive gear, and we'll see all y'all —oh, say—around two o'clock."

The three older adults left after agreeing with the teens to rendezvous at Ralph Hale's fishing boat at two o'clock. The six teens stood in front of the museum soaking in the warm sunshine and talking in generalities. It was finally decided that Harvey would drop off the two younger boys at Jorge's house, and then he would join the three girls at the malt shop for lunch. They were just about to leave when Eskil Rosendale appeared in the doorway.

"I've been listening to what's been going on," he told the half dozen, "from what I've heard from your dad, Anne, and scuttlebutt and such." He paused. "Be careful."

"What do you mean?" asked Harvey.

"Like I said, I've had my ear to the ground," Eskil explained in a quiet—though still gravelly—voice. "Talk of treasure gets some people excited. Just be careful."

"We will," Anne promised.

The six-feet-four-inch veteran handed her a slip of paper. "My cell phone," he told her. "Put it in your contacts. Call me if you ever need help."

"We've got it covered," Harvey said with just a bit too much bluster.

Eskil smiled ever so slightly at the nineteen-year-old. "I'm sure you do, Cadet," he said evenly, "but it never hurts to have help when you need it, does it?"

Harvey blinked and shed his momentary bluster. With a touch of a sheepish grin, he replied, "You're right. Mind if I get your number, too?"

"All of you," nodded Eskil. "I insist." And with that, he returned inside the museum.

"Well," murmured Tammy, "I don't know about all of you, but *I* feel better knowing he's got our backs."

ଓଓଓଓଓଓଓଓଓଓ

Business was booming at the Ordinary Malt Shoppe that Friday when the white 1967 Mustang convertible pulled into a just-vacated parking spot on the Common side of the street directly across from the eatery. The three teens got out of the car and looked at the line that had formed.

"Wow!" declared Connie Bascomb. "Old Man Dunlap's going to have to expand … or relocate!"

"They are busier than usual," admitted Anne Hambaugh, nodding. "I wonder why?"

"I'll go over and case the joint," offered Tammy Coleman.

"Reconnoiter," corrected Anne with a chuckle. "We're not looking to rob the place!"

After the older teen had left, Connie turned to her best friend, asking, "What do you think we'll find on the sunken boat?"

"Provided we *find* the sunken boat," replied Anne, "I don't know. Very possibly nothing."

"That would be a bummer," sighed Connie.

"Yes, which is why I don't want to get my hopes up," agreed Anne. "I mean, just finding Angus MacLeod's ketch would be quite exciting—a piece of local history and all—but whether we find anything else ..."

"It would be something else to attract tourists," said Connie, a touch of sadness in her tone. "I know Ordinary relies on income from the tourists, but it's getting to where they're everywhere." To prove her point she gestured to the growing line outside the girl's favorite eatery.

"I know," sighed Anne. "Here comes Tammy. Perhaps she will be able to shed some light."

With her auburn hair bouncing and her hazel eyes bright, the seventeen-year-old came up to her friends with a huge grin on her face. "Word does get around!" she exclaimed.

"What do you mean?" asked Connie.

"Our treasure hunt!" laughed Tammy. "That's the buzz in the malt shop! Everyone in there is talking about the treasure!"

"Oh, dear," sighed Anne.

"No kidding 'oh, dear,'" Tammy hooted. "It's craziness!"

"But why's the malt shop so busy?" Connie pressed. "I've never seen it like that ever."

"I heard Anne's name mentioned several times in conjunction with the treasure, and MacLeod, and the manor," explained Tammy, grinning. She put an arm around the Anglo-American's shoulders and gave a friendly squeeze. "We have a celebrity in our midst!"

"Oh, dear, oh, dear," Anne sighed again, this time shaking her head.

Harvey Freeman pulled up in his patrol car at that time and stopped in the street. He looked at the trio, and then looked over at the queue outside their favorite eatery, and then returned his gaze to the trio. With a sigh and a shake of his head, he said, "There goes lunch."

"Let's go over to O'Brien's Ordinary Rock Chapel," suggested Tammy.

The sports bar and grill owned and operated by Sean O'Brien—a founder descendant and member of the town council—was located near the entrance to Ordinary. It had gotten its name from the unfinished local rock that his ancestor had used to construct it. While the buildings along restaurant row were built with brick and finished stone, the Irish pub had a rough exterior ... much like the builder.

"Climb in," said Harvey. "I'm starved."

They made the Circus Maximus circuit and found a parking spot within yards of the entrance. Stepping inside for the first time, Anne was suddenly transported to her beloved England and the old-world public houses there. The wood interior was dark from the multiple decades of smoke—though there was no smoking allowed now—and the floor planking was worn smooth. There was a full bar against one wall and a dozen tables for two-to-four patrons carefully positioned throughout. Along the wall opposite the bar were booths for four-to-six patrons, and this was where the four teens found themselves.

"Not very busy," remarked Connie, glancing about the half-filled pub.

"The lunch crowd will be showing up soon," explained Tammy. "We got here just in time."

"Come here often?" quipped Harvey.

"Mitch and I have been here a time or two," she admitted with a grin. "The food's really good. I love their bangers-and-mash."

"Their what?" asked Connie, eyebrows raised.

"Pork sausages and mashed potatoes," clarified Anne, smiling. "I must admit that I do miss a good pub lunch since moving here."

"O'Brien's does a delicious Cumberland sausage that also comes with onion gravy, fried onions, and peas," Tammy told them excitedly. "It's the house specialty!"

"Oh," sighed Anne, "that sounds lovely!"

"Let's keep this simple and have four of those," said Harvey. "I've never been in here and it does sound yummy!"

"I'm game," agreed Connie, nodding. "I've lived here all my life and I've *never* been in here!"

It wasn't long before the foursome was enjoying their lunches. Anne rolled her eyes happily with almost every bite while Harvey and Connie commented favorably between almost every bite. Tammy appreciated her bangers-and-mash in blissful silence. When they were done and their empty dishes had been cleared away, conversation turned to the afternoon's upcoming adventure.

"The way word has traveled," said Harvey in a low voice, "I wouldn't be surprised if we weren't the only boat out there."

"True," admitted Tammy, "but hopefully we'll be the only boat in the right place."

"If the treasure hunters catch on," Connie told them, "they'll just follow us."

"Yeah, and the Chief can't keep any of them off the lake," Harvey agreed with a sigh. "It'll be a mess."

"What if they went after the wrong boat," suggested Anne in a whisper that even her friends almost missed.

"How's that?" asked Tammy. "Everyone knows Ralph Hale's boats."

"Yes," added Connie. "Something to do with 'Ordinary Guided Tours and Fishing Expeditions' written on the sides."

"Exactly," said Anne. "Let everyone see that loaded up for the hunt and go off to—oh—the south end of the lake. All the while, we—along with my father, uncle, and Ralph Hale—take my uncle's boat …"

"Aren't you the sneaky one," chuckled Harvey.

Once outside and away from prying ears, Anne made a call to her father and proposed her plan. The police chief agreed to it immediately—saying that he wished he had thought of it—and reached out to his older brother and their treasure guide. Everything arranged by telephone. It was agreed that they would meet at Raymond's sixteen-foot fishing boat, which was parked at the private mooring on his property, at two-fifteen, and set out at two-thirty.

Ralph Hale rolled up in his truck alone. "My boys be takin' my boat out. Made a good show with all the scuba gear and all. Lots of talk about the treasure prob'ly bein' at the south end of the lake, or thereabouts." He grinned. "You shoulda seen folks scrambling for boats! Cracked me up!"

"That's good," said Nathan Hambaugh, nodding. "Hopefully, that will keep people out of our hair long enough to do what we need to do."

"Well, I been goin' over in my head that picture window," Hale went on, "and I think I can get us pretty close to the spot. The fish-finder may or may not help, we'll just have to see."

"How deep is the lake?" asked Harvey.

"Deepest spot is a hundred feet, or thereabouts," answered the fisherman as he tossed a small bag of gear onto the boat. "Where we'll be … oh, I'd reckon on less than eighty or so."

"Deep for a free dive," murmured Raymond.

"Not for me," scoffed the sixty-three-year-old mariner. "But anyways, I've got my own diving gear in the truck. Gimme a hand."

It was not long before they were ready to head out. There were seats for six on the fishing boat so it was decided by the boat's owner that the four teens should join the chief of police and the fisherman. Pushed away from the small pier, the boat's seventy-five-horse-power engine was started, and the vessel was steered onto open water. With directions from Hale, Nathan steered the boat to a position on the lake, and then idled the engine. Hale looked at the manor on the distant bluff and recommended moving to a new position close by. This went on for the better part of half-an-hour before Hale was satisfied.

He was looking at Raymond's fish-finder and scratching the graying stubble on his chin. "Well," he sighed, "I reckon we're about as close as we're going to get."

Nathan glanced at the instrument. "Seventy-five feet to the bottom," he said, concern in his voice.

With Harvey's assistance, Ralph Hale donned his diving gear and made himself ready. In one hand he held an end of a rope. "Two tugs mean I've found the wreck," he told the others. "Three tugs mean I'm in some kinda trouble and to pull me up."

"What about one tug?" asked Connie.

"That means something done et me!" laughed Hale, and over the side he went. In the water, he rinsed and donned his mask and put the mouthpiece in his mouth. He gave them a thumbs-up, and then slipped beneath the surface.

"He's an odd duck," murmured Harvey.

"Odd though he may be, the man knows this lake," said Nathan.

"Now comes the fun part," sighed Tammy, settling back into her seat. "The waiting."

Anne, with binoculars to her eyes, was looking to the south. "There's quite a gathering down there."

"Good idea you had," her father said affectionately, "otherwise we'd be in the middle of that mess right now."

"How long before they catch on that they've been duped?" wondered Connie.

"Hard to say," Anne replied, lowering the binoculars. "I suppose it depends on how long it takes them to figure out that it is Sergeant Nielson on that boat with the Hale boys and not Pater or Mr. Hale."

Harvey chuckled. "And are they going to be mad when they finally figure it out!"

Thirty endless minutes later, there came two tugs on the rope which brought everyone out of their seats. The five went to the starboard side of the boat, causing it to list precariously. The chief of police quickly ordered everyone back to their seats—or within close proximity thereof—while he stood near where the rope went over the side. Long minutes passed before the diver's head broke the surface. He was helped aboard and out of his tank harness.

"She's down there all right," he told them as he briskly toweled off. "Mostly in one piece," he went on. He looked at the lawman and added, "She looks to have been scuttled."

"Sunk on purpose?" gasped Anne.

"Looks that way to me," admitted Hale, accepting a cup of coffee Tammy had poured from a thermos. "Sitting mostly upright," he went on. "I figure the storm knocked it about a bit, did some damage, but I'm willing to stake my career on this lake that she went down afore the storm hit."

"Any … remains?" asked Nathan.

"Naw," said Hale with a shake of his head. "Mind you, by now, after all these years, were there anything they'd've been washed away."

"What about the treasure?" asked Harvey anxiously.

Ralph Hale turned to look at the nineteen-year-old. "There's a strong box down there," he finally admitted. "In real good condition, considerin'."

"Wooden?" asked Connie.

"Yep."

"With metal straps?" added Tammy.

"Yep."

"Mr. Hale," said Anne gently, "can we recover the chest?"

He shifted his gaze to the seventeen-year-old. "I reckon with some help I can get it up."

"I'll radio Sergeant Nielson," Nathan said to the diver, "and have him head this way with your boys."

"Pater," said Anne urgently, "that will bring everyone else."

"Good point," nodded her father. "I'll have them return to the Ordinary Pier, make it look like they're calling it quits, and then Brad can drive them up here."

"Sounds like a plan," said Ralph, accepting a second cup of coffee. "In the meantime, we should mosey away from here before anyone gets suspicious."

Nathan Hambaugh steered the boat closer to his brother's private pier. Fishing poles were brought out and for the next two hours, the boaters had fun with a catch-and-release fishing experience.

A call on the chief's cell phone brought the fishing to a close and they returned to the pier. The four teens were put ashore while Raymond Hambaugh and the two Hale boys boarded the boat. Under Ralph's guidance, Nathan returned the boat to its place above the wreck. Marty and Biff Hale, kitted out in their diving gear, went over and down. They were not down long before a boat was observed speeding toward them.

"Who's that, do you suppose?" wondered Harvey.

Anne raise her binoculars. "Even with these," she said, "they're too far off."

"Do you think they figured out what was going on?" Connie asked.

"Could just be coincidence," said Tammy hopefully.

"Maybe," murmured Anne as she dialed her father's cell phone number. Moments later, she put her phone away. "He sees them," she told her friends.

From the shore, the four teens watched as events unfolded on the lake. The approaching boat made a sweeping circle around Raymond's fishing boat. The sound of a shot cracked the air, and the teens winced involuntarily.

"Pirates!" Tammy declared in disbelief. "We've got pirates on Lake Ordinary!"

Anne watched through the binoculars as her father, uncle, and Ralph Hale raised their hands. On the pirate speedboat were four men, three armed with rifles while the fourth was at the helm. She looked more closely at the helmsman: short and portly with a receding blond hairline "That's Mr. Bernbaum!" she exclaimed incredulity.

"Are you sure?" queried Harvey doubtfully.

Handing over the binoculars, she said, "Look for yourself!"

He took the glasses and peered through the magnifying lenses, adjusting them only slightly. "Holy cow!" he gasped. "I don't believe it!"

"He must've caught on that the key we showed him was to a treasure chest," said Connie. "Who would've suspected Mr. Bernbaum of being a pirate?"

"Can you tell who is with him?" asked Tammy.

"No one local that I can tell," replied Harvey as he lowered the binoculars. "This isn't good."

"What do we do?" inquired Connie nervously.

"Who do we call?" added Tammy with worry.

"Hello, Mr. Rosendale?" Anne said into her cell phone. "I'm sorry. Eskil. We have a situation on the lake." And the she proceeded to tell the veteran what was happening. She finished the call only a minute later, saying, "Thank you ever so much!"

Turning to her friends she said with a smile, "The United States Air Force's Special Operations is on its way!" They looked at her uncertainly. "Well, one of them, at any rate."

ଔଔଔଔଔଔଔଔଔଔ

Nathan Hambaugh watched the speedboat approach. He had hoped that no one would show up until they had recovered the chest but understood that things did not always work out that way. He told his two companions top-side who reflected his disappointment. The other boat did not slow much as it circled them, came nose-to-nose, and settled in the water. It was the rifles that caught his full attention, and he flinched as one was fired, the bullet going over their heads. He recognized only the driver: Theo Bernbaum.

The portly man with the receding hairline stood up, holding the boat's wheel to maintain his balance. "Drop your gun over the side, Chief!" he bellowed.

Nathan let his sidearm drop to the fishing boat's gently rolling deck, a minor act of defiance. He could not risk the lives of those with him, especially when two were still down below on the lake's bottom. "That will have to do," he responded, a hint of anger in his voice.

"All we want is the treasure," Bernbaum said. "Give us the treasure and no one gets hurt."

"It's still below," Raymond Hambaugh replied. "I cannot *believe* you're doing this, Theo. I've known you for years—"

"Years stuck in this one-horse town!" snarled Bernbaum. "The same thing, day in and day out. The annoying crowds of nosy, rude tourists every day of every year. I'm tired of it! This treasure is my ticket out of here! I'll be able to go *anywhere*!"

"You're sharing equally with your crew, I suppose," said Nathan. "Or did you offer them a measly five percent."

"Nice try!" laughed Bernbaum derisively. "They're family and they're from out of town, and their share is equal. Even with a quarter of that loot, there will be plenty for me start over elsewhere very comfortably!"

"You're assuming there's something of value in the chest," Ray said. "That's a pretty big assumption. Because if it's empty, the only place you and your kin are going is prison … for a very long time."

All during this conversation, Ralph Hale was watching the rope, and watching for his sons. "Here come my boys," he said quietly.

All eyes shifted to that one spot on the lake. It seemed to take a very long time before two heads broke the surface. The Hale brothers looked wordlessly from the occupants of one boat to the occupants of the other boat.

"Did you get it?" demanded Theo Bernbaum excitedly.

The brothers looked to their father.

"Well, did you?" he asked with a sigh.

They shook their heads.

"Why not?" Bernbaum almost screamed.

"The chest's empty," replied Marty, the older of the two.

Except for the speedboat's idling engine there was quiet. Everyone seemed to look from one to the other in surprise.

"Empty?" choked Bernbaum in disbelief.

"Yessir," replied Marty.

"But ... it can't be!" he exclaimed angrily. "It can't be! I ... but ... No! It can't be empty! You're lying!"

"Now, hold on right there!" declared Ralph Hale, turning his full attention to the former owner of the Ordinary Lock & Key. "*My* boys don't lie! Just 'cause you *assumed* there was some kinda treasure down there—and the fact that there ain't—don't make them liars! Best you lot skedaddle afore I come over there and knock the tar out of each and every one you!"

The four in the speedboat looked to one another with perplexed expressions which quickly turned to fear. They realized that they had made a very bad mistake which now cost them everything they had. They realized that—at that moment—they were all wanted men.

"What do we do now?" cried out the man who had fired his rifle.

Bernbaum took a moment before responding. "We've got to go! We've got to get away from here!" He snarled at the police chief who was still standing calmly with his hands casually in the air. "Don't follow us if you know what's best for you!"

With an amused shake of his head, Nathan said, "I have no intention of following you, Theo."

"Smart man!"

"I know who you are," the lawman continued, "so it won't be long before you and your kin are caught."

"Better to get going while the getting's good," added Ray, a small smile touching his lips.

With a curse, Bernbaum pushed the throttle forward and spun the wheel. The speedboat jumped forward, almost colliding with Raymond's fishing boat, before turning southward and roaring away. The three on the fishing boat lowered their hands, and Nathan recovered his sidearm.

"Well," he sighed, "that wasn't any fun."

"Theo Bernbaum," Ray said, shaking his head. "Who'd a thunk it?"

"Not me," admitted his brother.

"Never liked him no how," grunted Ralph. And then he turned to his sons. "So, the chest's empty, is it?"

"Well," said Marty, a grin slowly forming, "when we went to lift it the bottom fell off. Rotted through, and the weight from all them coins—"

"Wait!" declared Nathan. "What do you mean?"

"All them coins …" started Marty.

"… they spilled out the bottom …" continued Biff, his grin even wider than his brother's.

"… so, the top part of the chest is empty," Marty finished.

The three men on the boat laughed aloud, and the police chief waved to those on the distant shore.

"Well done, boys!" declared Nathan happily. "Well done, indeed! There will be a reward in it for you!"

Raymond Hambaugh clapped their father on the shoulder. "You have an amazing pair of boys there, Ralph! You should be proud of them!"

"Oh, that I am," replied the grizzled fisherman, smiling broadly. "That I am."

"Hand us a sack and we'll start bringin' 'em up," said Biff.

"One question, boys," Nathan said quickly. "Was there anything besides the coins in that chest?"

"Like what?" asked Marty.

"A figurine. A small statue. Heavy, about the size of a shoebox," he explained.

Both boys shook their heads.

"So," murmured Ray, "that search continues."

"I have to wonder," sighed his younger brother, "if there ever *was* a stolen statuette. Maybe it's all just a story."

❧❧❧❧❧❧❧❧❧❧

The four teens watched the drama unfold from where they stood on the shoreline. It seemed to go on indefinitely until, quite suddenly, the pirate vessel wheeled about and went south at top speed. The foursome was too stunned so say anything at first. They were at a loss for words for what they had just witnessed. They did manage to acknowledge the wave from the distant boat.

It was Tammy who finally spoke first. "They just left. Just … left."

"Do you suppose they got the treasure?" inquired Connie, frowning slightly.

Anne shook her head, lowering the binoculars. "No, nothing was passed between the boats. They just … left."

"Something must've been said to scare them off," Harvey deduced.

"I agree," nodded Anne, "but what?"

"At this point," said a relieved Tammy, "who cares as long as they're gone?"

"And very possibly into the waiting hands of Eskil Rosendale!" laughed Connie. "I'm sure glad I'm not any of them!"

"So, what do we do now?" Harvey asked.

"We wait right here," said Anne. "And in the meantime, I'll call Eskil and give him an update on the situation."

"I expect your dad has called the county sheriff's office about that boatload of pirates," Harvey told them with a mild air of authority.

"I expect you are right," admitted Anne with a small smile, "but I'm going to update Eskil anyway."

For the next hour they sat on the private pier watching the distant activity on the lake's surface and chatting about all that had transpired over the past few days. The sun was settling behind the far western tree line when the fishing boat started toward them. They watched in silence, excited about what had been found.

When at last the boat was brought to a gentle stop beside the pier and the tethering lines—fore and aft—had been secured, those aboard stepped off one at a time; Nathan remained behind. "Fetch your wheelbarrow," he told his brother, "and several bags of coarse cloth if you've got any."

"I'll check the shed," Ray said, "and I'll be back in a few."

"Ralph, I sincerely thank you and your sons for helping with this … adventure … today," he continued, addressing the fisherman. "I'll see to it that you're generously paid for your time, and for going above and beyond the call."

"A pleasure, Chief, a pleasure," said Ralph Hale with a genuine grin. "Any time you need business done on—or under—the water, you call me."

Returning the smile warmly, Nathan said, "You can bet on that!"

The Hales gathered their gear and left.

Anne, unable to restrain herself, blurted impatiently, "Did you find it? Was it there? Oh, Pater, say something!"

With a laugh her father replied, "I will if you give me the chance!" During the quiet lull he told those gathered, "We found the chest, and we found the treasure within—" The teens whooped with unbridled joy. "—but there was no statuette of Tlaltecuhtli." The cheering stopped as suddenly as it had started.

"So … no treasure?" asked Tammy disappointedly.

"Oh, there's treasure," he said. "The chest was full of coins—gold, silver, and copper—from MacLeod's time, there's just no statuette."

"Then … it's elsewhere?" queried Connie.

Nathan Hambaugh shrugged. "I don't know. It may be just local lore."

"Was there anything else," stammered Harvey, "you know, down there?"

"No bodies, if that's what you mean," was the chief's reply. "And after this much time, finding remains would've been unlikely."

Anne glanced in the direction of the manor on the bluff. "So, they may still be up there."

"But where would we start to look?" wondered her best friend.

"Someplace no one else has looked, I suppose," sighed Tammy. "Wherever *that* may be."

"Well, the fact that Angus MacLeod's fortune was found on the *Banrigh na Locha* from the clue left in the stain-glass window confirms that they were still around after she sank," Anne said thoughtfully. "Now, they disappeared at some point after that event, and after the window was made and installed …"

"I expect the business that made the window is long out of business," her father told her. "Here comes your Uncle Ray. We could use some strong backs to help shift this treasure."

"Where's it going to?" asked Harvey as he handed his boss a small burlap sack from the wheelbarrow.

"Lock it up in evidence," Chief Hambaugh said. "I'll contact the Treasury Department tomorrow—and probably the State Department—to start the next-of-kin ball rolling."

For the next half hour, the six filled small burlap sacks with the wet coins and placed them into the wheelbarrow. This done, Harvey—being the strongest of the group—wheeled the treasure to Chief Hambaugh's patrol car. There the sacks were transferred to the trunk, the wheelbarrow was wrangled onto the backseat, and then the two lawmen left. The car was definitely riding lower now.

Raymond Hambaugh and remaining three teens went to his house where Andrea and Emma Hambaugh patiently waited to hear of the day's excitement. Neither were thrilled about the rifle-wielding pirates, but they were excited by the treasure find.

"Well," said Emma, "quite a day for all of you. Quite a day, indeed."

ଔଔଔଔଔଔଔଔଔଔ

Paul Harkness came off his cot at the sounds of men struggling with something heavy at the stairs. His face pressed against the bars of his cell, he watched as his former boyhood friend manhandled a heavily laden wheelbarrow into view with assistance of the red-faced cadet. Officer Carl Newberry, who had been the nightshift guard, unlocked the door to the evidence/property room and stepped aside.

"What's that you got there, Nathan?" sneered Harkness.

Ignoring the man, Nathan Hambaugh and Harvey Freeman maneuvered the wheelbarrow into the room, parking it as far to the rear as it would go. The interim Chief of Police then locked the door with Newberry's key, double checked that it was secure, and pocketed the key. Looking at his silent officer, he said, "I'm going home to freshen up, Carl, and then I'll be back."

Newberry nodded. "Take your time, Chief. Nobody's going anywhere."

The sneer was out of the prisoner's voice when next he spoke. "What did you lock up, Nathan?"

"Nothing that concerns you, Paul," said Chief Hambaugh. "Not anymore." He turned to leave.

"You found it!" Harkness murmured incredulously. "You found my treasure!"

Nathan stopped and turned to face the man behind the steel bars. "*Your* treasure, Paul? Do tell me how you're related to Angus MacLeod."

"It's mine!" the man snarled, his face twisting with rage. "You *know* it's mine! I've been looking for it since we were kids!"

"You, and everyone else within a hundred miles of Ordinary," replied Nathan levelly. "It goes back to the MacLeod family as it's rightfully theirs."

Spittle formed at the corners of his mouth as Paul Harkness reached in vain through the bars for the irritatingly calm police chief. "I'll get you for this, Hambaugh! I'll get *all* of you for this!"

From the other cell, Hortense Grimes laughed grimly, "Oh, be quiet, Paul."

"*You* be quiet!" was his bitter retort. "It's *my* treasure," he sobbed softly. "It's mine … my treasure … mine …"

EIGHT

Saturday, July 10th.

They had all gathered at Anne's house on the Old Mill Road north of town. It was late morning. The sun had long since burned the mist from the lake's surface. The waves sparkled like diamonds as the gentle west-to-east breeze moved the expanse of water. A dozen or so boats could be seen, distantly, in the general vicinity of where the *Banrigh na Locha* lay. Word had gotten around quickly about the recovery of the treasure somehow … but then, this was a small town …

"It's a good thing your dad decided to be out there to talk to the curiosity-seekers," Connie Bascomb said to her best friend.

"Yep," agreed Tammy Coleman, her hazel eyes resting on the crowded scene. "Letting folks dive—those who can—but telling them not to touch is a good idea."

"There's always someone who will push it," grunted Harvey Freeman.

"Ralph Hale's boys are out there, too," Anne Hambaugh reminded the cadet. Seated beside her was Benbow, the Hambaugh family's stocky brindle rescue mutt. She was absentmindedly scratching his ears. "They're taking turns diving on the site with the tourists to make certain that everyone behaves."

"Can't do it forever, though," he reminded the redhead.

"Well, there isn't much down there worth stealing according to Pater," she responded back. "The novelty will wear off after a bit, just like the crashed fighter plane."

"True," he sighed. "True."

"I heard on the radio this morning that Theo Bernbaum and his cousins from Clovertown were apprehended by the county Mounties," Tammy said.

"Sort of," admitted Harvey. "Truth be told—and it'll get around quick enough—Eskil Rosendale met the—er—pirates at the boardwalk's pier and held them at gunpoint until the deputies showed up."

"Gunpoint?" Connie asked.

"Apparently he had a Colt .45 pistol on his hip and an AR-15 in his hands," chuckled the cadet, "and several spare magazines for both. A little more firepower than the pirates expected. Needless to say, they surrendered as soon as they set foot on the pier."

"Good," said Anne firmly.

After a minute of peacefulness, two fourteen-year-old boys emerged from the house to join the older teens. George Hambaugh and Jorge Bustamante seated themselves in the remaining two Adirondack chairs and joined the others in looking out at the lake.

"That Studebaker's going to be a beaut when she's done," George told them, a touch of pride in his voice.

Glancing over at her younger brother, Anne said with a smile, "Enjoying yourself with the restoration project, are you?"

"Rather!" he nodded emphatically, his British accent coming through strongly.

"The car is in fine shape," Jorge added in his quiet voice. "Really, it's mostly just taking it apart, cleaning everything, and putting it back together."

"Mitch helps us as he can," went on George, "and Mr. Lechter has been a great teacher."

Marcus Lechter was the owner/operator of the Ordinary Car Care Center. He also took on the role of auto shop teacher at the high school. The car being discussed was a cream-colored 1934 Studebaker President convertible roadster that had belonged to the mysterious Anja Matthaus. She had been involved in espionage and murder in 1943 and had disappeared under mysterious circumstances. Anne and her friends had recently wrapped up that mystery.

"I am glad you're enjoying yourself," Anne said, "and that you're learning so much!"

"Not to mention staying out of trouble," added Harvey with a grin and a wink.

"Well, mostly," interjected Tammy, chuckling.

"Can we get back to the subject?" Connie asked.

"What was that?" inquired George.

"The treasure," she sighed.

"That's been found, I thought," said Jorge.

"Connie means the statuette," Anne clarified.

"And let's not forget that we still don't know what happened to Angus and Eleanor MacLeod," added Tammy. "They're just as important to this little mystery as the treasure."

"That's true," admitted Anne. "The treasure may or may not exist, but we know that *they* did."

"Ralph Hale says the ketch was scuttled," Harvey speculated. "Do you think that crazy old sea captain did that?"

"But *why* would he do that?" Connie asked, glancing his way.

"Well, if his workers—or even just a few of them—were getting restless," the cadet explained, "and they were starting to talk more about his treasure, and starting to look for it, he might have scuttled the boat with his fortune on board to prevent any of them from swiping it."

"Could very well be," admitted Tammy. "I suppose he could have kept enough to continue paying the workers' wages, their own living expenses, and stuff like that."

"I agree with all this," said Anne. "It is all quite feasible, and certainly worth accepting until we learn otherwise."

"But the statuette of what's-her-name, oh sister mine," George pressed. "Do you think it was all just a story?"

"Very possibly," she sighed.

"So, assuming the statuette story is just that," Tammy went on, "what do we do now?"

"I suppose we find them," Connie suggested, a slight shudder going through her.

"Yes," Anne nodded. "Something happened to Angus and Eleanor after the boat was sunk, and after the window-map was made …"

"The stained-glass window could have been made *before* the boat was scuttled," proposed Jorge quietly. "Captain MacLeod was an experienced seaman. He may have chosen the spot to scuttle his treasure ship and had the window made as his treasure map, and *then* sank it." Five sets of eyes went to the soft-spoken Hispanic boy. He looked back with his large dark eyes. "*¿Hay algún problema?*"

Anne laughed warmly. "No, Jorge, there is no problem!"

"It could've worked that way," admitted Harvey, nodding. "I'm also thinking that Connie has the right idea: finding the MacLeods. *If* the statuette does exist, it may very well be with them. So, if we find them, we also find the statuette. Maybe. If it's *with* them, I mean."

"Okay," said Tammy, "I'm game. But that manor—and its property—has been gone over with a fine-tooth comb for the last million years or so without them *or* it being found … or even hinted at."

"True," sighed Harvey.

"So," sighed Connie, "we're back to square one."

"We need to come at this from a different angle," murmured Anne thoughtfully. "We need to come at this as if it were *not* a treasure hunt."

"Looking for dead people," suggested George, a ghoulish grin on his youthful freckled face.

"Yes," agreed his sister, giving him a somewhat concerned look. "So," she continued, "If you were a good Christian and you came across a … oh … murdered couple, what would you do?"

"Call the cops," answered Tammy.

"Ah!" Anne said dramatically. "But the local authorities—including a majority of the townsfolk—don't like this murdered couple and wanted nothing to do with them. What then?"

"Give them a proper Christian burial as best I could, I suppose," murmured Connie thoughtfully.

"Where?" pressed Anne, a small smile on her lips.

"In the churchyard would be the logical place," Harvey chimed in.

"But there is no churchyard at the manor," countered Anne gently. "And it's unlikely the townsfolk would be keen on their internment in

Ordinary's cemetery." After a momentary pause as her friends—and brother—pondered the problem, she proposed, "*But* … there is a small private chapel …"

They looked at the wavy-haired redhead. Her gold-flecked green eyes were sparkling, and she wore a wide smile.

"I suppose, then," Tammy posited, "that I'd bury them in the … chapel."

"More accurately?" Anne urged.

"*Under* the chapel," answered Jorge, now sitting fully erect.

"Do you really think so?" Connie asked, uncertain.

"Well," replied Anne, "like we've been saying, the place has been searched for over a century."

"Surely someone else thought about looking in the chapel," George said.

"As we talked just now, I got to thinking," explained Anne, "that when we were up there the other day—poking around—I remembered looking into the chapel. I think it was the shadow of the cross from the stained-glass window that was cast on the doorway which drew me. But my point is, I looked in that little chapel and saw nothing."

"So, what makes you think there's something there now?" Harvey asked.

"Because I saw *nothing*," she answered, leaning forward in her seat.

"You lost me," Connie sighed.

"There was nothing disturbed," interjected Tammy. "Right?"

"Precisely, my dear Watson!" declared Anne as she became more excited. "There was nothing to indicate that the room had *ever* been disturbed. No holes in the floor or walls. No piles of dirt or displaced furnishings—"

"Not that there are any furnishings to speak of," quipped Tammy, grinning.

"A couple of pews," said Harvey.

"And the dais," added Jorge.

"Query," inquired Connie. "Wouldn't this … someone … this good Christian … wouldn't he fetch the local preacher?"

They all thought for a moment, and then Tammy said, "Pastor Archibald's family has been preaching here for as long as I can remember."

"Same here," agreed Connie.

"If his family has been pastoring here since the beginning," proposed Harvey, "there may be—should be—some kind of record."

"And with the rest of the town not being keen on the interlopers," George added, "he wouldn't necessarily have shared that bit of news."

"I have to wonder," Anne murmured, "*who* might have found Angus and Eleanor."

"Could very well have been the pastor himself," Jorge suggested. "He may have come up to the manor for private Sunday services."

"A good point," admitted Anne. "It wouldn't have been unheard of. And as long as the … interlopers … stayed out of *their* church, the townsfolk probably wouldn't have minded much."

Tammy came out of the Adirondack chair she had been occupying and stretched. "Let's go find us the preacher," she said in an exaggerated Western drawl.

ଓଓଓଓଓଓଓଓଓ

Archibald Pettigrew, pastor at God's Ordinary Church, ushered his young visitors into his office with a smile. "I'm afraid I don't have enough chairs for everyone," he told them apologetically. "I don't usually have so many bodies in here at any one time."

"Funny you should mention bodies," chuckled Tammy Coleman.

Pastor Archibald looked the seventeen-year-old inquisitively. "I don't quite follow."

"Oh, you will," Connie Bascomb assured him.

With everyone now taking up the limited office space, and with the door firmly shut, Anne Hambaugh said, "As you probably know, we've been working the mysteries surrounding Angus and Eleanor MacLeod."

"I know!" he said enthusiastically. "I've been following it as best I can, and I find it all quite exciting! Discovering the sea captain's sunken treasure yesterday must have been exhilarating!"

"More so for my father and uncle," agreed Anne.

"Ah! Yes! The encounter with the pirates!" declared the pastor. "Pirates on Lake Ordinary … how extraordinary! But I would think that more terrifying than exhilarating!"

"It was that," she admitted.

"My word," he sighed with a shake of his head as he took his place behind his desk. "All right, then, you young people came to see me about …?"

"Well," began Anne as she scooted to the edge of the chair she was occupying, "we were discussing the case—specifically Angus and Eleanor—and trying to work out what became of them. We assume—from what little we do know—that they were probably murdered by one or more of the workers, which is why the manor is unfinished. We know that their remains have never been found over the many, many years of treasure hunting." She paused for a moment, and then continued, "And then it occurred to us that—perhaps—their remains *had* been discovered, but sooner rather than later."

"I … don't quite follow you," Pastor Archibald said as his fingertips came together in the shape of a steeple.

"What if they were found soon after their deaths?" asked Anne.

"Okay," he agreed with a small nod.

"Let's say they were found on a Sunday," she added, watching his face.

"Okay …"

"Let's say they were found by Ordinary's pastor at that time," she finished.

Archibald Pettigrew looked at her, the picture in his mind becoming clearer. He looked at the other five expectant faces. "So, you think that—possibly, very possibly—Angus and Eleanor Macleod were found by the town's pastor, and that he took it upon himself to give them a proper burial?"

The six young heads nodded in unison.

The pastor sat back in his chair as his eyes drifted thoughtfully over their heads to the cross above his office door. His tipped slightly to one side. "Well," he finally murmured, "they weren't welcome here in town … so it only stands to reason that the local pastor would go to them for services …" He looked at junior investigative journalist. "You may very well be on to something there!"

"The pastor of that time," inquired Anne, "was an ancestor?"

"Yes, indeed," was the anticipated reply. "Jacob Pettigrew was one of the town founders, which is why I am part of the council. He would have been the pastor at the time the MacLeods came here." He hesitated. "But Jacob was in his seventies so he would have needed help burying the couple."

"Who would have helped him?" Connie asked. "None of the townsfolk liked them."

"True," Pastor Archibald murmured. "True. Who, indeed?"

"Would there be a record somewhere?" Harvey Freeman asked helpfully.

"There would *have* to be," answered Pastor Archibald. "But, because these weren't church members, their deaths wouldn't likely be entered into the church's official records."

"Personal records?" asked Anne. "A diary, perhaps?"

The pastor smiled. "Jacob *did* keep a diary. It's in his old trunk in my attic. Boys," he said, addressing the three teen boys, "if you will be kind enough to assist me."

The four left the office and were gone for almost half an hour. The three who remained behind were getting antsy by the time the others finally returned.

In his hand, Pastor Archibald carried a worn, leather book which was held shut with a narrow strip of leather. Resuming his seat, he placed the ancient item gently on his desk. "This," he told the gathering, "is Jacob's diary. I apologize for taking so long to find it, ladies. As the boys will tell you, the trunk wasn't easily accessible."

"We had to rearrange the whole blooming attic!" declared George Hambaugh. "Oh! Sorry, Pastor."

With a dismissive shake of head, the pastor continued, "I've never actually read it, you know, so I really don't know what's in it."

"There could be all sorts of dirt on the townsfolk!" laughed Tammy, and then quickly added, "Sorry, Pastor."

"You could very well be right," he sighed with a nod. "I certainly wouldn't be surprised."

"All we're interested in is the time frame for when the MacLeods went missing," Anne said. "We're not interested in any … 'dirt' … on anyone. Unless, of course, there's mention of who might have done the deed."

"Well," said the pastor as he carefully untied the leather strip and laid it out, "let us see what we can find." He gently—almost reverently—opened the small diary and began to turn the pages to the time frame in question. "Here," he said, "the fifth of November in the year of our Lord 1795 …"

"Guy Fawkes Night," murmured George.

"What's that?" asked his best friend.

"You know, the chap who was part of the Gunpowder Plot of 1605," George replied.

"I don't …"

"'Remember, remember! The fifth of November, the gunpowder treason and plot …' and so on and so forth," explained George. And then, with a sigh, he added, "I'll tell you all about it later."

"Well, *this* happened one hundred ninety years later," his older sister said, steering the conversation back on topic. "Go ahead, Pastor."

"It's a bit difficult to read," said the older man as he squinted through his reading glasses at the spider-like script. "This entry is more than two hundred years old … the ink is faded in spots …" He went quiet, and the others went with him. All that could be heard was their collective breathing. Finally, he broke the silence saying, "Well, well, well."

"What well-well what?" asked George eagerly.

Sitting back in his chair, Pastor Archibald Pettigrew looked at the fourteen-year-old and then to his sister. "The name of the man who helped my ancestor bury Angus and Eleanor that day is reasonably legible …"

After an uncertain pause, Anne inquired in a soft voice, though she suspected that she already knew the answer, "Who is he?"

With a small nod, he replied, "A fellow Scotsman to the deceased: Nathaniel Hambaugh."

The other youths looked at Anne and George in silent surprise.

"Why didn't you tell us?" declared Connie.

"I didn't know!" Anne responded, defensively. "How was I to know?"

"It makes sense, though," said Pastor Archibald in a calming voice. "No one from town would help, certainly, but someone who had been cast out probably would." He hesitated, and then continued, "Pastor

Jacob knew your ancestor's character, Anne … and George … and would have known that Nathaniel was someone whom he could rely on to help, and to keep it secret."

"Why should he want to keep it secret?" asked Harvey.

"I'm inclined to think that—back then—he wouldn't have known who had murdered them," the pastor explained, "and an investigation was out of the question because of the attitude of the townsfolk toward Angus and his wife."

"So, Pastor Jacob—your ancestor—and Nathaniel Hambaugh—Anne and George's ancestor—buried the sea captain and his wife," said Tammy contemplatively, "and told no one."

"I never saw any mention in the *Ordinary Outlook* for that time frame," Anne informed the gathering. "It was only mentioned—after the fact—that they were gone, with some of the townsfolk speculating that they had returned to Scotland. There was never anything to substantiate that, of course. But one got the impression that the townsfolk were glad the MacLeods were … gone."

"Not an altogether welcoming community," sighed the pastor. "So, now the question is: where are they buried? They wouldn't have been buried in Ordinary's cemetery—no way to pull that off—and there isn't a churchyard …"

"We think," replied Anne somberly, "that they may be buried in the manor's chapel."

Pastor Archibald thought for a moment, and then he nodded. "That would make sense."

"And I am inclined to believe," continued Anne, "that they are beneath the dais."

"Yes," he agreed, "I am inclined to agree with you."

"Back to the manor," Tammy said.

"We need to bring in your dad, Anne," Harvey said. "It may have happened more than two hundred years ago, but it's still a murder investigation."

"Oh, yeah," Tammy muttered. "There's no time limit on murder."

Nathan Hambaugh sat in silence as he listened to Pastor Archibald Pettigrew and his daughter tell him—and his wife, brother, and sister-in-law—what they had deduced. When the two had finished, he looked slowly over at his older brother. "Did you know?" he asked, stunned.

Raymond Hambaugh shook his head. "I had no idea," he replied, equally stunned. "I mean, it makes sense that Jacob would recruit Nathaniel, but I never knew. Dad never mentioned it to me, at any rate."

"I wonder if Dad knew," murmured Nathan.

"It may have never been discussed," Andrea Hambaugh told the brothers. "Something like that … they probably swore each other to secrecy."

"The secret would have died with them," admitted Emma Hambaugh sadly. "It's rather bittersweet, isn't it?"

"So," said Nathan, "we think we know where the couple are buried."

"Yes," his daughter said with a firm nod.

"But we can't just go in and demolish the place," he continued, "digging holes and hoping we find them."

"I'm certain they're beneath the dais," she insisted.

"I'll call the county sheriff in the morning and ask if they have one of those ground-penetrating radar gizmos," he told the gathering. He smiled at his daughter. "Although I have no doubt that you are correct, Anne."

"Should we post someone there?" Harvey Freeman asked. "I mean, word might get out, small town and all."

The police chief glanced at the cadet. "Part of me would disagree with you," he said, "but another part of me would strongly agree with you." He looked at each of the six youths in the family room. "Are you lot up to spending a night in the manor?"

"That would be so cool!" declared George Hambaugh before anyone else had a chance to speak.

Jorge Bustamante sighed as he slowly shook his head. "Why me?" he asked. "Why me?"

"It was my idea so I'm in," the cadet said, though his voice was not quite in agreement with his words.

Anne Hambaugh was nodding her head. “I’m game,” she said. “It would be a shame to have gotten this far and something happen because we weren’t there.” Glancing over at her two quiet friends, she continued, “Right?”

Connie Bascomb and Tammy Coleman sighed together as they looked to one another for support.

“Yes, of course,” said Connie.

“We’d love to,” finished Tammy.

“In that case,” said Chief Hambaugh, coming out of his leather recliner, “go home and get whatever you need: sleeping bags, flashlights, water, snacks, so on and so forth. Make certain that your cell phones are fully charged. I’ll talk to your parents; they may or may not agree. Be back here in an hour. I’ll go up with you to scout around. Harvey, since you’ll be the one representing the law you’ll be in charge. I know you’ll have your phone but make sure you take your walkie-talkie, and make sure it’s fully charged.”

Pastor Archibald stood up and turned to the six youths. “You are remarkable young people,” he told them with a mix of pride and admiration. “Know that my prayers will be with you, and that you will never be alone.”

“In a way,” murmured Anne, “it’s hard to believe that this adventure could be over by this time tomorrow.”

ଔଔଔଔଔଔଔଔଔ

The sun was setting across the lake in a splash of color that drew the attention of the six teens. It was just them at the decaying manor, surrounded by darkening woods and the emerging sounds of night creatures. Chief Hambaugh had gone … it was just them. There was still some discussion as to where to set up camp.

“Not in the chapel,” Harvey Freeman said firmly, his arms crossed.

“But that’s where they are,” insisted Tammy Coleman, a smile tugging at the corners of her mouth.

“My point exactly!” the cadet affirmed inflexibly.

“Well, that’s where I’m bunking down,” the seventeen-year-old told him.

“By yourself?” he asked.

She hesitated for a moment, and then replied, "I'm sure I won't be by myself." She glanced to the others standing nearby. "Will I?"

Connie Bascomb gave the exterior of the brooding edifice a worried look. "I don't know, Tammy."

Anne Hambaugh chuckled at her two friends. "What if we were to set up our housekeeping in the grand hall?" she asked. "That way we're close by without being too close."

The others, after giving the proposal some thought, nodded in agreement. They filed inside, closing the heavy front doors as best they could, and with the aid of flickering light from oil lanterns cleared space on the cold stone floor. They used a cast-iron hibachi as their campfire, feeding the small fire from a bundle of wood brought from the Anne's house. Night settled in around them quickly, and an eeriness seemed to join it.

"It is all in the imagination," Anne told them dismissively. She hoped that she had sounded more at ease than she felt. "This is nothing more than an empty old house."

"With dead people buried in the next room," added George unhelpfully. "What could possibly happen?"

"There are times when I despair of you, oh brother mine," his sister sighed, to which he grinned.

Jorge Bustamante rummaged around in his backpack, bringing out a large bag of marshmallows, chocolate bars and graham crackers. This brought a multitude of 'oohs' and 'aahs' from the others. "Just because we are in primitive surroundings," said the well-read youth, "doesn't mean we can't enjoy a little taste of civilization."

The group settled into fixing their delicious snacks around their little fire. Their topics of chatter were wide, with the two youngest excitedly discussing how work was progressing on the 1934 Studebaker. Eventually, however, the conversation came around to where they were, and why they were there.

"You don't really think there's anything to this ghost stuff, do you?" Harvey asked, rescuing melted chocolate from the corner of his mouth.

"I thought you didn't believe in ghosts," Tammy said.

"Well, as a general rule, I don't," he told her. "But being an open-minded kind of guy ..."

"If you're referring to what George and Jorge saw—or thought they saw—the other night," Anne told the older teen, "I am confident that that was an owl they had disturbed. I mean, when we came to investigate the following day there was nothing to suggest otherwise."

"It's not like a ghost would leave footprints," he muttered.

"Harvey!" declared Anne, not sure if she should laugh.

"What?" he responded vociferously in return.

"Can we *not* talk about ghosts, please?" Connie inquired nervously. "I mean, I don't believe in them either, but do we have to talk about them?"

They went quiet for several minutes, lost in their own thoughts as they enjoyed their treats, and then Anne got to her feet. "I'm going into the chapel for a look around," she told them as she turned on her flashlight.

"Me, too!" whooped her brother, scrambling to his feet. "Come on, Jorge!"

The Hispanic teen looked at his best friend for a moment as if contemplating his next move, and then sighed and resignedly got to his feet. "*Someone* has to keep you out of trouble. Lucky me."

"You're all nuts," grumbled Harvey as he got reluctantly to his feet.

"It's okay, big guy," Tammy told him reassuringly, "in all the best scary movies nothing hardly ever happens before the old clock chimes the midnight hour."

"You're *not* helping, you know," he growled as he glared down at her.

With a long sigh Connie also got to her feet. "I'm certainly not staying out *here* by myself!"

Together, the group of six walked the dozen or so feet to the open doorway of the chapel. Their flashlights cast long shadows in multiple directions. The five younger teens fell in behind the bigger, older, uniformed teen; Harvey was not amused and told them as much. Crossing the threshold, they fell into a line shoulder-to-shoulder, allowing their flashlights to play over the dusty interior. The four small pews that existed were set up two—one behind the other—on either side of the center aisle. Ages of dirt, blown in by more than two hundred years of winds, was deep enough in some places that vegetation had taken hold. Leaves that were blown in had decayed, creating a natural mulch. There was a strong dirt-like smell. The chapel's scent seemed more like a garden than a place for prayer.

"Nothing here," said Harvey, "let's go."

"Very funny," Anne countered, and she began to move into the debris-strewn chapel.

As she neared the cluttered dais, Anne swept the beam from her flashlight across it and its altar. She thought she had seen something. It had been fleeting … it may have been nothing … but it may have been *something … It was an owl*, she reassured herself, *that's what it was.* Mustering her courage again, she took several more steps toward the dais. She wished she were not alone.

She turned her head to call to the others only to find them directly behind her. She started involuntarily at the discovery. "Oh!"

"Well, we had nothing better to do," Harvey told her, smiling. "Shall we?" He walked the few paces to the foot of the steps of the dais. He shined his light on the altar's ancient stonework; he could just make out some kind of relief beneath the layers of grime. He felt a sudden urge to wash the filth away. Turning on his heel, he hurried past his stunned colleagues and back to their campsite and grabbed his water bottle and a handful of paper towels. These in hand, he returned to the altar and began to clean it. Seeing what he was doing, the others did the same and soon the six of them had it looking as clean as its first day on the bluff above Lake Ordinary.

When they had finished and had stepped back to admire their collective handiwork, Anne asked him, "What brought that on?"

"What do you mean?"

"That sudden urge to clean the grime and gunk from the altar?"

He thought for a moment, and the replied, "I don't know, really. I was looking at what was beneath the … grime and gunk … and thought it looked … pretty."

"It is made of marble," said a voice behind them.

As one the six teens spun around to face the speaker. It was Pastor Archibald Pettigrew, but now he wore jeans and a flannel shirt. "Michelangelo worked with blocks of marble," he told them as he walked toward the dumbfounded group, a smile on his face. "The story is that he would see an image in the marble and—in a manner of speaking—release it." He went quiet for a moment. "A long time ago," he explained as he went up the steps of the dais, knelt, and placed his hands upon the altar, "I was struggling with my calling. My father wanted me to follow him into the evangelical ministerial profession, as he had followed his father, and so on and so forth back to Jacob. But I wasn't so sure that was what I wanted to do. There was a whole world out there to be discovered." He paused for a moment, and then went on. "I was as curious about this place as anyone else as a boy. And while everyone else was scouring this wreck from basement to attic in search of that elusive treasure, I was in here." He looked at them with a sad little smile. "Oddly enough, I felt peace in here, and I was able to think. I came here several times over the course of a few months—whenever I felt uncertain—and I spoke with God. He listened, and here I am today: the simple pastor of a quiet little town." He patted the altar lovingly. "Anyway, this is made from thick sheets of marble. The inscriptions—different prayers in the ancient language of the Scots—are hand-carved. Beautiful workmanship." He rose and turned to face them. "You are wondering why I am here," he said.

"Well, we *are* just a wee bit curious," admitted Anne, having recovered her senses first.

"It's simple enough," was the man's reply, "and nothing ominous at all. Your father and I spoke when he returned, and we agreed that—while you're all quite capable and nothing untoward was expected—having an adult around was not necessarily a bad idea."

"And you lost the coin toss," Tammy said.

"No. Believe it or not, I volunteered," chuckled the church's pastor. "I have not been in here in a very long time … and considering what we may find tomorrow, my being here isn't such a bad idea."

"Care to join us for a squishy, chocolaty treat?" asked George.

NINE

Sunday, July 11th.

Anne Hambaugh opened her gold-flecked green eyes and for a moment was startled by her surroundings. *This is not my room*, she thought, and then she remembered. She found that she was a little stiff from sleeping on the hard, stone floor. She glanced at her wristwatch and sighed: six o'clock. She pushed herself into a seated position and stretched out some of the kinks. In the process, she looked about at her companions. All were still sound asleep … except one.

Pastor Archibald Pettigrew was beside the hibachi, feeding kindling to the small fire. Glancing over at her, he smiled and nodded. "Good morning, Anne. Sleep well?"

"The bed was a bit too firm for my liking," she replied with her own smile as she got to her feet, "but well enough. You're up early."

"I have a sermon to give this morning," he reminded her. "And I must say," he continued with a sigh, "that it won't be easy."

"Oh?"

"I suspect I'll be a little distracted."

"Ah!"

"Your father should be here with the fellows from the county's crime lab about noon," he went on. "I feel that I should be here when the dais is excavated … just in case remains are found, you understand."

"Quite," she responded with a firm nod.

"Well, then," he said as he stood up, "I'll be off. There's a pot of coffee brewing on the Coleman stove. It should be done in a few minutes."

"Oh, thank you!" she beamed.

He laughed lightly. "Your father told me about your addiction."

"He's one to talk!" she chuckled.

"I'll see you all about mid-day," said the pastor. He gathered up his gear and left.

Anne's eyes went to the chapel's open doorway and she pursed her lips in thought.

"What thought is rattling around inside your head?" inquired a sleepy voice.

Anne glanced over at her best friend who was up on an elbow and looking at her with drowsy brown eyes. "Good morning, Connie."

Connie Bascomb sat up, stretched and yawned, and then replied, "Morning, yes. Good? We'll see what sort of mischief you get us into."

"I?" Anne responded in faux surprise. "You cut me deeply, Connie. Very deeply."

"Ha!" was the sarcastic laugh from another source. Tammy Coleman unzipped her sleeping bag and stood up. "It's a wonder anyone can sleep with you two making such a racket."

"Another ray of sunshine," smiled Anne. "Coffee, anyone?" The other two shook their heads. "Then I shall partake of my morning elixir alone," she sighed, and poured it into a metal cup. She inhaled the steamy fragrance and sighed contentedly. "There is just something about coffee brewed over a campfire."

"Hand me the skillet," said Tammy, gesturing toward the cast iron skillet that was with their cooler of food, "and I'll get some bacon started."

"That ought to wake the boys!" laughed Connie as she delivered the heavy cookware.

And she was right.

It was mid-morning by the time they were all sufficiently fed. The three male members of the party volunteered to clean the cookware, plates and utensils and put it all away. Their campsite was tidied up and all the gear returned to the back of Harvey's 1978 primer-gray Jeep Cherokee Chief.

"Now what?" Harvcy Freeman asked as he closed the tailgate.

"We explore!" said George Hambaugh excitedly.

"Oh, wonderful," sighed Jorge Bustamante.

"That's fine," said Anne, "but I think a couple of us ought to stay here in case of visitors. And, Harvey, as you're the law in these parts, I think it should be you and at least one other."

The cadet nodded in agreement. "Not a prob."

"Well, I for one want to poke around a little," Tammy declared. "I'd get bored out of my mind sitting around here waiting for things to happen."

"I'd have to agree," admitted Connie.

"You four go ahead and do your exploring," Anne told them, chuckling softly. "Harvey and I will hold the fort."

After the four others had wandered off in two different directions, Harvey turned to his fellow guardian, "What happens if there's nothing to be—you know—found?"

With a glance toward the chapel, she shrugged. "Then the mystery surrounding Angus and Eleanor MacLeod continues, I suppose."

"We did find his treasure."

"Yes, though not Tlaltecuhtli."

"Mind if I ask you something?"

"Ask away."

"Do you believe all that stuff about the stolen statuette, and the curse, and all that?"

Anne thought for a moment. "Well, I'll tell you," she finally replied, "I don't know. I mean, does—or did—the statuette exist? Very possibly. Was it stolen back in the midst of time? Also, very possibly. Was Captain MacLeod the thief and most recent holder of said statuette? Maybe … or maybe not. It certainly makes for a good story, and it's also entirely possible that he put that story into motion to—perhaps—boost his status back in the old country."

"I suppose," murmured the cadet thoughtfully. "After all this build-up, it'd be kind of disappointing to find nothing."

"True enough," admitted Anne. "But," she added, smiling, "think of what we *might* find!"

"Two really dead people."

"Well, yes," she laughed, "but we *may* also find Tlaltecuhtli!"

He glanced from the seventeen-year-old to the chapel, and back, a look of skepticism on his face. "Do you really think so?"

"You know, Harvey, I've struggled with that," she replied. "I mean, a part of me hopes we do, but then, a part of me hopes we don't."

"That's what I like about you," he quipped, "you're so decisive."

"I'm serious," she said, her eyes on the chapel entry. "It would be nice to wrap up all the aspects of this mystery, but at the same time, it would be nice to leave a part of it intact. A little something that would continue to draw the tourists."

"Yeah, I suppose," he muttered.

"What are your thoughts on the subject?" she asked.

"I guess my thoughts are a lot in line with yours," he answered with a smile.

"Brilliant minds," she told him with an elbow to his ribs.

"Well," he drawled with a grin, "I don't know about that!"

ঙঙঙঙঙঙঙঙঙঙ

The six teens were standing at the open door of the MacLeod manor when an Ordinary Police Department vehicle and a Sheriff's Office Crime Scene Investigations van rolled to a stop. Chief of Police Nathan Hambaugh stepped out of the patrol car and started toward them. From the van emerged two women in deputy's uniforms. They went to the back of the van from where they brought out a boxy-looking device with handles which they carried to the manor.

"Kids," said Nathan, "these are Deputy's Arlene Smith and Zoe Jones. They've been kind enough to offer their assistance with our curious little problem."

Deputy Smith, of average height and with dark hair, smiled at them. "We don't often get a chance to use this gizmo."

"Usually," added Deputy Jones, slightly shorter and with blond hair, "it's the ground-penetrating radar that looks kind of like a big lawnmower."

"The thing in this crate is handheld for use on walls and such," continued the first deputy.

"It's a bit weighty and awkward so it takes two to operate effectively," finished the second deputy.

"I'm looking forward to seeing it in action!" declared Anne Hambaugh.

"I think we all are," admitted her father, grinning. "And here comes Pastor Archibald, right on cue." He gestured to the deputies to step inside the centuries-old edifice. "We can start anytime."

"My apologies for my tardiness!" stated the pastor as he hurried up the path to the others. "I got involved in a rather lengthy conversation with Mrs. Martel regarding her cat!"

Nathan laughed as he ushered the minister inside. "You're right on time."

The ten went to the open entry to the chapel where they filed in, Chief Hambaugh leading the way as the senior law enforcement representative on hand. They walked down the center aisle to the steps of the dais where the deputies put their crate down. While Deputy Jones opened the top of the crate, Deputy Smith stepped up onto the platform and walked with slow deliberation around the altar.

"Ready, Zoe?" she asked, returning to the open crate.

"Whenever you are, Arlene," replied the shorter deputy.

Together they brought the instrument out of its crate. It looked like a black box with two sets of handles on either side. The deputies took it up the dais and placed it on top of the altar, at one end. A coaxial cable was run from the device to a monitor on top of the crate. They glanced over at the police chief who stood beside the pastor.

Nathan Hambaugh took a step forward, took a moment to glance at the teens, and then nodded for the deputies to begin. "Let's get it done," he told them in a soft voice.

Deputy Jones flipped a switch, and a faint hum could be heard emanating from its black metallic shell. After nearly a minute, the two took hold of the handles and began to move it across the smooth surface. A black and gray image appeared on the monitor's screen and the others crowded around it in hopes of seeing something. The problem was that they weren't sure what it was they were looking for … or at. The image changed very little for the first few agonizing minutes, and then, gradually, it showed a cavity of sorts.

"I think we have something," said Nathan.

The deputies stopped moving and the taller hurried down to look at the monitor. "You're right, Chief," she said, grinning. "The altar is hollow. The lid is about six inches thick; the walls are probably closer to twelve. The radar is bouncing off something below the top, about six feet long and four feet wide, I'd say." She tapped the screen. "But that baby is hollow, and there's something there!"

They all converged on the altar and began to study it closely, looking for an opening of some kind. After several minutes it was George Hambaugh's young eyes that found what was sought. There was a seam, almost indiscernible, on the side that faced away from the chapel body. It was on the side where the old wooden cross still hung.

Using tools from the crime scene van, the deputies began work on the seam. Slowly, the seam became a slit … and then a narrow opening. It took the team the better part of an hour to find the accompanying seam and work that into a narrow opening. They gently pried the thick marble slab away from the altar and laid it carefully down out of the way. This done, they stepped back to allow the police chief first access.

With a flashlight in hand, Nathan Hambaugh approached the dark opening. He shined the light and panned it downward. "There's a large box in here," he said in a quiet voice. "You can see where the dirt has settled around it, exposing some of the top. I need a broom to sweep away the remaining dirt," he added, "and a pry bar."

Handed these items by the deputies, he went to work clearing off the wooden lid. It was old but had been protected beneath the altar from the elements. Done with the sweeping, he set to work with the pry bar removing wedge-shaped nails, moving gradually around three of the four sides. This task completed, he used the bar to begin prying up the lid. The nails on the fourth side screeched in protest as they were forcibly pried from the wood.

"They're in here," he said in a quiet voice, as if not wanting to awake the couple. He looked up at the silent, inquisitive gathering. "They're in there together … holding hands." Stepping back, he gestured to the minister who stood nearby. "Pastor, I think this might be your bailiwick."

With a nod, Pastor Archibald moved into the space vacated by the police chief. He looked upon the skeletal remains of the couple, made the sign of the Cross, and said a simple prayer. He was not the only one who murmured 'amen' afterwards.

Standing before the others, he said, "I am inclined to agree with Chief Hambaugh. There is no logical reason why these two souls should be anyone other than Angus and Eleanor MacLeod. Their clothing—what is left—is consistent with their time and position. That these two bodies are interred here, in the MacLeod Manor's chapel, holds with the proposition made yesterday: that they had been found murdered, and that Pastor Jacob and Nathaniel Hambaugh buried them within the altar."

"Pastor," said Anne, taking a step forward, "is there … anything else?"

He smiled down at her and shook his head. "No, nothing else."

Relief seemed to touch her face as she nodded her thanks.

"With the assistance of the Chief and these fine deputies," he went on, "I would like to re-inter this couple where they have spent the past two hundred and fifteen years."

The coffin's lid was replaced and nailed shut. The dirt was re-placed, and fresh dirt was brought in to completely cover the wooden box. The heavy marble slab required several able bodies to lift it back into place, with a fresh caulking to secure it. More than hour was spent reburying Angus and Eleanor MacLeod, and when the task was complete, everyone silently exited the chapel.

The deputies loaded up their gear in their crime scene van, bade everyone farewell, and left. Pastor Archibald Pettigrew informed the Chief of Police that he would arrange for a proper marker to be placed on the dais at the foot of the altar to mark the final resting place of the couple, and then he departed. Shortly thereafter the black-and-white police cruiser, the primer-gray Jeep Cherokee Chief, and the white Mustang convertible followed suit.

The MacLeod manor was once again empty … except for the dead.

ƆƷƆƷƆƷƆƷƆƷƆƷƆƷƆƷƆƷƆƷ

It was late that afternoon when sixteen people met in the comfortable family room in the home of Nathan and Emma Hambaugh. A buffet had been set up by Emma and Andrea Hambaugh, and Raymond Hambaugh was handing out the age-appropriate beverages. The conversations in the family room were quiet and varied, and the chiming of the grandfather clock was noticeable without being disruptive. Off to one side of the large bay window seven teens were huddled, chatting while nibbling food off their plates. Nathan, Raymond, Eskil Rosendale, and Pastor Archibald hovered near the ornately-carved liquor cabinet that Nathan had acquired while on a diplomatic trip to Singapore; the pastor held a small sherry. Emma, Andrea, Elisa Rialdi, Maude Raynes, and Charlotte Pettigrew were relaxed on and near the leather sofa.

It was Nathan who finally steered all conversation to the subject of the gathering. "Last week," he said, "I suggested to Anne that she investigate a haunting up at the manor." She smiled her acknowledgment. "And I had Harvey—my able-bodied cadet—investigate a trespassing incident that involved George and Jorge being carted off in leg-irons." The older teen nodded his acknowledgment as the two younger teens grinned a little sheepishly. "I had *no* idea at that time where it would lead." A chuckle rippled through the room.

"Through brilliant—and joint—deduction and determined investigation, these young people solved a century's old missing persons case: the whereabouts of Angus and Eleanor MacLeod. They found a sunken treasure ship: MacLeod's ketch, *Banrigh na Locha*. They were instrumental in the capture of several desperate criminals: Paul Harkness and his partner, Hortense Grimes; and Theo Bernbaum and his three cousins. Now, I'll tell you that I'll be the first to admit that I never expected Theo to do anything criminal!"

"And be a pirate, no less!" exclaimed Charlotte Pettigrew, the fifty-year-old wife of the town's pastor.

"Once that got about," Andrea chuckled, "the curiosity-seekers rolled in!"

"It wasn't all smooth sailing, though," pointed out Raymond seriously.

"True enough," admitted his younger brother. "Both Anne and George were kidnapped by Harkness and Grimes. It was Anne and her friends who worked out where George might be, and—indeed—was. It was Eskil"—the Air Force veteran gave an abbreviated nod to the room—"who followed the kidnappers when they had snatched Anne, and it was Mitch"—the nineteen-year-old aspiring illustrator and part-time landscaper/gardener flushed—"who figured out where they might have taken her by the getaway car they had used."

"I'm just grateful no one got killed," said Emma. "*This* time."

"Yes," agreed Maude. "That's always a plus."

"But we didn't solve an important part of the mystery," said Anne.

"What is that?" asked her Aunt Andrea.

"The *real* treasure!" declared George.

"Tlaltecuhtli?" inquired Elisa as she sipped her sweet *apéritif.*

"Yes," nodded his older sister. "Finding the MacLeods and his ship and all … they're certainly important, but the elusive jewel-studded gold statuette … that would have been a wonderful wrap of the case."

"But …" added the former librarian, a touch of a smile at her lips.

"Yes," sighed Anne, "… but …" She looked around the room at all the faces of those who had played a part in this latest mystery. "I am grateful to everyone here because everyone here contributed—"

"Except me," quipped Charlotte Pettigrew. "Thank you for the inclusion, though!"

A chuckle went through the room.

"A part of me—as some are aware—is sad that we did not find Tlaltecuhtli," the teen continued, "but—at the same time—a part of me is also glad we didn't. That piece of local folklore will continue to tantalize—to tease, to entice—the imaginations of future generations of young people."

"And trespassers," added Harvey.

"Yes," laughed Anne, "them, too."

Tammy Coleman playfully nudged the cadet in his ribs. "Look at it as job security."

"Ha!" he responded sardonically.

"Regardless," Anne went on, "we've done our best to find all the answers. And, sometimes, not all the answers can be found."

"Like why Harkness did the purse snatch thing," suggested Connie.

Nathan smiled. "They needed some quick cash, apparently," he explained, "and, unfortunately for him, he picked the wrong target. As it turned out, Marjorie Nielson didn't have anything of value in her purse. And he didn't mean to run over Harvey, that happened as he avoided someone else. The only thing he managed to do was draw attention to himself."

"And that ugly car they were driving!" laughed George.

"They had stolen that some days earlier from another part of the state," the chief explained. And then, with a sigh, he added, "Paul was never the sharpest knife in the drawer, though he would tell you otherwise. Growing up, we did a lot of stupid things that were his idea … and I wasn't very bright either because I went right along with him." He paused for a moment. "I'm pretty sure I gave my parents all of their gray hairs."

"Well, my brother," said Raymond, "I'll tell you this: they were proud of you, and they loved you. You turned yourself around and you served your country honorably. I'm just sorry you never gave them a chance to tell you that themselves."

The room became very quiet.

It was Emma Hambaugh who finally broke the silence. "This may sound selfish," she said, "but I am grateful for how things went for Nathan in his youth, because, otherwise, he may have followed a different path and I would have never met him. He is a good man, a loving husband, and a wonderful father."

"And he'll make a crackerjack Chief of Police!" chimed in Pastor Archibald. This brought laughter roiling through the family room.

"Thank you for that vote of confidence, Pastor!" chuckled Nathan Hambaugh. Turning to his wife, he said, "And thank you, my dear. I, too, am grateful for how things have turned out, and that I met you. You are my better half, and I love you more than words can express."

"This is getting mushy," muttered George, just loud enough to be heard by everyone.

"Ah, the innocence of youth," sighed Andrea Hambaugh dramatically.

Elisa Rialdi looked across the room at the seventeen-year-old with the gold-flecked green eyes and wavy red hair, and asked, "What's next for you, Anne?"

She smiled broadly. "I'm going to get my driver license!"

"And I'll teach her!" declared Tammy Coleman.

"Oh, no," groaned Harvey Freeman.

Made in the USA
San Bernardino, CA
23 May 2019